Last Taxi to Nutmeg Mews

Sarah Murphy

PEDLAR PRESS | Toronto

ACKNOWLEDGEMENTS
The publisher wishes to thank the Canada Council for the Arts and the Ontario Arts Council for their generous support of our publishing program.

LIBRARY AND ARCHIVES CANADA
CATALOGUING IN PUBLICATION

Murphy, Sarah, 1946-
Last taxi to Nutmeg Mews / Sarah Murphy.

ISBN 978-1-897141-28-1

I. Murphy, Sarah, 1946- --Childhood and youth. 2. Murphy, Sarah, 1946- --Homes and haunts. I. Title.

PS8576.U67Z472 2009   C818'.5403
C2009-904141-3

DESIGN
Zab Design & Typography, Toronto

ILLUSTRATIONS
Sarah Murphy

TYPEFACE
Auto 2, by Underware Type Foundry

Printed in Canada

The Canada Council for the Arts since 1957 | Le Conseil des Arts du Canada depuis 1957

ONTARIO ARTS COUNCIL
CONSEIL DES ARTS DE L'ONTARIO

To Rosemary –
Enjoy the ride!

Earl's

So there i am sitting in earl's with my friend leila telling her some kind of story or maybe not maybe what i'm doing is something more like taking out a little package we both do this a lot and placing it on the table maybe we're talking about violence again not so much violence against women as violence and women or for that matter violence and children and who knows what it is really oh yeah i understand violence oh yeah you remember the time mickey's head the black and white cat the nights in the closet and she's answering oh yeah the baseball bat and it's like we just kind of turn the package over in our hands

///to admire the wrap the shine of the paper the accomplished precision of the bow but we never open it not anymore never get beyond that we could if we wanted open sesame moment with its magic words oh yeah that's what opens the door oh yeah oh yeah we acknowledge with our eyes our hungry looks knowing this time for sure the wrapping the little special twist our tone can give the bow the edge of the hidden words is worth so much more to us than the contents more pleasant anyway so leave it there in the middle of the table leave it in the air between us a pretty package wrapped like that open sesame and turn away

///so maybe the magic in the words is more like a secret password a sign or countersign *consigna* they say in spanish though that's more a slogan or maybe it's more a countersigh a long sigh anyway while we're just kind of looking away from both package and words only then she laughs laughs and says you could do it that way you know you could it's possible do your whole life like that all these little stories we never actually tell after a while and now we're onto that describing without ever quite telling them again how these are the ones we just write headlines for and leave alone make them into the who goes there who goes there of the middle of the night of our lives the open sesame of a dark cave we don't want to look into just know who's passing by just enough to remember ourselves and i just laugh oh yeah oh yeah that would be good i say really good write them down and then because i don't know if she means me or some kind of any you any you at all i sort of say well *one* could *one* could i suppose but i wouldn't i certainly wouldn't though it's sort of inspiring i tell her one's autobiography my whole autobiography this life i've been thinking too much about as headlines

///just make a list and let the reader write the story what a novel way of dealing with the novel or even the memoir i say and besides what a great way to get out of this constant pondering to escape trying to look at the questions contained behind the words to never resolve anything and i'm even starting to like it when she says oh no not at all you have to actually do it write them down first the headline then the whole story the story to match the headline write the whole thing all the details gory or not remember the headline then write the story one two three four and she counts with her fingers beginning to end and i say yeah right yeah right then oh no

///oh no no way and just laugh again not me not me and besides i couldn't i really couldn't you don't understand i say i couldn't

///and by then it's true and that's what's strange maybe a moment before it wasn't but the minute i say it it's true as if this truth too was hiding there behind the headlines the passwords the countersighs because no matter how much i try to hide behind that pretty packaging the minute i think about doing it actually telling all these stories this is what happens all the stories are gone there are no stories left behind the headlines what were those stories anyway i find myself thinking there's nothing inside the package it's not just my laugh that's hollow it's my life like the cave is open the cave is open the open sesame cave that's supposed to contain not that storied treasure but those treasured stories all hidden right inside and instead it's just hollow and echoing and full of stalagmites and tites and things to slip on i can't even see and i've already fallen even in that restaurant back into the darkness and now i know that's what i've been avoiding that's what i've been wrapping in my pretty phrases my bright ribbons of storyless words it's the stories i've forgotten i have no map no x marks the spot for the darkness no longer contains stories or headlines or passwords or anyone who goes there who goes there at all not anyone who can lead me out anyway so i just look up

///from the table and out to the windows and out the door and try to see it how the sun is still shining the sun is still shining it's the middle of my own bright day and the sun is still shining i haven't opened anything this isn't a cave or the dark inside of an empty package and leila i say leila touching her hand leila i say look out there that's not a headline or a story look out there look out that window you see those leaves you see that sky all that brightness that's my autobiography that's my autobiography out there that's my autobiography you can write that headline if you want the sun still shines it's a great password the leaves are green is the countersign because that's all it's ever been it's all that effort to keep the day bright forget the rest and keep the sun shining that's my autobiography my only autobiography only i can't you see i can't i can't even say it i can't.

Stuck finger blues rrrrrrr rrrrrrrr rrrrrrrr

Like i said the truth is i don't want to do this at all you know what i mean i'm not the least interested that's what i keep telling myself it's just not where i'm at conversations in restaurants with their little headlines are one thing telling the whole story any whole story something else altogether that's what i think and not for the first time as i sit down at the computer at the computer again always again

///you want a whole story well i'll give you a whole story that's right a whole story maybe i'll just write a novel instead that's right like a real novel you know what i mean storyline and setting and point of view and above all those consistent characters consistently constructed i've done that before or at least i think i have more or less consistent anyway done that always in never out of character thing only even as i think it try to make that plan try to find a story place with a logic of its own lifting my right hand to thumb my very real nose at an imaginary leila i can't i already know i can't

///the stranger truth overcomes the consistent fiction and the inconsistent just ride it out if you can darkness descends so sitting at the computer with my thumb on my nose not even waving is just about all i can manage these days there's no letters on the screen responding to my fingertips it's all i can do to get a pencil a chalk crayon into that hand to make myself draw in fact the only place the sun is shining is out my fingers i can't seem to get the day colours back at all that bright sun i spoke of in the restaurant there's just this thing of sitting in the dark and pouring the only colour in the universe out my fingers like a little light through a crack in the door that i'm slowly opening to see if the coast is clear until there's this one morning i wake up and maybe i'm just too caffeinated from the morning coffee or too hung over from the night before or maybe i'm just so very very tired from work or conversations in restaurants i don't want to have but too shaky anyway far too shaky

///for the discipline of drawing so i figure i'll just do it just do it the way leila said just do it just make my list and begin just begin that's right begin it should be fun i tell myself i need something to do so begin just begin i'm too wired too awake just begin and there's my fingers on the keyboard and doing that thing sort of like a piano player shooting back her cuffs and fingers across the keys letting my fingers float across the letters asdf gh jkl semi-colon qwer ty uiop zxcv bnm comma period back slash

///only that's all that will come out you see no matter what i tell myself i've got no list no list at all absolutely none not a single one of those headlines will allow itself back into my mind there's no restaurant and no sun and no one to finish my sentences or for that matter to begin them no one no interlocutor but myself and i'm silent i'm hiding in the dark so it's just the dark just the dark the longest time just the dark that's all the dark the dark and my fingers moving making nonsense instead of music or even words asdf qwer ty uiop bnm comma period only i can't think of anything else to do not even get another coffee so i just sit there in the dark that isn't dark it's bright out my window and let it happen asdf gh jkl semi-colon qwer ty uiop z until my index finger comes again to the r and sticks rrrrrrrrrrrrrr

///rrrrrrrrrrrr rrrrrrrrrrrrr rrrrrrrrrrrrr

///and suddenly it's that rrrrrrrrrr rrrrrrrrrrr jiggle jiggle buncha phoneys buncha phoneys thing mickey always did my mother mickey and then it's mickey in the cab and this voice saying something and it's my voice my voice only much younger and you see there it is right there right there in that voice you've got your first headline in that voice your first password sign or countersign twenty-six nutmeg mews my voice says only it's more than that it always is

///rrrrrrrrrrrr rrrrrrrrrrrr jiggle jiggle and i'm telling the whole thing reciting the streets of how to get there that's right how to get back to twenty-six nutmeg mews telling the driver the way home the way i'm sitting in the dark and telling myself the way back even if it's not home never was not a real home really but still it's how to get back through the dark how to get back rrrrrrrrr rrrrrrrrr rrrrrrrrrr

///and how to get back and how to get back over and over the way it was over and over that cab ride over and over not last exit but last taxi to brooklyn that's right to brooklyn brooklyn i tell the guy brooklyn over the bridge the brooklyn bridge and i don't know why i'm doing this at all i just am not the tunnel now the bridge i say and maybe it's that little yellow light on the top of the cab maybe it's just gleaming in the dark and i have to move toward it you know the one i mean what does it say i can't even remember what it says

///*libre* they say in spanish *libre libre* free free it's an old joke from my days in mexico you ask the cabby are you free and he gives you that mexico city that new york cabbie look and yes on bail he says and switches off the light as you get in and isn't it strange how i can remember that but not what it says on the top of a cab in english in new york when it's free i know it isn't vacancy that's a motel and motels are from a whole other time and place i don't even think they'd invented motels yet when i was getting into that cab with mickey or only just because they were so new no one had stayed in their like before on our one trip back to mickey's hometown along for the ride we were with car blessed cousins and a dog that would only pee on the new york times

///vacancy signs by the road remain a country western song a road trip like that one wisconsin June only one i was ever out of the city so this sure isn't country no headlines for country at least not for a long time and no road trips either just cab rides so let's just go back a moment to where that one bright light is because it's the only colour among all the grey shadows the yellow light without any words even that simple *libre* maybe it's just numbers on the signs numbers or nothing maybe it's an absence just a question for wanting to be a millionaire which i always did for getting out of there wanted to win the lottery or some contest which is what it was in the end that scholarship though this question was likely the cheapest the first one right there the way it is at the beginning for sixteen or is it sixteen hundred dollars what does it say on the top of a cab in new york when it's free only i'll just remember

///rrrrrrrrr rrrrrrrrr rrrrrrrrr so no matter what it says i'm not free or for that matter *libre* not at all not with mickey's twisted face grey above me and a new colour now the red slash of her smeared lipstick and pushing her into the cab and rrrrrrrr rrrrrrrrr and my own voice repeating the words repeating

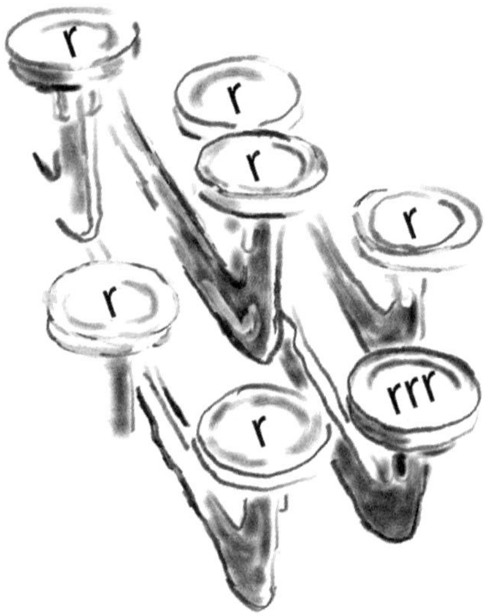

the streets it's a map now and no one's free no one at all not the cabbie and not me no one's free that's right to brooklyn to brooklyn last taxi to brooklyn because they never want to go to brooklyn they always tell you they can't get back at least not with a fare so i want to tell those cabbies i can't get back either and it isn't fair can't get back or even out there's no exit not first or last just no exit at all from brooklyn not my brooklyn so i just smile instead the way i am right now over the keys my nicest pasted on little kid smile and i say don't worry

///don't worry it's just over the bridge

///don't worry with mickey rrrrrr rrrrrrr and trying to hit the cabbie buncha phoneys buncha phoneys whaddaya mean it's too far while i try again it's very close i say very very close i don't want to try to find another last taxi i really don't not me very very close i repeat first exit off the bridge not the tunnel the bridge that's right the brooklyn bridge and talking and talking i finally get her in talking and talking so he doesn't get another chance to say no before i'm in myself and i've closed the door and maybe he feels sorry or maybe he knows it really is close who knows but there we are and rrrrrrrrrrrrr rrrrrrrrrrrrr rrrrrrrrrrrrr

///mickey's snoring or maybe still singing buncha phoneys buncha phoneys and we're on our way he's starting to move no more chance to be told no and all i have to pray for now is it's not one of those rides when she pees and not on the new york times all polite like wolf the dog but on the seat like that one time on the subway the seventh avenue express with tim when we had to leave her because she wouldn't get off no matter what we did she wouldn't get off we passed our stop and she wouldn't get off i hardly remember it but tim sure does being the man of the house at ten instructed to take care of me and mickey too and to ignore the social worker type who tried to save us as mickey sang rrrrrrrr rrrrrrr rrrrrrrr while for me it's just a vision of the puddle looking back from the subway door and a flaring of the nostrils for every time i stand on the platform of atlantic avenue station the echo of the smell of alcoholized piss down the years from elevators and car seats and beds and floors so who really cares if she pees or not except the cabbie this time the shame will be brief because the one thing i know is she'll have to get out he'll make sure she gets out no matter the condition of his cab so this is better especially since tim isn't here the air is solid with summer heat and tim is at camp so who cares if she passes out on the front stoop not a stoop at all really just one stair and the two stones to the sides like railings or like seats where we will hunker down back to the building legs to the sun or moon so many days so many nights so what can i say if she collapses into that hollow before the door except it's better than holding her up singing on the street so already i feel the relief as the little light that once said free or whatever it is whatever magic numbers that light turns off and i'm in the dark with my finger still stuck rrrrrrrrr rrrrrrrrrr rrrrrrrr

///the rrrrrrrrrrrrrrr of the cab and the rrrrrrrrrr of mickey as it starts to move rrrrrrrr rrrrrrrrrr rrrrrrrrrrr until my voice resumes

///all over again that's right you got it over the bridge and the first exit that's right you take the first exit the first exit not the last exit the last exit and you've gone too far so first exit to brooklyn the first exit off the bridge in any case the one to your right then straight through and a left down henry if you get to hicks it's too far again you'll have to circle and who wants to do that my best child being grownup voice my imitation sober mickey hail a cab voice while drunken mickey keeps it up the rrrrrrrr rrrrrrrrrr rrrrrrrr the stuck finger chorus rrrrrrrrrrrr rrrrrrrrrrr rrrrrrrrrrr

///it's down henry to state and a left on state you can't take jerolemon because it's the wrong way you take jerolemon from clinton when you come up atlantic from the tunnel but the bridge is better it's closer that way and i don't tell him how i love being inside its metal shell passing below the girders and imagining myself in the clouds the bright views of the buildings the water that goes on forever out the narrows and into the ocean so that sometimes i can think i'm free too not like the claustrophobic white of the tunnel with its marking for every hundred yards you pass to let you know inch by inch how much closer you are to the end of the ride but either way never free even imagined free for long so just do it who cares which way if you come from the tunnel it's columbia to atlantic a right on atlantic and a left on hicks just one block to state if you go too far you can take clinton but you have to circle clinton to jerolemon jerolemon to state and there are too many circles i've been circling for years so let's keep it clear keep the instructions clear to unstick my finger it's back to the bridge and henry to state then left again on sidney and sidney to nutmeg our own small mews those three houses opposite the school that's right nutmeg mews our own street our nutmeg mews and be careful it's only one block and no you can't come up the other side it's just one way one way to nutmeg mews last taxi first exit first exit to brooklyn clinton to jerolemon henry to state up sidney and only one way only one way only one way only one way one way home only it's a dead end

///a dead end

///one way home and no way out so up nutmeg to opposite the school that's right so i might as well tell it tell it like it is tell it like a headline tell it without words tell it without colours tell it like a long dark taxi ride but tell it tell it tell it dead end last taxi first exit over the bridge clinton to jerolemon jerolemon to state state to sidney sidney to nutmeg

///nutmeg to twenty-six that's right twenty-six old twenty-six we always called it old twenty-six and who cares whether or not the fog of the night or the fog of memory is clearing because here we are and i can see it the old wrought iron door and i'm getting the money out and i'm paying the cab and i'm opening the door hoping mickey will follow and that she'll just get into her bed and go to sleep she won't try to go out or get to the bars but just go to sleep while i stay awake at least until the singing stops the rrrrrrrrr rrrrrrrrrr rrrrrrrrr while my mind tells itself stories the way it does now stories of a brighter future the stories i once followed to leave that place even if i left part of me behind so maybe it's true maybe i can do it maybe since i've done it i can do it again maybe to get out of the dark maybe i just have to say it write my headlines on the paper the way that girl once wrote her future in her head write them down and follow them up and this time when i turn around that last time to give those last instructions maybe i can take them too

///because all you can do from a dead end street is turn around the way i tell the cabbie how half way up the block there's a new street that's right the beginning of livingston where you take a right take a right and just keep going keep going till you see the sign for the bridge that's right the sign for the bridge unstick my fingers qwerty jkl semi-colon and the sign for the bridge nm comma period back slash and just keep writing keep on writing because maybe that's all they are all they've ever been all these headlines are just the instructions for leaving so maybe this time if i just do it i'll get it right not the bridge or the tunnel take the first exit then go across to henry left on henry henry to state left on state to sidney up sidney to nutmeg nutmeg to old twenty-six open the door but just back in the cab back in the cab with all my headlines held in my hand like the new york times and no more mickey to pee on it no more baggage asdf take that one right turn that one right turn uiop and just keep going just keep going watch for the sign the sign for the bridge zxcv let it begin.

Sunday morning with li'l abner and kickapoo joy juice

and daisy mae of course what do you expect that was mickey and maybe if cherokee bill you'll find out about him soon enough was around there was even some sort of diatribe about the kickapoo and what happened to them really and what was that awful little indian doing there ugh how what did hollywood think it was about as all of them recovered from a hangover but i never identified cherokee with that character he was way too thin and handsome so he had nothing to do with that comic outside commentary even if mark and mickey were daisy mae and li'l abner and i loved the funnies but mostly i loved that it was a calm time sunday mornings mostly really it was and all the newspapers were there all of them the news and the post and the times and we never looked at headlines or the times at all for that matter passed them by for the post and the news for the comics in sunday colour the way me and tim loved new yorker cartoons even if they were in black and white and everything else too felt li'l abner warm and the funnies bright and i don't want to write anymore about it i don't want to explain about any of these characters come to any conclusions or morals of my story even take the more mature astute moral high ground of anti-racism explain how i could feel the meaning of racism in cherokee's pain as he looked across the room at mark and mickey explicate the horrors of kickapoo joy juice and how later understanding must have been born even then no i don't want that or any explanation any understanding at all i would give up understanding just about anything to have that back the feeling inside that image that bright sunday morning funny paper peaceful image the five of us perfect my two fathers and mickey and tim i want to sit there forever and look at it as if i could be inside funny paper bright colours and that's the way i feel about a lot of this list as i write them down headline after headline because sometimes there's something too good to be true and sometimes it's too true to be good and others it's too awful to contemplate so i don't always want to say much i don't want to say anything and maybe sometimes i won't say much i won't say anything i'll just sit there inside that moment or i'll get up and walk out not just of the story but of the room because sometimes it will just be too horrible right up front no image needed comic or coloured or otherwise at all just too horrible right on the surface from the very beginning of the words.

Cobblestone small feet

Woolly bear caterpillars in the rubble

Sliding the bannister

Sails on the model boat pond

Kyoko of the yellow kabuki slippers

She was mark's mistress and lived near the model boat pond i don't remember much besides the slippers i've always remembered them buy that kind of slipper again and again love to pick them up and look at the way they close around the ankle with those three little metal tongues you reverse into cloth strips cherokee bill would buy me some later too in japan where he was those years he was away with kiko his japanese wife i don't think they knew about each other and their japanese women beginning with k him and mark it doesn't matter if those slippers are never quite comfortable not with my feet and their pushed over big toes it hurts the way those slippers separate the big toe from the rest to fit into the thong of those platform shoes you know the ones she wore them too the ones with the two small boards at front and back underneath the sole to raise them up and make them clack on the hardwood floor she wore a brocade kimono too i remember that the hanging sleeves mostly i must have been sitting on the floor that one time we visited i can't see any part of her above the obi around her waist i don't know what tim was doing.

Still life with closet

Hard as it might be to imagine and still halting or not at some point it just becomes easy to brainstorm the list one after another item by item down onto the page though writing them out that's yet another matter and just like i said hardly ever another story mostly it's that stuck finger blues all over again so maybe it's time to stop the hesitation and just get started only what i come up with instead is more like a stuck incident blues the same thing over and over a generic headline for casual conversation maybe for the restaurant maybe to comment on one of those silly stupid stalker movies with the heroine screaming from inside the closet the way i will say with a kind of sophisticated laugh the last thing you want to do from inside a closet is start to scream and then look around to see if i can be serious or just cover it up with nothing in my wardrobe is quite that horrible though either way whether i say it or not it's still true why would you scream from inside a closet the whole point is to disappear and really for hiding and being hunted if not hiding and seeking closets truly are the best down on the floor with the snuggly clothes on top or even the one with the exit to the roof it had a shelf i fit nicely on me and the towels so yeah yeah and it doesn't even have to be leila just did i ever tell you about being hunted and not screaming well ready or not here it comes

///and it's not really at the beginning of the story either but you know how that is no matter what anyone says except for the particulars in a court of law you ever hear of anything that actually begins at the beginning well neither have i and let me tell you nobody really knows how any story truly begins this one for sure began a long time ago a long time before me maybe even before mickey even if i was its obvious target in the house now and out of the cab though often as not there's still the rrrrrrrrr rrrrrrrr rrrrrrrrr to avoid getting stuck on always i must avoid being rendered immobile by that sound the way tim will be that last time he sees her in the hospital stuck before i can find my hiding place as mickey starts her hunt get to the closet or the window box or the dumbwaiter shaft and maybe it's the same night as the cab that really is possible but there are a lot of other nights as well rrrrrrrr rrrrrrrrr rrrrrrrr and don't look now here she comes home from the bars or just from downstairs an hour or so after charlie arrived to deliver the cutty sark and maybe at that moment of decision it really does feel like the beginning room after room of potential places to hide in a house of inescapable and continuous beginnings though really it's probably more a middle a permanent middle a moment in the middle of what won't go away the hiding place chosen and now to the waiting the same moment over and over the moment between when you hid and when you're found or if you're found so its kind of like a chorus imagine this is a song and it's the chorus rrrrrrrrr rrrrrrrr rrrrrrrrr and you're hidden somewhere maybe the closet maybe the dumbwaiter shaft so it's sort of like a rule or maybe even the rules the rules the rules for how i live my life

///so any time you want to know what this story is about this whole story that is all these stories that are one story well you can come back here to the chorus and oh yes you can say that's the story that's the story that fits in between that's the story that's always there the one that always echoes in that moment that fits between all the other moments so it really is as good a place as any to start and maybe better than most the moment between

///the period between the one that can be a lot of periods the times when mickey is the only one around the only grownup anyway those times when bill is away or at sea mark in africa or manhattan or dead paul garcia still alive but thrown out or just out for the evening all the people i'm going to tell you about all gone all gone maybe even tim at camp again so there's just me me and mickey

///mickey and maybe some guys she just happened to have lying around really that's what it was like it's the mickey chorus rrrrrrr rrrrrrrr rrrrrrrr and the mickey chorus line only believe me they weren't exactly kicking up their legs though maybe they were opening hers or mine and none of it just one time either one incident or anecdote but any time any time at all any day or night weekend or weekday winter spring summer fall and you never knew when it would be which day or which night which hour which trigger but any time that felt like all the time because what else could it feel like if it was always there and waiting now and then and forever the perfect headline to begin the chorus to come back to not the moment after or the moment during but the moment before so it's never specific it's generic not just permanent but generic hardly a headline at all then this closet thing maybe more like a classified ad a department like sports or city maybe it's the children's page you can find it under hiding or hidden instead of for sale or wanted let your fingers or maybe your mind do the walking this time to that closet to this moment that is the moment that always lurks behind all the headlines all the compressed incidents permanent and aching and always there

///did i ever tell you about the closet the shelf the dumbwaiter shaft what waits at the turning of each corner the ending of each day the edge of each dream between the step and the stair the dumbwaiter and the rope the shelf and the box in the shadow of the shoe the hollow of the hat the holes in the lace always waiting to resume to encounter its power to become something else the needles at the doctor the guys in my room a hand grabbing a penis a pussy in my face so i am always in the closet always under the bed in the dumbwaiter shaft no matter where else i go and mickey is always hunting me hunting me though she hasn't caught me yet and i don't know if she will as i shrink down and make myself tiny and she comes humming and singing singing and humming to some strange tune her own made up words her rrrrrrrrr rrrrrrrrrr rrrrrrrrrrr or her buncha phoneys buncha phoneys or just come out you little shits you little shits wait till i find you you little shits or maybe it's just you you little shit or even you you little cunt because maybe i'm the only one there in this permanent moment earlier and later and in different versions so for little cunt little cunt it's just me and for little shits little shits tim is there and for buncha phoneys it could be anything or anyone man or men or just me or giving up drunk on the floor in her own piss but either or any way it's always the same story the moment before story there i am repeating it and repeating it my long chorus same story line

///which is maybe allowed in this writing business i'm not quite sure i haven't figured that out yet i don't really get the rules certainly not for writing the truth is how to live my life is hard enough making these headlines part of it harder still a lot harder than that novel i promised so it's a mystery to me whether or not it's permitted if they let you write the same stuff the same story over and over i mean if this is a novel which is a good question in itself can it still have a chorus a story that repeats and repeats it doesn't seem fair when you have to live it repeat the same story over and over and it's damn obvious you've had to do that for the longest time that's definitely a rule hey i just found one rule i understand wow i've learned a rule or maybe i'm lying maybe there are some rules i've always known knew it even in my closet you have to live the same story over and over so my question is if you have to live it why can't you write it the different versions the multiple nuances the same titles with different footnotes or bodies of text or of evidence or whatever it is only the truth is writers

///or maybe it's publishers or editors or even readers but certainly somebody seems to favour having different stories really different stories like completely different stories with different consistent well-rounded characters none of these human storm systems these roaring deus ex machinas for each one so it doesn't seem to make a difference that nobel laureate garcia marquez or maybe it was someone else and garcia marquez just repeated it said each one of us has only one story just the one so we tell it again and again the fact is it's still not what anyone sets out to do it's not like anyone ever sits down at their computer or their typewriter or even pen and paper in hand and says hey i'm going to sit here and write the same story again and again for the rest of my life even if you might kind of like the one you've got the way i like this one given the choices this is a definite favourite all those sweet snuggly blankets there are a lot of things worse than sweet snuggly vaguely musty blankets for a chorus a chorus line or lineup one after the other will number three please stand forward the blanket or towel or old newspaper so that's what we'll call it celebrate that i haven't been caught yet that maybe i won't be caught at all this time

///it's worth telling again and again just for that small possibility it's even worth singing sing the hallelujah i haven't been caught yet hallelujah chorus the moment of the wall between present and future of the veil before the veil is torn the clothes at the bottom of the closet torn away the moment of the belief shining beneath the clothes the belief you won't be caught not this time maybe it's a series of fugues refuges anyway if not flights maybe i could just call it variations on a hidden or maybe it's a hiding theme maybe you're allowed to write the same one over and over if you kind of call it that fugue poem with refuge chorus poets get away with that sort of thing all the time so maybe just call these poems not a novel

///novel or not here i come just call them poems closet poems or poems from a storied closet i don't know then maybe i can get away with just a little story maybe you're permitted if it's a story so tiny it's hardly a story at all not even a headline just eensy teensy weensy a ball of fluff like dust under a bed cat hair on a blanket mouse shit at the bottom of a dumbwaiter shaft maybe you can repeat it then and besides it's always happening maybe they'll let me do that i can certainly make these stories that way eensy teensy as teensy weensy as me trying to disappear into them at least this chorus like that

///call it a suite instead of a fugue that's a good word too a suite of the sweetest hidden moments not drawings but images hidden in the mind the hide in the closet image suite each one grey except for the smallest crack the crack in different places different openings to the light make them sketches or one repeated etching done on the press definitely in black and white a dark grey page with eyes the story the colour placed by hand just in where that eye appears and the rest texture grey texture made with the etching point the acid bath not even headlines or passwords just etchings etchings or sketches perfect and small absolutely miniature and in their frames even the handdone sketches each one just about the same the in the closet as yet uncaught moment like a still life or sketches for a still life maybe a whole bunch of still lives the way you see them over and over in galleries or museums still life number one with roses still life number two with roses still life number three with carnations number four with marigolds number five with chysanthemums oh i love to spell that word the fingers dance across the keyboard for that one better than number six with rrrrrrrrrr rrrrrrrr rrrrrrr finger stuck on mickey's voice make that seven with apples eight with pears nine with dead quail or dead rabbit or dead fish their guts splayed out delicate and glowingly portrayed onto the cutting board i saw that at the louvre

///even spilled guts in still lives seem so calm so collected so precise so pretty maybe that's what makes them a reward for this waiting a reward with this waiting so pretty you can imagine them there in your closet even if it is more like studies for a crucifixion number one number two number three number four the feet comforting each other one on top of the other the arms resisting the moment of being stretched out tugged from under the clothes or maybe even it's the last supper the tension of the last bar closing waiting for the last drink to be finished the glass if not the chalice put down the this is my body and this my blood in the feel of the racing pulse the held breath the hugging of the knees in the last closet no exit to brooklyn though the fact is it's calm enough collected enough i'm collected and small and precise in that closet almost as small as a kitten in a box made for an iron i'm hardly moving hardly breathing and anyway forget the crucifixion you could likely make a case even in the stillest still lives for the horror lurking behind in the shadows seeping through from the underlay that grey energy its own stilled waiting for the falling of the petals the cooking of the quail the grabbing of my wrist the smell of the huffing alcoholic breath the rotting of the fruit or of the fish guts the smell of my pee or of hers always the getting ready to move the about to unfold the about to happen contained in the moment to come which is never there

///never in the drawing or in the painting or in these smallest of stories which is probably what makes this a good place to begin even if it's not the beginning makes the name fit still life in the implied horror in the shadows of the closet still life in the pattern on the blanket held by the hand still life in the dirt under the bitten nail and besides that i like the idea it was mostly stillness perfect stillness that was in the permanent moment the repeated chorus stillness i was learning stillness so still it could make the moment to come never come never come at all that was the point perfect stillness could make the future never come so whether it was a caught or uncaught moment wouldn't matter whichever moment it was whichever moment was to come i could still paper that moment over with my still life my still lives just holding one or another still life in my mind my own gallery like the filthy rich moving along their halls of pictures even the fallen aristocracy still life after still life so they never had to see what was underneath what the structure was that held it all together

///like the fact that i would always be in this house mickey would always be hunting me catching me showing me off to the men she just happened to have lying around while i would paper it all over with these tiny unbreathing incidents until it wouldn't matter which moment was to come all moments could be papered over the way you meditate through pain concentrating on just one image just one small space just one still life that's right still life with closet still life with blanket still life with bedsprings still life with dumbwaiter rope still life with laundry still life with drainpipes under the sink that probably works well enough in fact it works perfectly the way i would always isolate those objects pieces of those objects with my eye i would i would just the way a still life does pulling forward one special a few special objects especially those baroque chiaroscuro ones that pull the central forms from the shadows of the underlay the grisaille i think that's what it's called glazed over later with bright transparent colours the lights pulled out further pinks and greens and purples and yellows with a turpentine soaked cloth so that they glow

///that would work well enough those few highlighted spaces the crack of the door the edge of the shelf the little embroidered flower on the inherited pillowcase to halt my breathing my anticipation or the fact of my pain to make my life so still so very still an unstory a still story a stilled story still life with story right there in its frame plain wood or baroque stucco its little title at its bottom in glass just like these little headlines still life with headlines no more movement than headlines the story hidden in the dark of the moment to come

///hidden in perfected hiding i could do it sometimes even playing hide and seek during the day hidden in that house so that no one could find me what an amazing thing really it was what a privilege it is even in dreams to be able to hide so that the monster passes you over no one can find you making the surface of a blanket that you are hidden under just like a blanket that no one is hidden under or hiding under your bed all the way back where no one can see or amid the debris of the dumbwaiter shaft that seems too small for even the tiniest person until you can imagine that perfect moment forward into the future of its imperfection the seeker tagging you and touching base or mickey tugging your arm out of its socket until you no matter what happens you are always there among the dust balls the dust bunnies still life with dust bunny me a soft but giant dust bunny disappearing dust bunny

///even if i never heard that phrase not until i grew up saw the balls but never knew they had a name learned that only about five years ago it's not a rule that you should know that name dust bunny even if you are familiar with the dust accumulated there in layers or balls always there but never mentioned like so many more truly nefarious things that one probably really is a rule if not a still life you will not learn to name the events or what surrounds them but just to hide to hide and see but never name never seek more than your hiding at the back of the closet or on the closet shelf by the ladder to the roof under the bed or in the window box or the dumbwaiter shaft hunched up and made small a story too small to mention an event too little to name to bring to anyone's attention not even a sketch up on the wall to let them walk by so that it seems very warm in there under there up there very comforting where no one can see you no one notice

///so very still and warm your own still life your own life stilled until even when you're found you're still hiding and it seems the best thing in the world better than a mother's hug that little heat of your breath against your dirty old blanket smelling of solidity and use a place to go sunk deep inside that one place and this one rule finally this one rule that guides the mind if not the hand the biggest still life rule of all still life with rule i was learning about how to live my life so i learned it well even if i hardly knew it for years that rule that paints the still life that paints your life still the rule that makes this all a joke obviates the whole question really it's funny when you think about it because how can it matter how many versions there are or how many stories or how small they are or how often you are allowed to tell them because after all there is only this

///this still life still

///still this rule of silence that shrinking down that says you won't want to tell them big or little or the same or different a fugue or a story or a poem or a suite you won't want to tell them anyway tell them at all still life with apple still life with orange still life with dirty blanket because this rule will tell you how to only see the fragments the little fragments you can use to pretend to remain hidden always remain hidden in the moment before pulling each image forward out of the story to make it its own still life so you can stop before telling the big story the moment after story rest cuddled in that ubiquitous headline just savour it in your mouth your eyes never telling anything more as you make sure there is no story make sure you never see the story the whole story that the story never ends so you can't possibly tell it whether or not it's always the same and whether or not you want to still that's all it will ever be just that image that brief bright image and maybe that's enough or maybe it's just strange but whatever it is it's more beautiful than the bright curves of painted fish guts so let's throw them all up on the wall of the restaurant if not your room yes indeed i've been hunted but i've never been caught and if i have i wouldn't know so hey look

///still life with blanket still life with stuffed toy still life with frayed dumbwaiter rope still life with window box hinge still life with bedsprings still life with old sock still life with dirty nails still life with closet all the time any time on the wall over and over a suite of drawings a series of poems who cares about the rules who cares at all except for this one that says there will always be an image to cover the moment a story so tiny it will just be an unnoticed old title on a brass plaque told over and over like a glaze to make permanent the moment before always the moment before with me my breath caught way in the back under the dirty old smelling blanket with its edge held in my dust bunny fingers always in silence always in stillness always still life always still.

Stepping on ants

The fact is that sometimes it will be particularly easy to be specific take a story from beginning to end sometimes you might even get help the way someone will always come up with this question at a workshop or just playing around you know how it is people always do this ask what your first memory was *what is your first memory* they say *what exactly* as if that really meant something there was some terrible significance in how far back you remember though in truth there probably is of some sort anyway even if i have no idea what most of the time but it's always there *what's your first memory* they say and look at you in that hand rubbing oh i just can't wait to see what *she* reveals kind of way so the one i always come up with is that one about the ants *oh yeah* i say *my farthest back memory what's my first memory* sometimes they even ask you to do it to get sensory material produce feeling make yourself emote get a precise setting writing and acting exercises are like that so *ants* i say *ants* and kind of throw out my arm and giggle

///i think it might even be my first memory i don't know anymore the fact is i've been using it for first memory material so long it's kind of lost its oomph its *je ne sais quoi* texture i don't really see it anymore see them their six tiny legs moving not the way i used to though i probably could if i really tried maybe i should draw it or something wallow in the specificity of it to make it real again it's a comfortable enough memory really and a comforting one too there's a lot of memories i can't say that about and besides i can always add how i learned a lot from this one throw that in as i say *oh yeah ants ants are my first memory* my first memory and my first miracle ants you see ants ants are the ones you can step on and they don't squash the small ones anyway

///they're not like cockroaches i know i'd had experience with cockroaches by then you can't get around cockroaches in brooklyn the usual petite tan ones or the queen size blue black kind we called water bugs if you stepped on any of them they squished ucky ucky squished and then you had to kind of look at them all pinky yellow and gooey or scrape their ucky remains off

the bottom of your shoe but with those little ants there was stepping on them as we walked down the sidewalk in the backyard absolutely no goo on the rough old concrete of the kind we always called cement the kind i cut my hand on later falling on a glass when the blood was all over only this memory is much younger younger before a lot of things when there were just those ants always the littlest little black ones only slightly larger than the dark brown kind that crawl into the neck of your syrup bottle even when it's screwed closed and drive you crazy when they pour out onto your pancakes and you can't even manage a shrug and a *well the protein's probably good for you* as you look at all those little legs and you refuse to wonder how many you've already eaten as you throw the food away

///we only had the black around new york certainly i never saw any red ones we'd just heard the red ant legends bigger badder bites and how they hunt you down it happened to a friend of a friend out in new jersey though at the time of this memory i was too young even for *we'll bury you up to your neck in honey and the ants will eat you* i must have been all of two and really if i concentrate make it into a real memory again and not just the memory of a memory the standard answer to *what's your first memory* so as not to have to look to see if there are any uckier ones before that then that's my age maybe two maybe all of two or even eighteen months and there i am stepping on the ants with my little two year old shoes the white leather baby's first shoes you still see around the kind doting parents cast in bronze from a time someone in my family might have tried that a time i think life was maybe happy not with mickey and mark most likely though they were without doubt still pretending trying to cast the middle class life they imagined in bronze to keep the ground the house the lawn from moving out from under them

///but happy at least with the housekeeper who they could pretend to afford too the way they could look such a nice intellectual career oriented literary couple forties style even if likely as not i wasn't mark's daughter that was always something of a crap shoot but after all it must still have been the forties and the two of them already in terrible debt or mark was anyway that's the way mickey always said it later mark was always the one in debt according to her even if she was working too helping to bring in the bacon and to drink it up as well if that isn't too mixed a metaphor rather sickening really if you try to make it come to life sort of like ants in your syrup or cockroaches on your shoes or mouse shit in your post grape nuts that happened to my husband just once back in mexico and he wasn't able to look a grape nut in the eye for twenty five years the way i can seldom do it either for that matter hardly do it blind try to feel my way back into the texture of those days rather too much really like raw bacon sliding down the throat swallow after continuous choking swallow like that old saloon spittoon joke only thicker and with its added piggy smell the bitter bile filled nausea of so many of those alcohol infused days or even days after when mark would drink raw eggs and mickey milk the texture definitely worsening as time went by

///because in that first ant time even if it was the brief period when mickey was at home playing the late forties or early fifties after the war mom before she went back to work then lost that job to drink and mark to death and seldom worked again her one big job lost the same way still the housekeeper was there for those evenings the image broke apart so happy times with the housekeeper if not the parents though there must have been some sundays it wasn't pretend the way you can see me walking down that sidewalk in a dress a cute little pink or white one i hadn't had time to become a tomboy yet even if the tendency was already present i'm sure what with the way i would examine all the small animals in the grass and not be afraid of any of them so curious just the way you can see my eyes popping out the giggle rising in my throat just there

///there i go stepping on the ants stepping on one small black ant as it makes its way with its small piece of grass or cracker crumb there it goes walking out the other side out from under my shoe just walking out all six little legs and the antennae going and there i am smiling maybe even clapping my hands in amazement i know it's something i talked about strange as it may seem not with adults but with tim or aj maybe even cherokee bill if he wasn't already gone and i know that sometimes i would just sit and look and try to figure it out my first memory and my first miracle *look at that the ant just crawls out the other side look look* or maybe i just said *look look ant* or even *ook ook oooook* and bounced up and down on the balls of my feet and wasn't into sentences yet just figured out the sentences to go with the thoughts later as i played with cherokee rode on his shoulders because he was still there while tim rode on mark's and of course it was a miracle it was *look look look at that* with the ant coming out the other side even if i couldn't talk with adults about it about anything really still just repeated what they said mark saying i could say anything and me repeating after him *sas kat che wan* dividing it up into syllables like that the way i still did when i first got to canada though of course i never knew back then it was a place i would one day drive across all endless green purple blue yellow colours we seldom got in new york

///while all the people from the new yorker where mark worked were so impressed with the perfect child in the perfect home they practically clapped for the magic trick the perfected illusion with me its high point its *piece de la resistance* what mickey always said mark wanted the perfect house and the perfect wife and the perfect children then added bitterly i've seen her do it over trendy california cuisine salads bought easily what with old twenty-six rented that house worth its pretty penny hurray for gentrification to bring her back into the world she missed so long *i'd've had to cut out my heart and my head and my cunt* she always says she answered him but i always let that one wash over me even if i know it's a perfect feminist parable like cooking in the kitchen then running up the stairs to get the food off the dumbwaiter in the butler's pantry since the house was designed for the middle class in the time of servants before there was just no place you could get good help these days certainly not cheap help certainly even mark's and mickey's illusions weren't enough for a staff and there was nothing like that little jog up the stairs to teach the modern housewife her place still by the time i heard that story nobody ever went into the dining room anymore except to steal the silver and i'd spent my years wishing mickey really had cut them out cut them all out cut herself right out of the picture because by then there was no housekeeper and no mark and for the longest time no cherokee and certainly no middle class nothing at all except hunger and that terrible nausea that she orchestrated with its symphony of nightmare colours eggplant purples and mustards and olive greens all mixed together with the solid bright knowledge i had gained in the dappled sunlight of that peaceful backyard not even from archy and mehitabel and typing so fast and without shift keys mark's favourites the talk of all those writers but from the ants from the ants

///my first memory and definitely a first miracle to know that if you just make yourself small enough small enough small enough all six legs and your antennae still moving you won't have to crawl into the dark cracks like the cockroaches under the bar stools of montero's or even the ice cream parlour or how your small son will admire them too in a restaurant in cozumel a society of cockroaches babies and adults small infant triangles just right for jumping in your tea from the edge of the lid as you open the jar angular adolescents and rotund adult lozenges walking briefly out of the cracks then scurrying at his first movement into dark nightmare corners you won't be like that trapped forever in that eggplant dark never to leave not if you just make yourself small enough condensed enough armoured enough with your antennae still waving then you can still go out in the light and even if they step on you and the dark comes the dark boxes or closets or bedrooms or basements where all the horror happened and continued to happen over and over then even if they step very hard when they grind their feet down it doesn't matter if you're in that dark space under the shoe that terrible space on the bed then still you won't be crushed you won't you won't no matter what the weight on you or the stabbing pain you won't you won't if you hold your breath and make yourself small your antennae still waving you won't you won't you won't be crushed

///something you never thought you'd need to know when you first had that memory walking along that small sidewalk in the sun fascinated with everything your shoes the ants the waving grass the heat through your pink sundress a golden child the gentle universe spun around who no one would ever hurt not anyone which is how you remember it when you weep over that baldur myth how we were all once children and we were all once golden and if we weren't we should have been the universe for one brief instant spinning around us never to hurt us never and yes i was that child i was the sun of some brief solar system i shone gold and that's how i remember it the times i take it beyond a formula for a first memory it's all there in the sun and the lesson too that i needed for years when the sun was only inside me and i was in the dark and the shoe had come down what seemed like forever i knew still

my antennae were waving in the light yes i did i did i really did and i thought of the ants and i knew i was still there and i couldn't be crushed that if you make yourself small enough small enough inside your own little exoskeleton no matter how many times they step on you or how hard no matter with what ferocity they grind their feet the way tim and i ran along the sidewalk stepping on the same ant over and over that's right no matter how hard or how often they do it you won't die you won't you won't you won't be crushed small enough hard enough smart enough you won't be crushed you won't you won't

///and only years later will i figure this thing out for real and probably then only because i can let myself do it i will have learned the lesson that i needed and be able to let it go i'll be long gone from that house except maybe in my mind because i keep going back even when i decide to read this stuff at some event or other i dream i've left it at home and home turns out to be old twenty-six so maybe that's what i'm doing going home to rescue that golden child that child who knew the sun in herself rescue that lesson i don't know but i dreamed i'd left this there and my car had stalled and i had to get out and walk and i couldn't get to the house no matter how fast i walked and there was mickey coming at me up the street in her old blue jeans safety pinned shut i just couldn't reach the door just see its twenty-six carved into the stone lintel but it doesn't matter all that much after all i will have taken what i needed to know even if i go back in my dreams and the colours are still the same eggplant purple and maroon still i'm out here and most of the time i know it the nightmares don't invade my days much anymore that's right i learned that lesson watching carefully and biting my tongue to stop from screaming hiding in the backs of closets with my antennae moving to create a time yes a time will come a time when i can laugh and discuss that memory all casual and sophisticated giggling and throwing out my hand the way those writers must have done at those garden parties while i concentrated myself not on repeating after them but on stepping on those ants

///what an amazing thing to think i will say *so wonderful*

///my first memory and my first miracle the ants were so different from the cockroaches you could step on them and nothing would happen and then the laughter mine and yours only i'll laugh till i cry because in the end no matter what i thought or said or whooped running after them or told myself captured and thrown down hurt and humiliated it wasn't size or silence or antennae that saved me that saved the ant the tears pouring down as i say this thing finally admit it my own tiny cache of survivor guilt this small luck won that i never fought for because in the end it wasn't how small the ant or how hard its brown black shell or even how it kept its clever antennae moving not your size or your shape or even the bright reflective beauty of that carapace shining its own image back to the world that could save you not my intelligence not my endurance not my perspicacity not my obedience that brought me through but just the unevenness of the ground a final accident the gift of pockmarked cement.

Walking through pigeons

by borough hall in their hundreds moving grey like the grey water passing by the docks rainbow necks like oil stains on grey river surface parting before me me parting the waters knee level black metal fences marking the shore they flow by is this the first then really first perfect urban brooklyn memory in shades of grey with colour shimmer in corner of vision is it memory without language thought or moral is it i would like that an alternate first memory is it let it be before it becomes this flow of pigeons my first metaphor.

No more step catch up step catch up on the stairs

We all start by doing that but do we remember when we stop i don't know except i do maybe not my first memory maybe just my first intellectual memory really leg passing leg on the stairs it was a concept i swear a concept like standing up only i knew it then sequenced it then from crawl to stand to step to walk to step catch up on stairs to leg passing leg if only i could sequence this all these headlines make them solid make them uninterrupted make them narrative make them go somewhere so maybe i should just eliminate this talk about it later sense memory and intellectual memory and body memory and remembering remembering which already means forget it could hardly be the first.

Towel rides along the top floor

is a tip top top floor memory when all was bright in the house and the linoleum was old and i can see the broken edges as it reached the doors and we reached its edge on our towels coming so fast pulled by cherokee or mark or mickey fast fast in our pyjamas after the bath and right before bed.

Folding sheets minuet

one two step to tim arms raised sheet corners in hand three four hand corners to tim step back running sheet through hands five six reach end of sheet lean back come forward again time after time time after time over and over crashing together folding is done folding is done folding is done laughter remains

///with lonely pillowcases piled on top.

Peewee weewee peepee

isn't a tongue twister it's another alternate first memory located there at the tip top of the house the tip top top floor with the towel rides and another happy one too like scattering pigeons or noticing their necks peewee weewee peepee isn't just a rhyme but a reason to laugh

///the way we once all laughed at sensation that time of being so young we took baths together me and tim though not so young it was still thought we needed supervision today parents probably would but everyone agreed back then kids our age wouldn't drown if left alone so it was like that eddie murphy line from whichever film has him laughing in the jacuzzi it must be *trading places* and there he is saying where i grew up we were so poor if we wanted bubbles in the bath we had to fart and you're giggling again even if it wasn't from the time you were so poor you could make those jokes it was from the time before that when mark and mickey were pretending to be so if not rich then middle class they could afford to leave you with the housekeeper or as far as baths went just left you alone while what you remember from that line is the joy of farting

///in the tub not the smell you didn't even notice the smell but the bubbles leaving your body to come to the surface of the tub the delight in a body that could produce bubbles and then there was the peeing too a body that could produce water peepee out of your peewee weewee or the weewee of the peewee with both you and tim doing it and both of you using that unisex weewee word so maybe this is a gentle exemplary tale for the middle class surely you could make it that way no large consequential memory though yes a memory maybe first memory of consequences or for that matter penis envy because of course there's the fact that equal opportunities for water producing weewees or not tim had much better aim and i don't know that he bragged about it just sort of showed off so there's this time he's peeing in the tub and what you do before you know it before you can even think connect cause to effect is you take his legs and kwham you lift them up

///over his head and there he is making water all right he's peeing in his face and you're smart enough to know you may love that bodily make water sensation and he may love his aim but love has got its limits and the face must be one so in the next motion you're up and out and stark naked running down the stairs so no this can't be first memory you're running much too fast there's no step catch up step catch up here but taking the stairs two at a time from the fourth to the third floor only he's pretty fast too and he's got the magic weewee the one with the aim so he doesn't chase you down the stairs he's just quick to the railing and peeing through the spindles down after you and maybe it is penis envy maybe it is penis envy after all because you can't pee

///back at him all you can do is laugh so hard your own unaimed pee is now dribbling down your legs but no no there's no trauma here no trauma at all from that golden shower or for that matter later love of strange peefart perversions but just a definite delight in alliteration and tongue twisters the peepee of the peewee weewee the weewee of the peewee goes peepee how much peepee could a peewee weewee peepee if a peewee weewee's peepee should fall

///frighteningly fast over stubborn staircases while the weewee of the other peewee goes peepee along lightening fast lunging legs assonance consonance alliteration that's all just a lesson in prosody and a certain tendency

///to very pedantically instruct your children in penises and vulvas and even urethras and when it's human to always call it piss.

When the promenade was new

and there were the first fences first rustoleum red then copper green higher than my head the knowledge of fenced in a good alternate first memory except i've always known the woolly bear caterpillars came first that was the rubble from which the promenade was built.

Sawdust on the dockside barroom floor

Maybe how the highway destroyed that made just dust all dust not sawdust.

First rainbows

not bright on pigeon necks but on the water shimmering circles ovals growing jagged edges holding eyes holding them first then holding them for years eyes not to sky but burrowing down below feet at edge of dock eyes shifting focus to lap of garbage against old creosote soaked wood piling cartons bottles leaves newspapers orange rinds bobble of turds diaphanous drift of toilet paper wiggle of used condoms white eels the neighbourhood called them eyes moving outward along water to there there where all the colours are shimmering in circles against dark grey surface your eyes sticking there held there while what fascinates most far more than pigeon necks is not was this the first but when did i know they were rainbows and wonder how it was my rainbows were round and besides that floating oil on water so there could be no pot of gold at end or for that matter escape to somewhere over.

Sometimes a free lunch

Definitely not that i'll never know forget that forget it all forget this direction of inquiry forget this please forget this.

Flight to Tallulah

It always comes back this one image this one act one hand reaching out into air into water it doesn't matter just one hand and blue behind blue in front thick with colour thin of explanation until there's that one day far into adulthood walking with tim on nutmeg mews and there i am my one hand reaching out no blue at all to the old carriage house its gaping wood plank doors reformed long ago into pristine windows in the first round of gentrification but even now bringing back the early smell of burned gasoline the look of old oil stains black as the limousines inside all us kids on the block imagined as instruments of flight the exit to elsewhen elsewhere first exit out of brooklyn so is it true is it did they once pick us up i ask tim a carriage house limousine just for us is it true that envied story of our flight did we fly did we flee up through suburbs into hills out of city my first time on green surrounded winding roads is it true did we did we

///did mark come down from kyoko's or did he send for us

///i repeat only to notice the answer's right there in my hand reaching out how could i forget watching it move not into air but in through water blue before blue behind voices hovering floating high above circling tallulah's oh dahling caw not just the literatti but the glitterati of the time clinking glasses yes it's true we'd fled through trees flown briefly through air to splash into the pool earned the right to brag to the whole neighbourhood though who knows if mark really did throw me in played out that sink or swim literary cliché of so many a children's story on this his final flight to the country drunk before lunch and afraid of flubbing his last stateside interview his tallulah bankhead profile for the new yorker before he let his fear force him into so much further flight flee fled fled and fly flew flown across the ocean to south africa to cover the pass book riots of fifty-two

///only to drink himself to death in some fleabag hotel

///so why not throw this overly articulate three year old child he calls his daughter into the pool after she so precisely pronounces saskatchewan parrots perfectly some cheeky phrase before tallulah's ironic eyes why not just forget completely his children are in the water and as for me why not forget it all forget the trip forget the bragging forget the old carriage house forget the later lunch forget even who rescued me if it was mark jumping into the pool in his clothes or someone else reaching in to pull me politely out maybe my brother next to me shoving me forward or just myself flopping that hand flopping that hand to create just enough pull to get me to the pool's edge that's right forget it all because somewhere inside i know already not in the hand reaching into blue but in the sick mustard yellow feeling clogging my lungs the red purple dread dragging me down the water entering nose and mouth that no matter if i make that edge it will always and forever only be the edge of flight no safety at all between fly flew flown and flee fled fled the hand reaching out blue before and blue behind to an exile i do not know from what but from which like mark's over half a century later and i can still see it on his face

///there is no return.

Nothing nice dice mice

If you have nothing nice to say say nothing writes itself across my brain far too often when i sit down at my computer more like an old-fashioned tickertape light display than a headline really bright red yellow green orange blue white bright lights forming letters gleaming glinting in the space of the mind as loud as times square though as far as headlines go even if those words wouldn't make the front page in three inch letters they would be good for lifestyles at a modest oh so nice inch or so if you have nothing nice to say say nothing dragging your eyes toward one or another advice column dear abby or some such if you have nothing nice to say say nothing always a good one to answer some question from the lovelorn or just the bitchy

///do i confront him with his infidelity her with her failure to dust and really that phrase can silence just about anyone or anything big or small and not just me as i stare at the letters expanding to become not a bright lit news flash or a modest headline among many but the only headline repeated again and again big and bigger its letters marching by as it substitutes its magnificent and yes oh so nice repeated generalization and yes i could say cliché but that wouldn't be very nice either would it especially as those nice say nothing words repeat themselves to take the place of all the specific bitchy nasty unnice things i definitely did have to say always have to say if you have nothing nice to say say nothing obscuring at least for the moment the fact that you know as well as i do the unnice to nice ratio in what anyone will ever have to say much less want to runs at least ten if not a hundred to one in fact you could make a very good case for that being the purpose of narrative

///narrative is for bitching for the telling of the unnice things that's right narrative is for gossip for figuring things out for strategizing for analysing those latter two words probably invented for pretending it's something nice you're saying nicely clean and perky anyway since what we have to analyse to strategize about is usually what went wrong not what went right and even if we do go for right it's just as likely it's to crow over what went wrong for someone else besides which it's the newest theory in the origin of language the gossip theory of language they call it gestures and grunts are for tasks for the great hunt the great gather language is for who didn't show and as for nice well the need to admire the beautiful sunset or the proposed mate's shiny fur or for that matter the mother in law's keeping of the hearth can be taken care of the bonobo way with genital rubbing far more if not pleasant pleasurable than oh wow beautiful man much less that modern long distance perversion the thank you note the little card now you can even do it e-mail probably use a template repeat yourself over and over i am thrilled overjoyed in awe of your terrific wonderful lovely extraordinarily tasteful gift that's right language originates not in affirmation but in negation that first telling of absence into presence it's a hymn a paean to the power of negative thinking without negative thinking we would have no language no language at all and really i do like that i do language and the story that pushes it into existence as the power of negative thinking

///so come forget with me that dollar a letter mark's sister our aunt nola would pay me throughout my later childhood years for the thank you notes i had to write for the so very nice clothes i didn't want she was my personal niceness trainer the one who ruled the if you have nothing nice to say say nothing department and department stores for that matter maybe if she'd raised that dollar a letter to five or even better to a dollar a line i would have gone for it more often instead of sinking into rebellious and sulky silence nasty greed will breed niceness every time so really there's no denying the power of that if you have nothing nice to say say nothing it will get you ahead if you just learn to deploy it right keep the nasty underhanded strategizing part to yourself if i'd come up with nice instead of nothing more frequently i might be rich today inherited all that money that went to the church which isn't really truly it isn't what makes me think it might be nice to say something nice insert nice into these headlines perky perky pastel polished nice and it's not altogether the fault of if you have nothing nice to say say nothing overwhelming all the other headlines the other stories either because whether or not i feel like bludgeoning my way through that shimmering morass as a writer i'd still put my money on the nasty even for getting rich no what makes me think about nice about making nice is that sometimes things really are

///nice if you know what i mean nice there really are nice things out there nice really nice just plain oh wow terrific thrilling linguistically incompetent fucking gorgeous fuck me oh wow man nice so instead of leaving it alone the way i should just shouting or shutting down that if you have nothing nice to say say nothing phrase inside my mind and finding another headline i find i want to rise to the challenge i want to do it make nice make nice make something some small story some description nice so i start the search for nice a specific something something nice find something

///nice

///and i do mean nice just plain nice jujubes nice jello and eating it through whole summers with peaches nice m&ms turkish delight saltwater taffy nice lifesavers nice generic hard candy in bright colours through cellophane wrappers nice sucking on sweetness in the mouth nice safe and sweet and insipid nice green and red and yellow and blue and nice nice nice ice slice dice rice nice the tongue slipping as the mind moves to my first book my very first book that ever so very nice book and i don't mean the first book i ever wrote or even read either just the first book i ever fell in love with because of course i didn't read at all back then someone read it to me or i just held it safe into the night of its bright colours sweet bright colours bold bright colours hard candy bright colours nice bright colours the primary the complementary colours the yellow and blue and red and green of *goodnight moon* and with them can't you see them feel them taste them ripe off the tongue the first rhymes my first rhymes gooey soft or sickly sweet or sourly sharp or just plain nice nice spice splice lice mice vice on your tongue

//bears and chairs and clocks and socks until you could expand on them yourself lairs and hairs and tears rocks and locks and docks without ever having to get to any headlines much less the stories hidden in them savour instead those nice things to say nice nice mice ice dice make them up leap from the moon to the spoon in the bowl full of mush which rhymed with the brush under the lamp which might have reminded you of camp or that would come later when you could read that book yourself an ever growing legend in your thoughts even if you only would ever get to go once and hate it and damp and stamp and ramp your mind expanding beyond the pages but held in the bright sharp perfectly delineated edges of that world that calm contemplative bright coloured slow-moving world forget that this is a nothing nice to say say nothing attempt not to narrate the nasty avoid instead all narration and just say whatever you can pick up and touch whatever you can savour and limit with your tongue whatever enters through the senses the shape the words the worlds in words themselves like hard candy sticky toffee who cares if what you intended to tell was why the invention of utterance occurred in that well let me tell you the reason she didn't get her gathering finished is he tried to eat the kid today

///forget that debate entirely forego all the headlines stories anecdotes narrations for bears and chairs and kittens and mittens balloons and moons houses and mouses tripping giggling slipping off your tongue go with the flow the glow the crow of language language language language utterance unto itself just the vibration in the throat as you let go and mow and show and doe and what do you know chuckling to yourself because there's this thing about rhymes repeating rhymes and crimes and dimes and times one after the other that either makes you laugh or makes you crazy though never lazy or for that matter into a daisy which maybe makes you start to think about that too so that you can easily drift back to story in how it was the one thing that would make us laugh to pass the time and dime and slime mile after mile after smile after tile in the car the truck the camper except if our young son was along when only after a couple of minutes he'd start to scream out loud and shroud and crowd stop stop stop

///and mop and hop and slop and bop and crop we would answer no no no he would shout slow and go and row and hoe we would answer until he finally decided to do it himself cast himself adrift with us in that world of friendly or ferocious linguistic possibilities after i told him about my secret middle name why i never tell anyone my middle name sarah m you'll never guess what for i tell him not mary or myra or melinda it's sarah maloney the name's maloney and then when he looks at me blankly and says what's so bad about that i go buh buh buh and he says baloney baloney baloney starting to shout and he's right of course because three syllable rhymes are few and far between and there were years of it a childhood not of insipid baloney sandwiches but of ferocious baloney fights maloney baloney maloney baloney maloney baloney up and down the block and maybe too of mothers telling those same kids hush hush like a *goodnight moon* rabbit if they had nothing nice to say say nothing only maloney baloney must have sounded nice enough to them positively music to their ears when they saw me turn purple scream louder much louder than my son stop stop stop i think it's something tim's older friend aj invented probably long before mark maybe before even cherokee left maloney baloney maloney baloney so that even if it's just the one possibility it sure makes up for there not being more or sarah having none must be as bad as mark and bark and dark or lee and sea and tea and pea though perhaps not as bad as that other pee or for that matter art and fart though the trick of rhymes was that even with maloney baloney ringing in my ears and tears and smears i could still go there go right there so easily to the safety of those first rhymes even if later i would tear once more up the street true enough so very fleet on lightning feet threatening and often enough successfully to absolutely beat instead of meet and greet anyone who might ever repeat that maloney baloney full of baloney

///ever again so let's forget that brief confession refuse to repeat it even to ourselves any more fingers to lips hush hush and a bowl full of mush and

back to just savour the flavour of those one syllable first rhymes of that first book and our thirst for that rush slush gush crush mush so that it won't matter if we had no idea what mush was the mind the brain leaping from rock to rock and clock to clock and sock and lock and dock picking them up and putting them down sucking at them sweet like those hard candies balls or lozenges small bright lollipops or multicoloured twisting all day suckers forget to think of the hidden bubbles that will suck into sharp edges to cut your tongue the acid in the sugar that will dissolve the skin of your lips run away run away to something that won't betray the ease sneeze please of those small rhymes mittens and kittens and nearly writtens doing it still with your mind with your fingers at the keyboard with no thought to which words you would have known then which were far into the future just feeling the texture of that mental movement chairs and bears and cares and the stairs you climb up to that one big horsehair filled leather covered armchair in the study at old twenty-six to pick up that book and feel the rhymes over and over and rover and clover and white cliffs of dover or moving to mickey and mark's bedroom book in hand to look into its gas fireplace warm and glowing and certainly showing itself so utterly identical to that *goodnight moon* room if not in its red and green then in the cone of its light the warmth of its fire and spoon and moon and mush and hush and cow and how and sow that
52 perfect bright room green and lean but never mean that repeated that scene as the colours just got darker and darker but never starker its gentle colours moving into grey to pray to say that's right good night to kittens and mittens and bears and chairs and noises everywhere so that at some point of grey you could believe that the yellow and white of mickey's of mark's room contained no gloom was that *goodnight moon* room believe that you too could snuggle down with that bedded baby bunny that that was where you slept with the old lady rabbit sitting and knitting the big yellow mellow bedroom even had a rocker and a brush if never the unidentified mush and mickey never knit anything not even a long an interminable scarf the way you would in sixth grade so you could believe it too whether or not it was ever true yours was that calm world that never said boo or shoo or who's cuckoo that had stars instead of bars that closed at three and lee and pea

///in the morning so that you might even keep doing it time after rhyme as you instruct your son on rhymes and limes and dimes and chimes and remember how you imagined yourself into that perfect world of that red green yellow blue room as if you had shifted through mickey's mirror in those through the looking glass years of that bright good night book and of all the stories not held in the hand to be rhymed in the mind but read out loud by mostly mark just so stories and alice stories nice if slightly twisted stories nicely said so that by the time mark had walked through his own looking glass to the permanent bar bye and goodbye in the sky and the bar guys barflies had moved into the house i had developed enough imagination to want to be there always inside my hush mush bears chairs book so what i'll tell lee next is how i would get there if not the reason no more baloney maloney but how and cow and prow to ward off the attack of the mad and sad and glad rhymers beat and sheet and fleet them at their own game and frame and shame and name offer some practical advice and mice and rice not if you have nothing nice to say say nothing but a way to keep on talking instead of balking when we start this rough tough stuff that after all has kept us going and showing and flowing along the road and goad the toad mile after smile after guile in the car the truck the camper so what he should do is use the alphabet trick and slick and sick and brick after all i do and goo and brew and stew even to get to sleep so deep better than counting sheep at night that's right you run through and blue and phew the alphabet i say just go and slow and blow through the alphabet so that whatever anyone says he just has to hop and bop and slop and skip and rip and slip and jump and bump and rump his way through the alphabet a good trick and brick and stick and slick way i thee pray to do it to find a rhyme and slime and crime to prevent having to shout

///out and sprout and rout you lout stop stop stop and mop and top you can just look through the alphabet in your mind you don't usually pay and bay and day and fey and bray attention to the vowels since initial vowels change the sound of the ones after them so if you start with stop you skip that a and go to bop and cop nothing for d so skip e to fop no g so hop skip i no j to lop and mop no n so pop no q or r to sop and top skip u no v and stop it right there so you don't have to explain the without papers of wop and you know there's nothing left with x or y or z though you can go then to the consonant clusters you even use that word this is you at your language teacher best or worst and pick up the stop even the stop stop stop you started with as well as shop and chop and drop and crop and prop and strop though that last's certainly obscure you have no idea if he's ever seen one but still the method's great not just for sharpening straight razors but the mind and blind and kind with its rhymes and besides when you're desperate you can just do it without meaning to keep the ball and small and gall that is words in your court drown and bown and cown and down the others out rout sout slout grout gout pout nought nought nought this the best and vest and rest and chest and slest way of all to fight blight sight right shite mad dad rhymers just do it yourself i say and there's the two of us and bus and cuss shouting so tom can't even talk until lee doesn't want anymore to stop stop stop and bop and lop and crop so we're doing it too and boo and coo and goo and choo and hoo

///eeeeeee and maybe that's when suddenly there's the rabbit a real rabbit not a *goodnight moon* rabbit this time and in our headlights too only it's in our own back alley just as we're pulling in still rhyming and there it is the giant snowshoe hare half brown half white it must be spring or fall white head white stomach brown ears brown body and who knows what does it all that grabbit nabbit rabbit sunny honey bunny rhyming chiming miming crashing in your head but something is sucking you down some rabbit hole or through some mirror because you're remembering how and sow and cow you used those rhymes and dimes and limes not just to fall asleep but to disappear from that yellow and chequered kitchen downstairs or even that upstairs room when its yellow wasn't any longer mellow and its purple rhymed with snurple or gurple or burple something that made no sense but sounded grating and ugly in the ears that you wanted to cover but could not instead tried and lied and died to get out through and blew and slew that gold and mould and white and bright mirror mirror on the wall of that room above its mantelpiece where mark no longer leans just so with just so stories now as the jackrabbit dashes away ever faster no bunny hop there no sweet soft encounter no green and red blue and yellow *goodnight moon* room greets you but instead as you step down your knee buckles and you lurch against the truck and before you can say cherokee trickster because of course that's who rabbit is rabbit is the cherokee trickster and not of rhyme or even alphabet invention but world making and there you are trying to escape to dash away yourself again your other favourite way always to get into another world not rhyming sliming diming but putting together ideas only this time you can't even think about what relationship there must be between cherokee rabbit and that other trickster of the southern united states of african american not native descent but made equally cute by the white mind bre'r that's bro' to you late twentieth early twentyfirst century folks who don't know that properly read upper class north american english pronunciation once failed to contain terminal r's bro' rabbit and his damn briar patch and catch and snatch and don't throw me in but you're in already far too deep

///by the time you see the jackrabbit's tail disappearing down the alley this is no bunny you've come to encounter it's not that prim old lady no trickster bone in her shushing body it's the trickster himself but which one you might wonder as you notice you're in a different room altogether a darker starker room and the table does not hold a bowl full of mush or hush but just a lamp and a newspaper clipping and the woman rocking has no rabbit ears or even knitting she's rocking you in her lap sitting on the bed there's no room for a rocker next to her small small table it's mary the housekeeper with her tightly curled grey hair and her cocoa brown skin who is maybe about to leave because she's not being paid or because she can't stand the bars the fights the drinking anymore even if mark and mickey accused her of drinking herself or maybe it's you taking shelter up there at night and she doesn't have any just so stories on her mantel with the mirror or even a mirror or a mantel at all so what she's showing you is a newspaper clipping and maybe it's in her scrapbook or maybe it's just there on its own and yes it's under the lamp on the table and rat bites baby that newspaper clipping headlines rat bites baby

///rat bites baby in harlem right there on the table you're looking at instead of the brush and the bowl full of happy unknown mush there is this photo whose content is too easy to know your hand going toward the exact place on the baby's thigh where you can see the bites of those rat teeth and you don't really know why you're there in this room with this just so so very so story that so not comfortable even if just so story not like mary's lap just so comfortable even in memory as you hear her trying to explain so maybe the truth is she didn't show you that story that photo you found it yourself opening her scrapbook only it seems so much more talismanic than that you're sure she held this story deep so deep maybe it was the kid of someone she knew even if she didn't live in harlem she lived with you and when you went to visit her friends or relatives it was out into brooklyn along myrtle avenue under the el you've seen that area if you've seen *ghost* so maybe she's telling that story because she's leaving and it's a way of saying listen little white kid because how was she to even know about cherokee bill a trickster too in his own way or for that matter the black politician cherokee bill said was tim's father after all what was that about the attempted abortion the timing of the pregnancy with mark in europe but who cares about those rumours or whether in fact mary knew them all and their truth too the way servants so often do so whether it's listen little white kid or listen little off-white kid it's still a way of saying look things may get worse at twenty-six nutmeg mews but it won't get like this picture there's always worse than what this house can produce the future she probably already saw it bringing forth which might or might not be another way of saying

///so if you have nothing nice to say say nothing just remember rat bitten babies and say nothing say nothing and survive which is maybe a special lesson from her own life now that she's leaving tired of mickey and mark and no money and solving problems that aren't hers and doing it for the off-white kids just doesn't cut it so maybe you can see in that image of that clipping how there have always been two lights in that house two lights to take shelter in and how you knew right then that pretty soon they would both be gone and you can see them both blinking out the lights that were as close as you could get in that house and back then that house was your only shelter to that red green room of *goodnight moon* the light that lit mary's scrapbook or the one that lit mark's just so story voice so that all you would have left from that moment to create a shelter of your own would be your rhymes and chimes and grimes only now too standing in your alleyway regaining your balance about to enter the small backyard of your own grownup house the bounding jackrabbit already out of sight you see something you've never seen before about that room and zoom and gloom gloom gloom you so loved in your imagination there's a hole instead of a bowl under the bright yellow lampshade of that *goodnight moon* mush brush hush light too and even if there still seems to be an old lady in the room maybe it's mickey or maybe it's mary or maybe you've whooshed down the hole and bunny honey is a passenger on a subway in the same yellow bright light in a seat across from you whispering in a syrupy social worker voice hush little girl hush but suddenly you're sick to your stomach and not on mush or even brush but maybe on that hush hush if you have nothing nice to say say nothing and of course it's not happening of course it never happened

///not quite like this not ever not quite just almost and toast and host and what you know or maybe just feel what makes that hole in that room grow in your mind is how in some way it's always been there or been there back at least to that rat bites baby moment that sheltering with mary moment there has been that hole in those times you would be playing at rhyming or at climbing at looking or at cooking at something nice anyway something beautiful the smell of garlic and onions frying chili peppers roasting a sunset over the narrows or the rockies the sensation in the fingers of hands looking for a grip on building face or rock the gentle lap of ocean or birdsong of some kind maybe even a visualization of same something so very very nice to say or to see or to eat or to touch or to smell like thinking you were reaching out for those cookies under laughing gas at the dentist when they tried to put your front tooth back in after you knocked it out falling from the backyard fence those cookies that were this or foreshadowed by this the same hole growing maybe in the middle of the cookies as they would start to crumble because those cookies would appear on your wall your eyes open in the middle of the night to crumble and rot before your eyes while voices ordered you to get out get out out out the cookies coming back to you often enough over the years when you were about to eat taste that perfect brownie that chili con carne or right in the middle of making love in that nice nice more than nice more near absolutely perfect squeezed eyed moment before orgasm offending your lovers so deeply when you suddenly shook your head and not in oh oh oh oh oh but in stop stop stop stop stop stop like your son only it isn't rhymes or dimes though maybe crimes of some sort anyway as just stop stop stop

///you have to stop as the cookies start not just to crumble and fall apart but to rot and shrivel up with always these voices behind them somehow both sharp and flat at once like a shovel grating on concrete as they laugh at you laugh at you laugh at you your hands going to your head to stop hearing them only you never can so you learn to breathe deep calm the desire to move in your shoulders learn to hide the rotting horror in your eyes hide it all from your lovers or even from yourself the way you do in that room in memory or with your son when you've started with brush and gone to bush only it doesn't rhyme no matter how it's spelled so then the next one is hush as you walk up the sidewalk to your door forgetting the jackrabbit the colour if not shape shifting snowshoe hare long gone from the laneway as there's that sickness again and it's the rabbit lady who's turning to you and whispering hush

///hush hush hush hush hush really hush because the next word that rhymes is lush and suddenly she's laughing her finger still at her mouth but her mouth wide and there's lots of teeth hush hush and then you hear a giggle a high flat giggle and then those sharp cutting monotones those rotted cookies voices again as she says hush hush and giggles heeeeeee heeeeee long like a cicada calling hush hush mickey's a lush heeeeee heeeeee pass it on heeeeee heeeee hush hush pass it on mickey's a lush hush hush mickey's a lush and the huuuuuush gets longer and longer the giggle gets flatter and shriller her teeth get sharper and pointier her mouth redder and redder as she laughs at you laughs at you they're all laughing at you all those voices hush hush mickey's a lush mickey's a lush hush hush mickey's a lush pass it on pass it on and maybe it's the social worker type on the train or it's all the kids at school the time they pulled down your pants hush hush mickey's a lush hush hush as they laugh at you all laugh at you but more than anything it's that you can't get away from yellow light and shame shame in that yellow room and even if you can briefly rhyme and chime and dime and grime to move and groove and behoove yourself to that red and green safe *goodnight moon* room the yellow light will always take you back to eggplant purple rotten cookies in the stomach to that other yellow light that's always been there in that laughter that less than mellow yellow light and laughter that can follow you into the most beautiful the nicest of places things so nice you want to say them like walking through the woods by turtle lake coming out again from the depth of the green on green trees and purple shadows warm red berries and turtles on logs into sunlight depth of nice nicest of nice and still in the middle of nice of nice to say as nice as ice cream passionfruit chocolate banana vanilla on the tongue and ready to say it to hum it to sing it even there at turtle lake it's the voices again coming out of the rustling leaves hush hush mickey's a lush heeeeee heeeeeee pass it on voices

///laughing voices now less flat less high it's men's voices and you're in the kitchen with its yellow walls and you're *goodnight moon* young and you can hear them laugh laugh at you because mickey's staggering and laughing herself that giggle jiggle laugh that always makes you put your hands over your ears and her lipstick isn't perfect like getting ready to go out as mark leans on the mantel it's smeared and she's about to be out cold or maybe not it doesn't really matter to them they just want you to act like her with her skirt up around her waist and she's laughing at you they're laughing at you everyone is laughing at you laughing at you laughing at you and now it's in that room the big bedroom and it ought to be comfortable and it's not it's not at all and maybe you start rhyming diming sliming to not hear that laughter only it comes back to hush shush lush mush and the cookies are rotting and you've got to stop making love touch along your skin burns down there it burns and you need to get away and they're laughing at you they're laughing at you hush hush mickey's a lush mickey's a lush mickey's a lush and gush and crush and you want to put your hands to your ears and mickey's a lush a lush a lush and then this time as you enter your house still remembering the jackrabbit and the rhyming chiming liming that took you back into that green and red that blue and yellow room and once more you're there only it's overly bright and the yellow sickness is back in your mouth your stomach and hush shush mickey's a lush and you have to rush for the washroom the way you did the outhouse at turtle lake when the voices came out of the leaves and heeeeeee heeeeee hush lush rush lady bunny still has her finger to her mouth hush hush mickey's a lush and she's laughing even louder than all those other voices and her snout is getting longer and her teeth are getting even sharper as a tail uncurls from under her dress and look at that red smeared around her lips is it smeared mickey lipstick or where her mouth has met flesh you don't know and what is that photo doing there under the lamp where a bowl of mush should be and why is it blowing in the air now to land on the bed how come the rabbit baby isn't there the photo is

///that old yellow and purple black newspaper rat bites baby picture has taken baby bunny's place taken it as he's crawled out from under the covers not only to turn around to say good night to the three bears sitting on chairs or the brush and the mush but gotten all the way out of the bed and out the window out your window out mickey's window out mary's window to greet the moon and not the cow jumping over it and to slide down the drainpipe the way you always wished to do whispering hush hush mickey's a lush hush hush hush until he can laugh it out loud free in the backyard hopping lurching leaping away from side to side like the jackrabbit down your laneway out onto the street only moments before rush rush mickey's a lush rush rush rushing from side to side place to place the way you always do your whole life rushing from place to place and what's on that bed in that room now is that photo that rat bites baby photo only the photo is you it's that photo where mary holds you up laughing yourself laughing baby laughing at the things you can't know yet as the lady comes toward you with her long tail and long snout and out out out only you can't get out this time you can't you're not bunny light fleet on your feet as she whispers hush hush mickey's a lush and she laughs at you laughs at you just the way those men did before the pain came and there are her teeth her big rat teeth someone's big rat teeth about to bite into your thigh and lie and die rush rush to mickey's a lush hush hush only no one's hushing except you your hands over your ears in your own toilet you can still hear them there they're all laughing and you realize suddenly that everyone knew all along or most of them did because as long as mickey's a lush and no one says it you don't say it because it's not nice as long as if you have nothing nice to say say nothing rules anything can be done to you heeeeee heeeeeee mickey's a lush hush hush they've known all along so hush hush mickey's a lush and brush and mush and rush and gush and quick find something nice to say and bray and pray to say now to cover this up even there in your bathroom you want to cover it up again you do cover it up again just the way you want to right now at your keyboard you want to go to a green red room with a calm and balm grey and day knitting bunny a striped pyjama sleeping bunny all quiet good night noises everywhere quiet quick hush lush gush rush surely you can find it of course you can you know you can and ran and ban you always can only this time

///you won't not can't but won't because this time you may still be grateful for that green room that *goodnight moon* comforting book those rhymes and dimes and limes that took you away from crimes but not grateful enough you might have needed it but it's still a trap and lap and snap and crap that's right and might and light it's a trap and you know it and that's the way it's always been and maybe somewhere inside yourself you've always known even when you loved it said rhymes like prayers that room was a trap maybe just the best trap of all the traps you could have fallen into those nights or those moments of memory but still a trap lady rat was always in that room and always biting you sucking your blood or your strength sucking away all your energy the energy you needed to stay there as your world your whole world turned to grey and rotted like cookies and was sucked down that hole the beauty sucked like the substance the flavour from the cookies until they would break up crumble disappear until you felt like a shadow of yourself as you watched yourself walk down the street no more bright colours anywhere as the rat lady stuck her head through from the hole she had chewed in the wall or the wallpaper of that horror filled yellow purple smurple gurple rotten cookies room and so much energy going into keeping her keeping what she represented contained hidden just so you could remember there was somewhere there had been somewhere a red green shelter room even a rat bites baby in mary's scrapbook shelter room that contained something of yourself enough of yourself to keep going to go on from what's been hidden to believe that there was more than what's been hidden those laughing men the rat lady the laughing mickey offering you to them as you would sit and grit and hit and bit and nit burp and slurp and nice rice mice dice moon spoon goon any rhyme at all in your mind to get away only to discover that even when you keep them nice and rice and cute little mice you would never dice or slice or let rot amid snot that unbeknownst to you there has been a price lady rat has insinuated herself into all the nice things

///in that room or underneath sunsets running along beaches inside a new dress or shoes or underwear your first bra lady rat eats them into grey from the inside out and you'll never write thank you letters because you'll never know what you're thanking anyone for if it's gratitude for love or for abuse because you don't know the story if you have nothing nice to say and you always say nothing you'll never know the story you'll only have rotting cookies crumbling away because you can't know the story if you only know the rhyme and time and dime then what's the crime you'll never know the reason and season and what of the treason if you never attach one thing to another word to word not in rhyme and mime but in syntax follow the narrative out of that room unrhymed words like glowing stones guiding you so forget the nice things to say forget forget the feel of the nice words on your tongue forget even remembering the nice things much less saying them because maybe they were never really nice rice mice after all so you didn't have to tell mickey or aunt nola the things were or if they were really nice and you really loved them lady rat ate them away anyway from the inside out so they were no longer yours so every time you feel something nice at the end of your tongue ready to be said you see that it's hollow it doesn't belong to you so you can count yourself lucky plucky sucky ducky those rhymes didn't stick you in that room forever and that when they take you back there together with the high flat voices and the rotting cookies you can still get away shouting stop stop stop no matter what your lover says because mickey invited lady rat into that room the way she invited those men into the house even if hush mush lush you would never tell her so that now when you go looking for the nice things behind the headlines sure they are there all the nice things are grey and hollow so forget if there's nothing nice to say say nothing which rhymes with nothing absolutely nothing you may have noticed and only nothing and go back to the power of negative thinking and stay out and lout and shout

///of that green red room for as long as you can and ban and ran as you tell the story as best you can and then when you've done it when you've told it 61
and told it and told it told it until you can remember it as a separate entity out there where you can examine it from all sides the way language was invented to do you can pick it up and put it down and marvel at it or leave it alone and if it ever gives you something nice to say and bray and clay and day or if you ever find something nice somewhere else you'll wait with it inside your mouth or your abdomen deep inside where it can't be stolen by bullies or thank you notes or lady rats bringing eggplant rotten cookie nightmares where it can't be eaten away from the inside out but is just itself all small and concentrated and you'll keep it there till you can feel it you won't throw it away in finding something nice to say to say something when what you have to say is something else altogether that involves rats and laughter and violation of the flesh and that will allow you to keep that nice thing as itself just itself you won't plant any rats inside the way the world of that green and red room the world of that book is inside its cover on your desk and you'll be able to go there only for itself where lady bunny still abides and baby bunny has not left through the window and you'll only ever say nice things those wonderful nice things that yes even you can find often as not when you're not sitting and looking for them and you'll say them when and if and only if your smile forces them out of your mouth amid rhymes and dimes and times or

sunset oh wow silences and you really want to say them and otherwise we'll go back to that other old saw not if you have nothing nice to say say nothing but say what you mean and mean what you say no matter how mean

///or lean or green or keen or freein' it is so the niceness has a place to go because you've forced at least a bit of the meanness out so if you have nothing nice to say say something else tell the story until you have enough room inside for the nice things to take root and grow and be really nice and not just a cliché with rats and rotten cookies inside so say nothing nice until you're ready just tell the story or say nothing at all or crawl or bawl or brawl run with the rhymes and the dimes and the limes and the crimes in your mouth but don't stop at the words don't stop at all but connect the dots and rots and lots and cots and snots and pots and keep on telling until the end

///and send and spend and bend

///and rat and cat and sat

///and hop and flop and stop

///and stairs and bears and chairs

///and good night maloney baloneys making noises everywhere.

Good night sleep tight don't let the bedbugs

bite that's right bite there's another great children's rhyme for you and i remember it too i remember mary mark mickey saying that i thought it was intolerably cruel really i did intolerably cruel to say that to a child make them think of biting bugs all night long and believe me they do bite that is i've had bedbugs by now back then i had no idea what they were but it still seemed nasty so i'm sure i said it just like that intolerably cruel oh that rhyme that rhyme is just so intolerably cruel and curled up my mouth and my nose and it wasn't necessarily that i was smarmy nice oh we don't say those cruel bedbugs things to children in this house like the n word being refused for the catching of toes in favour of tiger even if tigers don't have any that rhyme's how you could tell you were middle class in our neck of the woods eenie meenie miney how moe middle class am i in that place where all the folks around who someone might plausibly identify by the n word were likely working for that someone in his her house and it would hardly do for the children to insult those people who were taking care of them especially if the parents were up in harlem listening to billy holiday not like the working class irish kids whose parents would still say it certainly allow the n word uncorrected into that rhyme that's who taught it to me there was no servant in their houses to stare them down or if there was it was sister mother grandmother a servant too but in the house of someone across the bridge the upper east side sutton place park avenue working not for the middle not even for the upper middle but for the upper upper class for the people who wouldn't hire coloured that's the way they said it no n word just we wouldn't hire coloured i heard them myself not in any of the progressive schools i was scholarshipped to people there might do it but never say it just the way they so seldom found any worthy scholarship students of any colour but white this was from the parents in the schools we played volleyball with then visited their servanted houses and oh no we would never hire coloured overheard often enough so don't let anyone tell you that blue collars around red necks are the mark of racism not hiring coloured was a mark of true upper class white pride you imported your servants from ireland or some more current underprivileged european place had done for as long as there'd been family money at least a hundred years maybe now you might grab them out of brooklyn but you never hired coloured so maybe it was mother sister grandmother great grandmother but someone in those families on nutmeg mews had come over on the boat the plane to work in the houses of others or maybe you could take their attitude back all the way to colonial beginnings and the purposeful separation of the desperate immigrant who had sold himself herself for seven for fourteen years for life but whose children would be free from those whose children would not no matter if they were the master's own the back of solidarity in slavery broken way back when by always giving the whiter group a one up they would never forget or forgive in the fear of becoming n word loving white trash but hey

///this isn't sociology class it's just me doing what i always will if you give me half a chance going all intellectual the same way and for the same not rhyme but reason i would say those words like that intolerably cruel intolerably cruel call that children's rhyme those children's rhymes intolerably cruel biting bedbugs and catching toes no matter whose and a lot more of them for that matter rocking cradles and breaking boughs ringed rosies and falling down on your posy-full pockets humpty dumpty in all his pieces while curling my lip to turn myself as best i might into an intolerable snot as the family fell inexorably that's a good word too isn't it almost as good as execrably which was true of us too at least according to the neighbours as we fell down the social ladder past the working class irish past the newer italians past the most recently arrived denizens of the hispanic rooming houses where i visited with paul garcia though maybe levelling off before reaching crazy mary down the block who all the kids regardless of class creed or national origin riled with our teasing walking by or the mad prostitute in the corner house who regularly threw all her clothes out the window of her small room under the eaves on the fifth floor believing there to be a fire screaming the aga khan gave me that the aga khan gave me that dress after unlovely dress after hat after stockings after girdle after shoes while all the neighbours laughed intolerably cruel intolerably cruel i would say to myself and try to believe i just meant that rhyme intolerably cruel as we became a rooming house ourselves and there was no longer even a nickel for penny candy and if you were invited into the back room of the candy store you weren't really getting it for free no food on the table and it was rats not bugs i dreamed of biting rats like the ones of the rat bites baby in harlem pictures mary showed us from the papers to note maybe like the difference between indentured and intergenerational servitude that there was still further to fall and make me practice even harder to be an intolerable snot the best middle class intolerable little snot i could be despite the hardened snot under my unwiped snotty nose i thought it grew there not a finger but a nose nail i really did i no longer had a memory of its absence as i learned to fight and wear my dirty blue jeans with an altogether different hey you yeah i mean you only a girl say it again and i'll kick your ass sneer intolerably cruel an indoor pastime along with inexorably and execrably practiced for the days i could deploy it again let it trip once more off my tongue intolerably cruel intolerably cruel straight from the mouth of the middle class babe i could pretend to be in that school across the bridge intolerably cruel from an intolerable snot of a bright girl designing at least that one piece of her identity sculpting her lips her words her memory to accommodate the real reason for her denigration of that rhyme those rhymes oh we don't say those things around here the sure knowledge that those words that diction repeated over and over instead of rhymes deep into the night would dictate her escape

///from her world's intolerable cruelty.

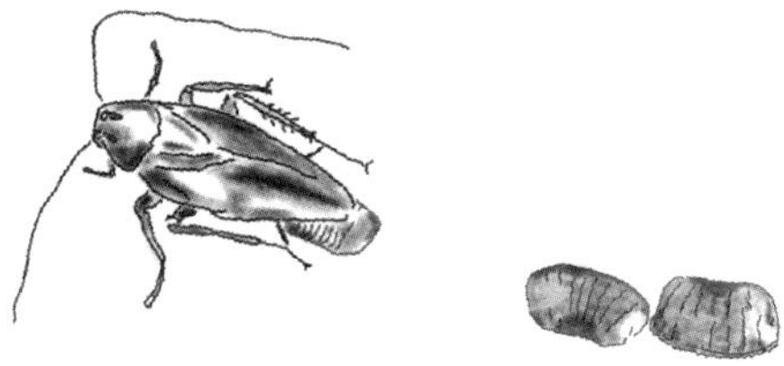

Brown

So i don't know if this happened before or after mary showed me that photo of the rat bitten baby in harlem which after all had if not more than one side more than one side effect besides its being for years the picture i measured horror against it was also somehow an act of utter revelation a gift of some sort that bound me to her in solidarity something i could never forget that carried me together with bill's stories into the civil rights movement just the way this incident did only this was so very different more like first lesson in white guilt far stronger than who or what should be caught by its toe that day i turned to mark or was it mickey and there's a part of me remembers it on a bus but i don't think it happened on a bus i think that what happened on the bus was that i was riding down to myrtle avenue and most of the faces around me were brown sort of the *café con leche* to ebony spectrum rather than the milk to *café con leche* of our neighbourhood so that i came home and i said to mark or mickey i think it was mickey why is mary's skin brown i said or maybe i said why is mary brown and then there was this quick looking away we don't say that they said or one of them did we say negro mary is a negro and maybe later much later during the sixty-eight olympics when the people i translated for from sports illustrated objected to those athletes on that podium with their black power salute and the word black said what was this calling themselves black they weren't black they were sort of tan to brown at best what was wrong with negro i would look at them kind of hard and say *negro negro* pronouncing it first in spanish and then in portuguese it means black and maybe even add something about pickaninnies being *pequeninos* the portuguese word for children that it was all just slave trade history we didn't want to see with our negro euphemism but that certainly wasn't what it was when i asked that question didn't even know my spanish colours from paul garcia yet though that brief moment without doubt got me into looking for contradictions maybe put me on the road to textual to linguistic analysis i don't quite know what it was that made me aware i had stumbled onto something big there's no retrofitting in that though there might be if i went on to say looking for silly childhood ironies how after all when i asked why my skin had brown spots they didn't tell me i was a freckle or that i had negroes it might be funny but it would trivialize the feeling that there was something in that leap from description to category closing down my attempt to describe a simple fact like red hair into a category of being that opened up this huge space put up this high wall something in the tone of their voices or in how they looked away that yes i could feel it you see i could feel it something like looking down the very long barrel of a very big gun five hundred years of history nestled somewhere in that space smaller than any freckle larger than a quarter of a million lynchings between the five letters of brown and the five letters of negro lay without my knowing what it was the entire history of american racism.

Raw potatoes

Is that a famine irish thing loving potatoes raw it can't be not during the famine anyway not with that one thing mark said about them i like to think of it as a secret message before he went away a kind of communion he never understood himself as he cut the potatoes and gave us each a flat round watery waferlike piece before he threw the rest into the pot and made his pronouncement just a little he said a small piece delicious but there's no nutritional value none at all what makes me imagine liquid raw potato goodness the first post potato famine luxury you can just see it can't you how it might start some irish canadian irish american potato peeling professional first job off the boat popping a slice into her into his mouth thinking not just of cheating the boss but murmuring mouth full of raw i can if i want if i want i can knowing there was no need anymore to think of what could be absorbed from that tiny sliver not caring for calorie or vitamin or any percentage at all of any daily requirement that's right i can if i want if i want i can maybe that's what writing is all about too i like to think so i can if i want if i want i can that's the way it is for me anyway now that i'm not starving not any more not for food or for affection or for safety or for a way into the world so i can tell it raw or cooked with or without salt or spices or for that matter nutritional value no requirements here daily or otherwise i can if i want if i want i can so who cares if the first time i tried cutting those raw potatoes on my own i opened my thumb and saw the white of bone and it was my own blood i ate raw on that slice of life it's not important it's still my choice that must have been their hidden meaning the raw potato message mark himself never got if i want i can i can if i want maybe there's no more to this storytelling just i can if i want i will because i can even if it doesn't change the facts or all the times it's hurt all the time it hurts this cutting or this telling or maybe they're the same and i can still see those potatoes off white and moist on dark pine stained cutting board against silver glint of knife with black handle and i love them i do fresh and oozing like nothing else in the world and better than most better than apple or jicama no fruit to match that first water fresh taste of first off the boat irish luxury eat your potatoes raw tell your stories raw no nutrition necessary i have that luxury too now raw raw enjoy enjoy.

Streetwalking

sometimes and it can be just anywhere a headline will write itself across my brain to be added to the list a headline that is just so obvious so very obvious so very this is such an important memory obvious that the truth is i've just kind of forgotten about it altogether forgotten even to remember that it's important and believe me in this particular case that's not because i haven't used it as a headline you can just bet i have it's extra extra read all about it big and besides that almost worn out with use if you want to know the truth used not so much with friends like leila in restaurants even when she's late i know she's coming and even if she doesn't come i know something just got mixed up and i call her on the phone and kind of go ahhe-emmm the way you do with good friends and she says oh shit was that today the way i would in her place so no this one about me and tim alone on the street the house empty mickey and mark gone this streetwalking memory is the kind you use with lovers

///lovers late at night like around the hour it happened or just when you're stupid enough to agree to meet them at crowded events or on subway platforms not that i ever did that as much with lovers as with members of one or another underground organization and then it's a different worry you have when they don't show but it's waiting up at night or watching person after person go by and the anxiety mounting to panic until you don't recognize your surroundings that sort of thing that makes you pull this out of your repertoire for use the next time you see them only you use this once too often with a lover this one where you underline it all i cannot stand people not turning up when they say they will it sends me into this horrible awful awful horrible space this is what happened to mmmmmmeeeeeee it was just the worst thing ever there i was on the street and i was so young and after a while you feel like such a manipulator and maybe you are maybe by the one hundred and forty seventh time you pull this out of the hat not that i've

had one hundred and forty seven lovers not nearly so you must understand that it could be i might use this more than once on the same one well by that time i'm telling you you feel like the manipulator of the century oh that bitch that bitch you imagine his her other lover saying the one she he wants to leave you for or you just won't let him her go to maybe it's the seventies and everybody just has to have other relationships that's the way we always said it and we underlined that ooootherrrr with our voices so maybe that's the way you lived your life then and you still might so it keeps coming up discussing each other's lovers or some such and you can just imagine one of your partner's saying oh that bitch that bitch she's so neeeeeeedy she's so manipulative can you just imagine the story that bitch told him told her well he well she told me all about it the bitch's exact words that bitch that bitch with her crocodile tears every time my lover says i just must get away and maybe it's not even to me at all she just wants some fresh air to walk the dog he just wants a round of beer with the boys or some such and there that bitch is again ooooooohhhhhhh don't leave me don't come back late don't stay out ohhhhhhh pllllleeeeeassse you didn't call last time and you knooooowwwwww what that does to me so you can just imagine how by the time you've done that enough times you believe it too exactly what you imagine that other woman that other guy that lover that friend that one that many of the boys of the girls that he's that she's gone to play poker pool curl have a drink watch the hockey game see a movie discuss a book with saying oh that bitch that bitch yes it's become a heartfelt conviction so you say it to yourself you manipulating bitch who precisely are you kidding ohhhhhhhh i can't stand being left alone not when i don't know when you're coming back i can't stand you being late why did you get in at three thirty instead of midnight like you said you would you know three thirty's when the bars close in brooklyn i've told you that you know what happens to me

///and i'm not even talking about hallucinating getting choked night after night once on my own in canal flats the guy at my throat and it wasn't a dream it was a full body engaged hallucination i even had the adrenalin response was getting ready to move quickly to break his grip get some sort of weapon into my hand maybe the bedside lamp it was lucky i didn't have a gun likely i would have shot myself but that came much much later even the bars' late closings came much later than this headline this story there were no bars in the picture yet when this streetwalking happened not in my mind anyway physically they must have been there we must have visited that one down by the waterfront with the tin ceiling and the big windows and the peanut shells mixed with sawdust on the floor maybe we'd even eaten the peanuts as we looked out at the old ferry landing we'd probably even visited montero's with its glass brick windows and bar or even gone to the one with the free knackwurst lunch at the corner of court and jeralemon but we hadn't spent any evenings any nights in barroom backrooms yet or waited shaking in our rooms for early morning drunken arrivals no matter how often i might roll that information right into this ohhhhhh don't go stuff you know what it's like if you come in at four that worry wasn't there at all when this happened this one is the seminal memory i always want to say though for once it's not about semen

///or even sex it really is abandonment it's about no matter if it's as overused as the security blanket the stuffed animal you won't throw away it's been performed so damn often and besides that the truth is you really are good enough at being on your own you bitch you bitch you manipulating bitch whoever those lovers those friends are they'll look at him at her at that lover of yours and say that bitch pulls that on you and then she goes off to where for how long on her own and does what but ooooohhhhhhh she can't stand to be left alone oh yeah right and by now like i said i'm saying these things to myself over and over oh you bitch you bitch until this streetwalking headline this on the street alone with tim story just makes me want to say oh yeah right sarah yeah right forget that one as part of the autobiography the little life stories just throw it in the master or maybe it's the mistress manipulator's handbook along with the tears squeezed out of the corners of eyes this couldn't have any value forget about putting this one down it doesn't even make the list it's just a technique to assert your needs over other people's it's just a trick it probably never really mattered never really mattered at all it was just an adventure you really actually enjoyed it it was really fun that's right fun to be out on the street alone with your brother like that until there's one day

///that you're saying it just like that just like a headline only this time it's just observation no lover anywhere in the vicinity not even making nervous contact with new information you're just talking with someone not about ohhhh this is why i hate it when you're late or even laughing about your own adventures in manipulation simply the various nefarious actions or inactions of parents the ones they were or weren't conscious of or maybe it's even talking with your therapist about abandonment maybe about how strange how almost fun this event was how you didn't even remember the arguments between mickey and mark never remembered a single one even if there was the one time they left the house so maybe it's even with a friend a colleague and it's all very academic you're talking about the protections of class about how if you're rich or upper middle or going broke pretending like mickey and mark up to their ears in debt to keep up appearances which had to include of course a live in housekeeper well a parent like that might be just as mean and just as neglectful but the housekeeper the nanny can do it for them so in that early era there was no noticing the fights there was never so much as a rrrr rrrr rrrr though a lot of raw eggs in milk and tomato juice for hangovers while trying to look back on it i'm sure that's why i was spending all that time in mary's room and then there's this one night this one night no remembered argument but there we are on the street and even so tim and i can still make a joke of it the same way we can about that night in the subway when we had to leave mickey which is even a bigger reason it is so stupid of me to agree to meet anyone in the subway just because it worked in mexico city was no reason to think it would work in toronto when it wasn't even necessary to set up a contact a second contact after a first contact to avoid the police because you had to make the first one on the phone so you do the second in a crowded place so the people following won't overhear but why do it that way in toronto just because it was a political meeting why a contact at rush hour and not even smart enough to be absolutely precise and then there's the minutes into hours of watching people come and go and disappear not the way mickey did that time on the train just melting into the tunnel still singing rrrrrr rrrrr rrrrr but people coming and going watching people come and go and trying to figure out where my friend was and not being able to and yes that panic rising to make the walls of the subway undecorated white toronto walls not even any mosaics making them shake and shimmer and go unreal and yes maybe for a moment it was rrr rrrrrr rrrrr and mickey disappearing the sound like the sound of the tracks echoing but more it was just like all those dreams of disappearing people disappearing mickey disappearing mark disappearing cherokee disappearing paul even if no one had disappeared yet when you had those dreams those days when i would swing between mark and mickey's arms lifting my legs to let them carry me over curbs over the long concrete or slate blocks as we went along the sidewalk only there were the days they would let go of my hands and i couldn't keep up and i would stop and sulk sitting on the curb the truth is i may stand being left alone in the middle of the night no matter how i wail at those lovers a lot better than being the last person on the path on a hike or skiing cross country or whatever it is when i've fallen out of shape and can't keep up i almost go crazy when the last person walks out of sight and sometimes too i stop and wait for them to look back and notice i'm not there the way i did with mark and mickey waiting for the parents to notice they'd lost a daughter which mostly they did only there were dreams and in the dreams when they turned the corner in the dreams they would never come back and the monsters would come instead so they would turn the corner and there they would be monsters monsters even the buildings turning into monsters monsters so that's what this was kind of like

///only this one was so much more of an adventure even if for years the dreams seemed so much brighter brighter and so much more threatening those sharply coloured dreams of day monsters with monotone hallucinated voices and besides all that oooohhhhhh i can't stand to be left alone had kind of mashed the last vestiges of colour of meaning out of this streetwalking night even if the colour was pretty new york grey and pink evening standard anyway the texture gone too until there's that day that who knows with whom day except back to that it's not a lover when i'm just kind of telling it not even using it for personal gain not even therapeutic personal gain and suddenly it's like looking down a dark tunnel and it hits me in the stomach deep and breathtaking so that i can't even cover it all with an oh how silly we were why did we ever do that the way tim and i would say to each other grinning saying it over and over why would we do that why not just wait the obvious thing was to just wait

///which was maybe a kind of strange comfort or a strange shame both at once really in how we could do that as if we had betrayed oh not them by our lack of trust in thinking they would leave us but ourselves by not knowing exactly what to do the appropriate course of action stranger than strange that when you consider how old we were and already we had that thing about getting it right getting it right more like for making a good impression than for survival and what an occasion for good impressions you have to understand how it works there we are one of those nights before bars nights before closets nights before fear though maybe it's after pictures of ratbitten babies in mary's room but still before we could imagine them nipping at the flesh of our young lives and god knows which one of us woke first but the next thing you know one of us has come to the other in his or her bed though doing that regularly was something more we did later when we were afraid of a full house and not an empty one so maybe we've just woken up and moved both of us into the hall all *madeline* something is not right and we're whispering against the echoing silence of the house and maybe i or maybe tim i never asked if he had them too has had one of those disappearing dreams and we're both thinking wow it's really happened this time who really knows or even why

///did we feel in this the quiet of the eye of the storm the way we would so often in years to come the quiet that awaits the return of noise sealed inside that eggplant and olive dark but other than that it's really absolutely totally too hard to tell exactly what it was but there we are both awake and the truth is i don't really remember much about the whole incident at all except that one scene that's been blocked up for so long by the words i always use to tell it ohhhhh you have no idea how awful it was i just can't stand to wake up and find myself alone and all that i've let it become some kind of an old bricked up tunnel always just that one scene the night sky pink grey dark we walk inside hardened to impenetrable stone and i'm looking at myself looking at both of us really but now i'm not far away any more it's like i'm there on that street and i can smell the air even if it is as if i'm plastered to the ceiling of the tunnel up high and far away and there are our backs in a small pool of light as we step forward into the night and into the future i don't even remember the moment of leaving the house but just there right there on the sidewalk the door of old twenty-six back and to our left only i don't see it there's just us and the surrounding dark and we're moving slowly toward the sycamore where the black fence is at the end of our row of houses there's us and the sycamore in front of us and suddenly it's like i've sunken down into my body watching and not watching at once the way i would watch myself crash into that same tree only from the other side as i came up from that one driveway in front of the black fence came up and failed to make my turn and crashed and almost broke my nose when i first learned to ride a bike so that i can still see every detail of the bark just the way i fly into my body as we walk and there it is every detail of the bark and of the bright pebbles in our new concrete sidewalk and would you believe i can suddenly hear us and we're calling out mark mickey mark mickey mickey mark

///not cherokee not paul not mary just mark mickey mickey mark i'm sure of that because besides the fact that i can hear our little voices this time it wasn't a question of who had really been in that house that evening if cherokee and paul and friends from the bars were really all there as they without doubt often enough were believe it or not there's evidence enough for that from all the stuff mickey left behind if you can imagine doing this there along with all the stuff in that oh so writerly traditional scrapbook with its acceptances rejections inquiries suggestions reviews of mark's book or her and mark's brooklyn anthology tucked right in there though not at least pasted down for posterity there's this note from this middle class couple who'd showed up on one of those nights cherokee's twenty fourth birthday it happened to be making it an evening rife for some kind of an incident maybe like the one i'm describing here or the one in the book right before cherokee left that birthday had to have been i'd have been about three just like for the streetwalking but there they are describing one of the guys going out for more booze and then it's the cops showing up and not only rousting the guys but beating on them these are the good old pre-miranda pre-review board days after all with the couple calling the station to complain these weren't really cops were they they said in their clear shocked middle class tones and there's the sergeant saying what does it matter to you anyway they're only sailors and who cares if there was an electrician a repairman among them all of them too lower class to complain and then of course behind the mystery of the letter's placement as i pick it up in my hand there in the basement over fifty years later there is of course the question of where the hell were mark and mickey that the couple was writing them a letter to tell them what happened making it obvious the couple was there and they weren't and then there i am back again right outside

///along that street that is still so much the same i'm sure i can go out and stare at exactly the same pebbles so none of this is about who was there at all anyone could have been there before that moment when the silence woke us up without doubt all sorts of people were in and out and out and in beyond mark mickey mickey mark but the fact is those parties or get togethers or whatever they were hadn't become known yet to me weren't part of my memory at all any more than closets were this thing is all about the couple the parents the sense of safety in their existence mickey mark mark mickey and even if cherokee comes in there somehow during the day not at all in the way that paul ever did but to foreshadow who he was or what he would become with me riding on his shoulders and tim on mark's or going down daytime again to that seaman's bar across from the docks him and mark sometimes like one presence in which tim was always mark's and me cherokee's still cherokee isn't in this part at all in those days a mark adjunct he may have been but the couple was for sure mark mickey mickey mark the way we shouted on the street mickey mark mark mickey the mom the dad who brought safety and membership in a world of moms and dads and sunday garden parties with mostly middle class couples and maybe the occasional sailor but never the other way around and we said mom and dad and smiled and i showed off my precocity and tim his masculinity and everything was the way it is ever and always and still supposed to be even if the lawn was already reverting to dirt and all the rest was just as invisible all those nights of sailors and maybe electricians anyway so that's what this is about something broken that was perhaps always and already broken but we're just noticing it mark mickey mickey mark along the street so there's no who was there question in my mind at all just who should have been there and that was mark mickey mickey mark or maybe mary in their stead but you can tell she wasn't the one we thought was supposed to be there once she wasn't it was just a matter of shouting mark mickey mickey mark for the parents who should have been there mark mickey mickey mark the order of things that should have been in place so not even any questions

///like who brought chiquita who brought my cat that kind of thing to try to fit the incident into a time it's obvious what time this was the time when there was still a mark a mickey a mickey a mark to keep the world in place that's all it's about just that resonance of mickey and mark mark and mickey or even mick and murph murph and mick the way they called each other in their letters that nice couple with the nice housekeeper and the nice house and the nice careers that resonance in mark mickey mickey mark mark mickey the way it was with those dreams as mark mickey mickey mark disappeared around the corner that's what brought on the monsters the lack of the parent couple the safety net and i was left among the monsters and monster houses so there we are out there in the dark mickey mark mark mickey approaching the sycamore calling mark mickey mickey mark maybe we even called out mom dad dad mom that's part of what without doubt made us think we were so stupid for so long mickey mark mark mickey mickey mark as if when your parents disappear and they're not in the house no one's in the house you just think if they're not there they're just going to be out on the street like a lost ball a lost top a lost jump rope a lost yoyo behind a stoop or a garbage can or that black fence maybe deep inside the playground of the school opposite who knows but mark mickey mickey mark mark mickey up and down that portion of the street that little mews with its three houses without even being brave enough to cross the street because the truth is we weren't supposed to you see we weren't yet allowed to cross the street by ourselves and there we are still ever obedient sort of like not stepping on a crack because even if later we might have wished to break mickey's back ten times over right then i'm sure we were sure that if we just obeyed the rules were good children didn't cross the street without a parent or at least an adult then those adults would show up and there we are mickey mark mark mickey mickey mark on our own moving slowly forward calling and calling mark mickey mickey mark all of three and five or four and six at most mark mickey mark mickey mickey mark up and down the street mickey mark mickey mark mark mickey over and over just there where the sidewalk widens out for those three narrow white stone houses without stoops mark mickey mark mickey mickey mark calling out just there in that small grey white indentation the grey shadows of the maple trees directly in front of our door mottling the sidewalk the sycamore just up where the sidewalk starts to narrow those shadows seeming to lean in toward us sheltering us or challenging us or threatening us in true repeated *madeline* you remember her something is not right something is not right fashion as we slowly walk forward mickey mark mark mickey mickey mark toward the sycamore and then the truth is the harcourts hear us

///the harcourts from two doors down we must have been just in front of their house mickey mark mark mickey the third in those three white fronted brownstones each one just like the one next to it us in the first the secretarial school with its a and b and c and d and the quick brown fox in the second the episcopal minister and his wife in the third next to the black fence the harcourts with their red headed daughter caroline and the skinny son giles or nigel or some such so very much the thin english young gentleman though i think they were from new zealand and then the grandmother who sewed rose petals to cloth dried rose petals on purses or runners or bags for linens and i don't remember which one of them came out hearing us call mickey mark mark mickey mickey mark maybe portly mr harcourt forever in black or maybe it was the mrs skinny too and always in flowers what is it that i don't remember their first names maybe they were some of the few people we ever 77
addressed that way mr and mrs no not even that it was reverend and mrs the reverend and mrs harcourt and what the hell i've just remembered his name though not hers malcolm it was malcolm remembering it not because i ever said it but because mickey did over and over the reverend malcolm harcourt stretching out malcom i don't know why the sarcasm maybe because he wasn't as reverent as he ought to be though chasing after cousin bootie's bootiful bootie often enough never after children as far as i can remember we liked him a lot in fact under that certain terror that children i think always have of that kind of portly authority and the house certainly the house was not at all like the house of the witch in hansel and gretel for these two small children walking in the sparsely wooded streets of brooklyn following the gleaming pebbles sealed in the concrete reflecting back the glow of the corner street light though we weren't lost not at all not really so no matter how much it can feel that way sometimes little gretel with her hand in her brother hansel's still it was nothing like that we weren't lost mark mickey mickey mark we'd lost them which is when i get back to that why the hell

///did we go out they would hardly suddenly appear from behind a parked car or for that matter from under one the way we looked for chiquita and maybe too i get to thinking about why this always or at least sometimes or at least when used over and over seems such a fake oh you bitch you bitch you manipulating bitch such a total con using it that way for ohhhhh i can't stand to be left alone because the fact is we weren't scared at all this was not about fear this was an adventure a strange adventure for two little kids maybe but an adventure nonetheless no matter that i can feel the shadows the witchy fingers of tree limbs reflected grey across the ground still there's that thing we had learned from books or from comics from somewhere anyway when you can't find things when you can't find people you look for them and who cares how we had both become aware we were alone in the house but we had and whether or not i remember it we had bravely made our decision so very hansel and gretel yes indeed to bravely go out onto the street which is of course all i remember just the scene on the street in grey from up high and then closing in like that with only that one time remember it's just the one time that's what i said when i tried to explain how silly it was no histrionics no moulding of the incident to my own ends just how silly we were how silly and look silly manipulative me i said look how i would use that that silly thing oh what a bitch to pretend at fear of abandonment isn't that something else i might have been saying when suddenly i am seeing out of my own child eyes the eyes of that child holding her brother's hand and then in front of us the sycamore tree when suddenly yes i can feel the fear but it's not the fear you might expect not a scared kid on the street scared of the street why would we have gone out if we were afraid of the street not fear of the street even dark it was a friendly street but fear of the future that's right i can feel it in that moment already there that movement beyond childhood safety to know that something is over mark mickey mickey mark maybe mickey mark over a red expansion in the gut like the lover leaving anyway as your hand reaches out your voice says please something wanted needed shredding apart like old roses falling to petals in a box waiting till later to be sewn into meaning their musty smells brought forward with the feeling so clear the way i can smell the night and mickey mark mark mickey know it was surely it was

///the fear of the future

///the future not on the empty street but in the empty house fear of what the house would fill with now that mickey mark mark mickey that mom dad dad mom that first couple mark mickey mickey mark that was over you could feel it over in the night in the silence in the empty house and maybe our movement outward to make adventure already a way of asserting ourselves beyond that awful absence into possibility who knows but there we are on the street and there's that moment of emptiness and then a harcourt comes out maybe it's the mrs the dark night greying out her flowers till she's leaning with the trees skinny and tall like a nurse like a nun like a nurse nun now for sure it's that *madeline* shadow something is not right what is wrong children something is not right and the next thing we know we are on a small couch in the smallest of the rooms there on the top floor it must have been maybe it's the room with the rose petals where the grandmother kept all the dried rose petals a room to echo mine in the other house only this one full of rose petals and mulberry roses printed on tan wallpaper and there's this little couch and there they are tucking us in we're going to sleep head to toe it's so narrow head to toe we'd never slept head to toe before only there we are my brother's toes wiggling my armpits on this narrow couch head to toe in the room with the rose petals so maybe it was more like the babes in the woods

///than hansel and gretel i don't know how many people know that babes in the woods fairy tale what it might mean really when you say they're like babes in the woods it's got a poem to go with it something that seems so perky hallmark down to the end when they die it isn't reproduced in books much these days it's not the kind of thing for twentieth century developed country kids with its boy and girl failing to find their fortune or their future or even their way back just lying down on the ground in the woods and the birds bringing flower petals flower petals to comfort them something that might even have been a comfort to the starving and the bereft and the lost the dying children even to their parents in the nineteenth century imagining birds bringing flowers strewing petals at the awful end something like those mexican angelitos dressed like kings like queens like fairies as they go to their final rotting rest something i hadn't imagined yet those rotting thoughts would follow mark's final absence so maybe it would be easy enough to imagine in that room a comfortable rose petal covered forever sleep to refuse time refuse future fear even if it would be years before that silly story would actually punch me in the gut and make me weep as i read again that poem with its perky bright drawing birds carrying yellow carrying red carrying blue flowers to drop on children that story tucked in among other ever so insipid children's tales so easy to lie not just with the blanket over us with the harcourts telling us we were safe but to imagine grandmother's rose petals me covered tim covered with rose petals forever like those kids among red yellow blue flower petals or at least to imagine being able to breathe rose petals forever breathe rose petals tender on skin and not old streets and mickey mark mark mickey mickey mark and a future we knew had changed had skewed was forever different we could smell it

///coming maybe in the scotch on their breaths or just her breath as she as they arrived to take us home no more mickey mark mark mickey just silly silly children you must have known we were coming back so very soon you silly silly children and who knows if the harcourts didn't just leave a note on the door but were smart enough to go to the bar to montero's to the j&e the ferryman to find them mark mickey mickey mark the way we would again and again years later only then it was just her or her and cherokee mickey cherokee cherokee mickey so that maybe we would wish to lie down again and again in rose petals the birds singing over us like the harcourts whispering voices not hansel and gretel following out the pebbles in the woods the way we followed out the pebbles nestled in the concrete always there always the same never disappearing like the petals of the roses or the crumbs left by hansel or was it gretel by the babes in the woods disappearing to leave them forever among flower petals but always leading back to old twenty-six back our eyes on the ground clinging to pebbles as if they could halt our forward motion back and back and back only this time the house we went back to would never be what we had left that night never again what we hoped for if not expected so seldom the woodsman comforting house of cherokee and mickey and wooden crafts brought back from around the world instructions in woodscraft from an oklahoma reservation childhood or watching him paint in his techniques from the art students league the sober mickey telling stories of adolescence or journalistic travel even amidst the perfect sad so genteel poverty but so often instead the witch's house over and over as if it had switched identities

///while we slept head to toe in the harcourts' house all redolent of wood and lemon oil musty roses and shortbread cookies the burgundy and kelly green feel of my secret garden and victorian hidden places hidden places and transformations that somehow let us return not to mickey mark mark mickey but to the witch's house over and over forever the witch's house from hansel and gretel hidden in a closet if not kept in a cage and the kitchen always warming up to burning with the sounds of incendiary subviolent when not overtly violent voices ready to burn us alive if not to bake us into shrivelled mummies like the ever forgotten thanksgiving turkey so even if the oven was never meant for him and even if i never pushed her in still there was wanting to as she came at him at me with her carving knife dancing her little rrrrr rrrrr witch's dance so maybe you can hear it too the birds singing smell the rose petals let yourself drift off even if not head to toe leave that feeling that was dark and growing in the back of your child's mind that already knowledge in that moment in the rose petal room that something isn't right isn't right isn't right mark mickey mickey mark isn't right calling out mickey mark mark mickey isn't right isn't right so that sleeping head to toe or no sleeping head to toe rose petals or no rose petals hansel and gretel or babes in the woods there is always and forever after as the thought of that moment arises that moment mark mickey mickey mark on the street not fear but that desire to just keep sleeping to just go away somewhere anywhere because the something that is not right is not a fear for now but a knowledge of the seeds of the future hidden in the smell of the night of liquor on the breath of too many secret evenings in mary's room with newspaper photos of ratbitten babies information coming together that you didn't even know was there a texture in the night the way authors foreshadow the unknown future known only to them with textures hidden between the lines so the fact is that this is not a literary technique but what the night was bringing to us in secret song mark mickey mickey mark mark mickey whether we are following thoughts or following pebbles this time there is a clearly marked pathway into the future we just don't want it we want absent breadcrumbs already eaten we want to be lost we want to cling to the gleam of the pebbles fail to follow them into the true story of hansel and gretel where the mother put them into the woods

///not the evil stepmother so forget for the moment the kind woodsman even if cherokee it turns out was my real father that much of the story is true forget those comfort days that's just the witch fattening you up for the kill making you forget so the next time will be worse so remember just the mother who is the witch of despair who put them in the woods who put us in the streets over and over to find her again transformed into horror following gleam of pebbles in concrete home again and again to the witch's house in nutmeg mews fear not in the night but in the house in that knowledge of time to come it's old twenty-six and we can feel it in the shadows feel it in our toes our heads to our toes feel it and feel it and feel it feel it mark mickey mickey mark mark mickey gone gone feel it even in the smell of the wood of the harcourt house the imagined victorian secret garden of the rose petals feel it and feel it right there feel it until we might wish to be not hansel and gretel at all but the babes in the woods smelling rose petals rose petals forever just not to go back because even if mark mickey mickey mark are both still there for those few days or weeks or even short months longer it's like it says in that other note to him left in those scrapbooks so long ago a carbon copy from mickey's typewriter when you get up i expect you to pack your bags and it's over mickey mark mark mickey mickey mark is over and it's back

///to the witch's house where from day to day you don't know if it's oven or cage or gathering roses but you will never be safe never be safe again in that house the street your new home comfortable in your trees climbing your fences which is when you know it's true mark mickey mickey mark and i want to be a babe in the woods i want to breathe in rose petals and never wake up except to dream the smell of flowers the smell of roses the smell of no tomorrow no witch's house much as i hated it the babes in the woods will always be better than hansel and gretel so breathe deep smell the roses no more mark mickey mickey mark no more anything except sweetness please no story no story no memory no story just brother feet and blankets and rose petals and babes in the woods no more mickey mark mark mickey just rose petals rose petals until that's what it is not fear of abandonment but postponing the future the rising from the bed head to toe or entwined in arms you bitch you bitch you manipulating bitch what you can still feel in your entrails is neither that pretend moment of abject fear nor that youthful moment of first adventure it's no proto abandonment soon made right it's the emptiness in the house that knew the future which is why you will beg again for the lover's touch

///to not be alone for the future not to come for the rose petals on the skin in the fingertips exploring your body telling you you're real please forever don't go don't put me in that place where i don't know what is real where monsters reach through walls don't leave me don't leave me don't let me go to that place don't let me go forward let me be forever a babe in the woods among rose petals that little death among rose petals fingertips on skin on rose petals soft forever rose petals please don't go you know i can't stand to be left alone give me that little death forever soft on skin rose petals rose petals you can't leave you see how i need you i'm so scared i don't want to be alone rose petals rose petals soft on the skin rose petals rose petals alone in my skin lost in my skin

///and still manipulating you bitch you bitch you're doing it again take me out of time rescue me among rose petals oh you bitch you bitch you manipulating bitch stay here don't leave me you bitch among rose petals you bitch here take me here to rose petals forever soft in the woods rose petals muttering soft like birds calling petals in beaks rose petals forever in this moment fingers on skin rose petals forever and ever don't leave me you bitch you bitch i'm so afraid rose petals.

Next rainbows

Still looking down past feet saddle shoes peeking over edge not of dock of curb eyes still noting surface of water where it bunches up into balls into drops eyes resting on black asphalt by black car tires after rain water on oil not oil on water this time forming shapes still round still shimmering still colour after colour circling ragged from the centre prismatic forms still tucked away in corners of darkness still years before sky would open bright above you your eyes look up to invite rainbow from side to side of sky into mind the way now you see them so often even outside your attic window go into the street to greet them while back there you like to think it was an invitation like to a birthday party you've seen those cards full of rainbows and this one left by the curb just for you glimmering there to give your foot permission to break the rules still no pot of gold at end but this this this reaching out this leap into street the street itself your one giant step escape to somewhere over.

Burned on the fourth of july

or maybe it was the third or even the second it's hard to remember it's not like there were fireworks i don't know how long it was before i saw fireworks even knew about fireworks it was just going out onto the stoop standing in the middle of the street setting off firecrackers or waving sparklers we did it for days stayed up the latest ever every night past eight past nine because even in new york it gets dark late though never as late as calgary where i am now much less northern england but that special quality of new york summer night damp and close wrapping you in its sounds noise lapping at you like water so it's definitely not the quality of the air that takes you back to brooklyn that time in yorkshire maybe it's the grey night grey thinking grey and white and silver as you move across the countryside meadowhall dodsworth penistone denby dale morley batley ravensthorpe mirfield marsden slaithwaite huddersfield different days of different train routes all mixed up and coming back through night or late afternoon november grey

///not night at all not really not yet just grey already grey late afternoon fall grey grey across the countryside grey back from sheffield back from bradford back from leeds manchester liverpool lancaster grey grey and then the bright maybe it's the contrast to the bright the bright lights in colours from everywhere and anywhere that takes me back it's more than just a little intellectual equals signs oh you have bonfire night we have the fourth of july as you stand and look down over the town of huddersfield and luca luca there so careful with his sparkler such a big sparkler maybe it's how we didn't have big sparklers back whenever that was that's crossed my mind that takes me from brighouse mythlomroyd new pudsey to cortland rector canal whitehall brooklyn bridge fulton wall montague court hoyt schemerhorn borough hall the subway stops of my brooklyn my new york city childhood not bright explosions across countryside but red orange green blue white ordered lights in tunnels and those little sparklers just those little sparklers in their flat cardboard boxes so that even when lit you had to hold them close to your body at least to your hand the pointed sparks shimmering down onto your wrist your forearm though i don't yet remark on that one time

///that it's physical it's in the body not colours on trains and conclusions to be drawn from journeys from bright lights in tunnels or out of windows don't even note the silver the white the sparkle that makes me shiver because i do find myself shivering as i watch luca three year old luca just turned three year old luca walk with his sparkler along concrete slabs much less do i note how i hold my arm close to my side i just chalk it up to the cool of the november night contrasted to july as i continue to use all those comparisons to still keep all this in the mind not the body make sure it hardly matters that i shiver as i talk about how you had to stay up so late to see the sparkles against the grey of night sparklers really were so fourth of july so very fourth of july i say which really was too close to summer solstice to be anything but a too late past your bedtime secret privilege

///not at all really like this late afternoon communication in the crisp late fall air communication of bright bursts of colour but late late past eight past nine maybe even to ten to eleven and there were never any colours either never these brief and brilliant bursts for days in anticipation against the horizon exploding flowers over buildings out the train the bus window shepley stockmoor brockholes honley lockwood because sparklers just kind of sparkle silver and there were never any personal fireworks not ever the buildings were too high and near though firecrackers yes lots of them the days the evenings of noise not light but the secret communication of noise what heralded the coming of the fourth of july the ear instantly attuned to noise and its direction the secret community of children setting them off and as for colour just those innocent dull tubes their only colour on the outside the cheap paper packaging that hid the internal undifferentiated grey of gunpowder the opaque explosions until white bright sparkler night when night finally came warm soft night so it was just noise until sparklers you never went to the public displays and there's no secret communication in them anyway just open and obvious and sleepy if beautiful with pinwheels but that was so much later you don't even remember when or where it was maybe once at jones beach when you first saw fireworks no it's the secret communication you love you're falling in love all over again with brighter or softer coloured sparks brighter or softer noise moving to moments of sparkly bright even if cool not hot certainly not sweaty hot the way always then it was too hot too sweaty hot and close sticky close steam bath close candy chocolate ice cream melted onto hands onto clothing close and now it's here that one time with the faces their hot breath closer still a circle around me spinning spinning as i twirled the centre of attention

///the night tumbled down around my shoulders and the dress sticking out from my waist that white organza dress tied at the back like little girls' dresses always are and now yes it's down to one time no intellectual speculation but once more communication centred in the body the body of noise or laughter or light and i'm outside in the shelter of the buildings and the night just gone grey with no blue left maybe a bit of pink reflected city street lights not sun on the clouds a grey pink way up high above the buildings and all of us not on but by the stoop next door in that little sheltered indentation in front of the house brown stone stoop to one side white stone balustrade of twenty-six nutmeg mews to the other and it's not the first time that you've done it

///not the first time at all not the first fourth of july not the first sparkler not the first spin and spin and twirl and twirl and faster and faster that you remember so it can't be a first memory anyway since it's not even a first fourth of july memory it had been years by then that you knew about the fourth of july there is an i am doing this again sense to this which i can never get out of there's a sense of ceremony repeated sparklers and dress up and firecrackers which would make me maybe about four about four for the fourth of july it could have been three for the third not the night itself but one of the many preparation nights of being on the stoop definitely not two for the second that's too young and of course not five for the fifth the tradition never extended beyond the day itself and besides you couldn't have been much older not in a dress or with mark still around even if it seems ridiculous to have such a sense of continuity of this is the way the fourth is done if you were only four or three so maybe i was five even if it wasn't for the fifth and six is out no six for the sixth or for that matter the fourth the third the second six is out because mark was in africa by then died not on the fourth of july but on his fortieth birthday at the end of the month on the thirty first maybe he was already missing the state department looking for him when i was six there certainly was no mark standing around with us celebrating even if there must have been firecrackers so it's easier to remember this in the body than calculate its occurrence in the intellectual memory of dates with that body so young so concrete there's no way i could have gotten this one mixed up

///not the dress not there having been previous sparklers i'm sure of that sure too of how i went not on the fourth but for the fourth maybe the first the second the third even the thirtieth and maybe not that fourth or first or thirtieth at all but some fourth first thirtieth before this one's not concrete this side trip had already become part of the story the tradition of the fourth and its environs by that one time i'm remembering twirling spinning with my sparkler this side trip's part of the ongoing story of fourths gone by and fourths to come so who knows if it was really that year i was finally allowed to go with mickey and mark i'm pretty sure it's mickey and mark up to get the firecrackers the sparklers behind the butler street police station something that might convince me i really was precocious maybe i really was like i mean really after all

///i couldn’t have been more than five that fourth which would make me three all of three maybe two for when that fireworks stand with all its colours it did have colours bright colours became part of the story at least for me not that i went then but i knew about it thought about it precocious child already old enough three or two or four to understand irony the way mark and mickey and paul weird as it was they did all talk together go places together maybe that’s irony too mark and mickey and paul that threesome and cherokee bill makes four irony all irony even if i didn’t understand that part maybe felt it somewhere in the gut to deepen my understanding of the way they laughed they all did tim and aj too at how the firecrackers were sold in the vacant lot behind the police station the butler street police station it was funny very funny after all fireworks of any kind firecrackers maybe even sparklers they were all illegal in new york still are without doubt had to be bootlegged in from new jersey and that was so silly so very silly wasn’t it hahahaha those little firecrackers those sparklers they were so safe weren’t they hahahaha so safe the cops probably bought most of them for their own children and i can still see it the whole scene

///the green grass the grey gravel the little tan wood stand amid the rubble see the multicoloured open cardboard boxes see the red brick back of the police station glowing with reflected sun the glowing rectangles of old interior paint that still marked the last walls of rooms disappeared into brick and painted plaster under foot crunching amid grass as you walked everything in bright colours everything in absolute detail though maybe that’s an irony too maybe it’s the story that builds the memory so strong as if it had been there forever and the truth is that i really didn’t get to go not that time but only later one time later before the police station was closed and maybe torn down too which doesn’t mean i didn’t understand irony at least that irony behind the police station it was just years before i actually got to go and to look

///at all those little blue and white red and white little firecrackers in groups like fish on lines attached together by their fuses their gunpowder hidden grey inside maybe it really was years before i got to see that in the flesh to walk up and to choose blue and white green and white orange and white firecracker or grey sparkler packages though maybe not because by the time mark was dead and paul garcia was gone i think the police station was gone too not just the fireworks stand but the whole police station or maybe just that empty lot so maybe it was some time in between mark leaving and paul leaving with cherokee gone already years before that i went once i am so sure i went once that brilliance of sun on brick must be as real as sparkler white against grey and spinning twirling as real as train lights in tunnels or fireworks across recent bonfire night skies i couldn't have made it up not all of it not from casual description even if maybe it was with paul and mickey and tim and aj or maybe

///it's possible it was just with tim and aj maybe it was that time i was riding on aj's bike that was summer too i know it was that was a summer and mark was gone so maybe i was returning in triumph from the firecracker stand when i stuck my foot in the spokes and we had that crash and i hurt my ankle and maybe mark was hurt then too already dying in africa or maybe just in manhattan with his japanese mistress the one with the yellow kabuki slippers and i just didn't know it maybe that was it maybe it was maybe that's all just one bright superimposed image of that stand from one unconnected time i went there and all the rest of the story the precocious tale of fireworks behind the butler street police station hahahaha and understanding irony all that is just like the sparkler all black and white and shades of grey words in the mind sparkle bright greyscale of words of words and story told to me all in the mind grey and white and the occasional burst of colour like fireworks across grey countryside to communicate something bigger than the usual view that memory its colours maybe they're extra vivid to cover the irony of its untruth the most vivid colours for the cover up or maybe it's the colouring in the colouring inside the lines of the black and white story i already had the story with its outlines fixed and me working on my part in it like working in a colouring book working the story and the irony as if while listening to it again and again telling it again and again over the years i coloured it each time brighter

///what an irony

///those firecrackers those sparklers right beside the police station and all of them such little ones that even the cops knew they were safe the ones sold there were safe definitely safe and sparklers those little sparklers the safest of all everyone knew that sparklers were safe just the way i did as i twirled the centre of attention the spinning faces so close the air so close the grey pink city sky so close i knew i was safe and the firecrackers too safe safe at least the ones we bought in their bright coloured red white and blue american flag or any other colour fourth of july paper safe too only the ashcans the cherry bombs dangerous and those just barely and we never bought them anyway or at least i didn't and tim wasn't supposed to though maybe aj did and sneaked tim a few he certainly talked about them with awe that loud loud noise even as he lit the match against the fuse of the red and white the blue and white little ones they were for him the way the sparklers so dull iron grey and safe were for me i'd been told they were safe so safe as we passed our hands through the sparks so magical too safe and magical as they converted iron grey to white pointed sparks with always the same perfect dimensions not at all like the chaotic leaping of a flame more like a saturday afternoon at the movies cartoon with their sharp outlines and transparent colours magic magic magic our hands passing through safe magic the way they still do passing my hand through the sparks of luca's much larger sparkler tiny pin pricks of sensation but never of alarm and still the same perfect identical sparks grey metal become sparkling white sparkles yes i was sure

///they were safe safe as i twirled in my stiff rayon white organza dress white to match the leaping white of the sparks the points of the sash flying outward i can see that dress too feel its texture harsh on the skin in the heat of july the fourth the third the second with aj there and tim and mickey too and mark for a last a second to last time a last fourth of july in brooklyn before the july in which he died puking out his guts in the heat not of new york but of africa so there we are and we're laughing and maybe i'll put paul there and cherokee bill too just for fun and because it might have been that way just once the never happy but for one moment together family that was mickey's lovers mickey's husbands mickey's children running and playing laughing and drinking our sparklers still unlit in our hands and the shadows of the trees folding over us as the final dark the final grey falls at the end of those hours spent waiting into the night not this five o'clock late afternoon shadow but long hours for just that grey just that dark that will make the sparklers shine more and more excited waiting for the pink grey dark of brooklyn night way past the coming of the ice cream truck the good humor man the melted ice cream still gooey on our hands our faces in the heat waiting for the moment our sparklers will be lit to light up bright against the grey even if without colour no red no pink no purple no green against the grey the only colour in the faces the bodies huddling around me to seem to spin and spin as so sure i'm safe i twirl and i twirl the centre of attention laughing

///the way kids always twirl and twirl the world the faces around spin and spin spin and twirl until they get dizzy you get dizzy i get dizzy and i start to stagger and maybe i lose my balance or maybe i'm just giddy as well as dizzy and i start to flap my little bird wing arms in my puff sleeve organza dress as the faces spin around me and maybe i laugh or maybe they laugh or maybe tim shoves me or maybe i just trip on the uneven pavement where it changes from slate to concrete and start to fall or maybe i'm just entranced with the safety of those beautiful sparks and i'm drawing with them the way you always draw patterns with sparklers patterns against grey against black night watching the afterimage waiting for it to glow red to glow yellow to glow blue to become its own firework so maybe i'm twirling and drawing drawing and twirling maybe i'm trying to outline the faces spinning but no matter which way the next thing you know i've brought that sparkler that safe safe sparkler into my side my arm into my side into my you could call it hide the later scar would certainly be hard like horse's hide it makes it easier not to remember soft skin child skin as i hold that grey metal sparkler so bright so bright with its perfect five pointed sparks into my side because who's going to notice who ever noticed the red red glow in its centre not an afterimage but a here and now and simple meaning i hadn't understood i may have understood the complexity of irony but not the simplicity of fire that even cool white pinprick sparkler sparks emerge from a red hot centre as i move the sparks to my side to my hide white sparks to palest pink never exposed skin inside my white white dress as i twirl and i twirl and the faces spin and spin and the next thing you know their mouths are open the dress is burning the dress is burning

///and so is my side my hide and

///that's the part i don't remember because it's not just fast forward from surrounding faces spinning to another still circle it's a fast fade and a moment's darkness darker than the night around me opening into that other circle only not of faces even if they're still there still now this circle's so much smaller only my utter concentration makes it big makes it take up all of my mind my mental space like a georgia o'keeffe flower what i'm looking at is the circular burn on my side as big as oddly round as oddly coloured as a nebula in an imax theatre the charred grey black cloth of the dress stuck in its middle as grey black as the curled over centre rod of the spent sparkler thrown now somewhere on the ground and then there's the raw purple red of burned flesh moving to a yellow edge as if of bruising black to blue black to purple to yellow and the greasy butter smoothed across it and once more black again of buttery burnt cloth and then dress buttery yellow before it turns again to dry white and strangely enough that's all there is

///this memory like a photograph as specific as the bright light on the brick side of the police station and just as empty of sensation without its terrible pain or even fear just my own burned flesh floating in disembodied vision and maybe i should tell you that i know the pain the fear was there bright bright in the moment the dress started to burn brighter than the sparkler and i know it was mark it must have been mark fast with something it couldn't have been a blanket the blanket came later it had to come from out of the house you can still smell its wool it must have been a jacket mark used something fast and to hand before the dress went up in flames to wrap around me something to put out that brief fire very quick super quick the whole dress never caught i never went up in flames i only have the smallest the hardest of scars

///on my side on my hide maybe my smallest scar to match this small memory with its hole in the centre so like the charred black centre of that wound the scarred black wound at the centre of attention still the centre of attention the circled faces from laughter to horror with no moment of action of sparkler to side and burning dress to make this new irony clear the moment's only memory as constructed or more constructed than stories of the butler street police station the irony of the safe sparkler in the unsafe centre of attention my wild laughter the circling faces that egg you on to greater and greater risks of waving hands that draw faces or bunnies or ducks or just patterns wilder and wilder patterns with in and out flapping armwings while everyone laughs because no one believes these should be risks and much less you this is safe safe circle and twirl so safe always safe which maybe makes it an object lesson not a story lesson always safe

///of sun on brick and red and white and blue and yellow paper but an object lesson in the flesh the irony of the flesh definite unique specific the pain of the flesh in this lesson of unsafety not of sparkler but of centre of attention another premonitory object lesson really it was or i can tell you that anyway after all i was precocious so why not have premonitions to match the understanding of irony some deep in the gut purple red feeling blooming into black purple pain at the surface of the flesh not for mark's hand putting out the fire but for the coming of his dying even if that would fit more with the properly orchestrated foreshadowing you see in the traditional novel the traditional narrative the kind that takes the reader till the end to figure out so even if i felt it that pain in the moment in the moment before the moment acted maybe on that feeling spun faster and faster my birdwing arms in and out faster and faster because of that feeling the way you laugh too loud when you feel something coming something you don't want to know perform more hysterically take up more space at the centre of attention until once you know it whatever it is whatever happens it seems as if you've always known it that the consequences were logical the way i'm standing here

///amid the fireworks in huddersfield just seeing it now as if i'd always known it even if it's more like the reader at the end of the book suddenly knowing what they've always known and not brought into mind because that's right precocious or not it's taken me till now to understand this particular irony this perfect if ironic warning death and pain foreshadowed in safe firecrackers next to police stations danger in safety next to authority figures danger made safe by their stamp of approval when instead it's unsafe authority figures the irony or maybe the iron fist of unsafe authority figures that they've been unsafe all along unsafe and unknowing whether drunk or straight or depressed or distracted or doing it for your own good this is for your own good they always say only never think they really know

///what is safe or what is sorry or what is pain and loss and sorrow even that they do have your good in mind no matter what they say never think you're playing it safe so safe when you're there at the centre of their attention think it so safe at the centre of attention or don't think don't think at all just assume this is where you're meant to be safe so safe like luca running running and believing more than anything in the attention of the attention to your own fun believing that you were meant to have this joy to draw in the air while everybody watched to make yourself known giggling and giddy till you fall down always safe forever safe especially safe at the centre of attention all those faces looking out for you without risk no risk to you with that perfect childhood innocence of safe ironies even the ironies are safe sun on brick safe hahahaha firecrackers by the police station safe and twirl some more safe

///safe ironies about to be broken forever in that lost moment that is pain and fear and burning and that image of your side all melded black and purple blue and yellow the broken irony the oxymoron of safe danger to become forever the sharp edged irony of dangerous safety the moment between circle of laughing faces and circle of purple burn imageless but incised forever in that oxymoron forever absent forever present as you feel yourself staring leaning feeling into its lack that absence of memory to learn over and over how it's not safe not safe that centre of attention is not safe and maybe that's everybody's lesson not the object but the subject lesson of the loss of innocence that twirling and spinning and burning and sparkling we're still on our own that's the foreshadowing the premonition of what's to come that you will have to learn to look out for yourself even if it's that one moment between action and rescue still it's enough for that hollow circle of burn and pain you were set up to create inside their attention as they egg you on

///so very strong for you that knowledge as you look back with mark's hand over your side mark's hand and that jacket and mark about to leave about to die and you about to enter that purple maroon nether world of mickey and her men precocious too in loss of innocence in learning what is contained in the absent moment the centre of this repeated lesson so maybe i can go back to the sparkler make it push the narrative forward into some other place enlarge on how it wasn't safe the way they said it was safe and how so many things that sparkle aren't safe the irony of my early life sparkling enough to get away to impress the pants off the right people or maybe i shouldn't use that cliché i never did want them to get their pants off that was the one thing to avoid which maybe could be done by never sparkling enough to bring on mickey's wrath or that other sparkle in those men's eyes so maybe i could just go with that talk about the sparkling that could never be safe too bright lights that wouldn't be safe where being the centre of attention the little girl centre of attention was always the least safe of all and there is never precocious enough to make it all right to make it anything but sickening absent purple maroon yellow moments with crisp black centres to be excised by doctors or therapists with mark gone and cherokee gone with mickey and all those men the terrible sparkle of light glinting off glasses and being admired don't look now but here comes that story again and all of it full of invisible scars like the scar on my side i can't see anymore and what can you say what can you say except that there too in those scenes it always seems yellow and purple like a nightmare mustard yellow and eggplant purple the way after that sparkling night centre of attention there was just that purple and then yellow circle and the smell of burnt flesh and butter somehow so much like movie popcorn with some child molester's hand on your knee so let's go back to the irony of that hidden moment the obvious irony of that hidden moment and what you had to do to get through to get past that hidden moment that would become a thousand eggplant and mustard moments to get past what you always have to do to get past those moments to come to stand here watching luca my arm to my side and think of the spinning

///and what's true for all of us

///running and circling and sparkling or remembering sparkling moments as we sparkle our words or remember sparklers and besides that if it's so damn dangerous if this sparkler firework thing is so damn dangerous the centre of attention so damn dangerous why are you here what are you doing that's right why are you here this bonfire night this late afternoon dark in this garden with its small its large its brief its continuous explosions keith setting off the rockets yes why have you been moving back and forth across the country slaithwaite marsden morley batley except to make yourself the centre of attention wakefield dodsworth huddersfield the centre of attention denby dale hebden bridge sheffield getting up on stage in the dark the faces circling like explosions across the countryside their own centres of attention so that maybe that's all it is all it ever is narrating yourself narrating ourselves bragging our way with scars and war stories into the centre of attention your voice your cadence even here twirling twirling into the centre of attention all the sparklers all the explosions the centre of attention the dancing the bragging the telling the centre of attention each one into the centre of attention setting off our own sparkler our own fireworks from our centre of attention setting them off across the countryside each one our statement from our centre of attention because after all that's where you are you're standing here your hand to your side bragging your war story and luca is running back and forth his sparkler in his hand and you're not stopping him you're not stopping keith from setting off the fireworks you're not hiding inside as spent fireworks fall heavy into the yard as roman candles explode green over your head why are you just standing here telling this instead not foreshadowing and preknowledge or even hidden meanings that bloom as if you've always known them but just setting yourself almost setting yourself on fire with a sparkler even as you laugh because why if it's so damn dangerous why don't you make it stop make it all stop instead of laughing

///hahahaha except that maybe that's all it is all it ever is all anything everything ever is laughing and crying and sending up our fireworks our firewords that's what you write and maybe it's an accident an accident like sparklers to sides but if it is why did it wait till now to happen but who cares because it's most likely true our firewords at the centre of attention the bragging firewords of your story our story anyone's story the story that gets you through that skips from sparkler to twirling to centre of attention to black blue purple burn to centre of attention to horror of the years with mickey to centre of narration that makes it possible to leap that gap to land again to circle with your sparkler to leap with your narration narrating our selves into still here still here our stories leaping from the circled mouths of our own attention centre luca with his sparkler you with your hand to your side keith stepping back from the rocket taking off with its dangerous bright hiss as you brag to di your small scar story all of you still here still here twirling running narrating circling as the fireworks the firewords explode and fall their own centres of attention the way it will always be always twirling always telling always bragging twirling and bragging and circling and leaping over the forgotten moment to keep moving keep getting through the way luca will soon have his own moments to keep getting through innocence lost to experience of narration maybe already has his own moments to keep getting through and maybe it's dangerous and maybe it's not or maybe it's the most dangerous place of all because maybe it's the only place of all and maybe to be human is to be the centre of attention of the only place you've ever got so maybe that's all we are running and jumping and laughing and singing and twirling and playing amid the circling faces that mean you well or mean you harm as you tell your stories the centre of narration

///to get yourself through to leap over the absent moments whispered to yourself or bragged out loud brag your way through so maybe that's the only danger because it's the moment you know you're here innocence lost you know you're endangered twirling and bragging bragging and circling circling and telling and still here fourth of july or third or second or first or bonfire night or fourth or third tending the small fires of our firewords in the sharp fresh burn of the sparkler or the ugly purple of burned flesh safely dangerous or dangerously safe it's still the only place to be because there's nowhere to go so why not brag in firewords about fireworks by the police station or burns on your side or the precocious understanding of irony even as your eyes drink in the bright explosions and your mind remembers heat and it hardly matters what the story is as long as you're here dangerously safe or safely dangerous in the centre of your story the centre of narration words weaving the missing centre of the story into presence so what does it matter

///if you were precocious or if you understood irony because you're still here and you're still telling and who cares about the safety or the irony we're still here we're still here as long as we can centre our attention to tell our way to somewhere else tell it into the cool the heat of the night and safe and dangerous and always ironic because being here and telling the story that's the biggest braggingest only safe who cares if you understand it dangerous irony of all.

Tartar steak

This was good moneyed days with mickey when for that matter there were sourest wonderfulest dill pickles from the deli at the corner which is the only place she would buy them or the meat either just the best round steak she would always say or rump the same as for a roast and she would watch them clean the grinder and put the meat through trichinosis she said there wouldn't have been mutant e-coli and all those things we worry about or for that matter thinking about that deli again for another forty years trichinosis she repeated you want to make sure the grinder is clean if it's just finished grinding pork and then it was home where we chopped onions and mushed them into the bright red meat with our hands red oozing between our fingers and put it onto baguette only we called it french bread and i can still remember the smell and the crumbs the sound of the shattering crust as you cut it and for that matter the smell too of the meat we never added raw egg or mustard or any of those other flavours others use to disguise the raw meat flavour or scent as for that matter i would stick a finger into my mouth to pick up the baguette crust crumbs and just stuff the raw meat into my mouth with nothing else but salt and pepper raw raw never disguising raw.

The hurricane

I'm not at all sure which one just sure enough i remember it really i do anne beulah carla i don't know but definitely from those many years when a hurricane was always feminine and long before i heard that terrible joke about why is a hurricane always a her because if it wasn't it would be a himicane and even longer before i knew the name comes from the mayan god of wind huracan which is how it's still said in spanish *huracán* for the god and *el huracán* for the storm so it really is a himicane or at least masculine maybe this one was hazel in any case neither the storm nor the story a metaphor for mickey it's just as usual about mickey mickey and mark and i certainly do remember it somehow down by that indentation between our ground level one step stoop and the one leading to the second storey stoop next door the same position as for my sparkler burning only i'm looking down on that space which maybe puts us between the black desk and the typewriter in mark's study definitely out of the wind while we watch mark go outside to batten something down i swear he did he didn't just stay upstairs and watch out the study window with us though i know we didn't board anything up no one did not on our block and things did get loose battening or no and they tore down the street making giant clanging noises and besides

///mickey if you want to know the truth no matter how much it might seem in this accounting that there are no characters just naturally occurring phenomena that it's a world where maybe the house is the character or maybe the street is while the people mickey anyway are weather systems something to be predicted not comprehended well mickey still wouldn't make it for a hurricane no matter what the damage she always caused there's just no way no easily forecast slow tropical oceanic buildup for her more like a tornado the real quick single afternoon even if oft repeated thunderhead piling up into absolute stillness then all hell breaking loose you never know where just concentrate precipitate dissipate suck up huge quantites of liquid though it usually wasn't water create vacuums drop down funnels rain rats or fishes throw tractors into your basement drive mattress springs through your brain that sort of thing the kind that actually happened that summer we drove to wisconsin with the new york times pissing dog not that we saw any funnels just went to the storm cellar on the real quiet days with the thick green clouds you could feel them coming just the way you could feel certain still mickey afternoons nothing like looking out the study window and mark going out into the turbulent darkness of what should have been a calm fall afternoon battening the basement hatch cover bringing in the garbage cans so they wouldn't blow down the block or come through windows while chimneys really did though maybe that image of mickey

///that mickey storm metaphor might just give this chronicle a theme make it a man against nature story you know that one man against the naturally occurring obstacle if there just were a real man around that's what mickey would say if you let her probably did say i can hear her voice her wanting mark to go outside to do something to do something who knows what it didn't matter if it was useful but to do something to somehow face the storm face down the storm just the way she wanted him blooded in the war like cherokee bill the war hero she used that word blooded the way you do for a hound it didn't matter if it almost killed him did kill everyone around him more than once so a man against nature story if only there were a real man around a real man which certainly wasn't mark not if you listened to mickey not in her thunderhead stage but why am i saying this why am i saying it what does it have to do

///with that very specific mark's study memory except maybe that if i look from his face to hers it was already too quiet too still with that real man never around never mark not even when he went down into the hurricane maybe not to save us but certainly to make sure we were safe no rescue definitive enough for mickey not even when he leapt across the burning stairs to bring me down from my room when i was six months old not when you can blow up the day with the spinning vortex of your voice instead of relaxing inside your celebrated safety the way we did on that pleasant all too brief hunkered down by the fireplace going dark and stormy benighted fall afternoon.

Black desk black chair black

typewriter
mystery mark's study.

Oak brown bookshelves brown oak hideaway

bedframe
more mystery mark's study

///take away mark and you'd have yourself a haiku.

Typewritten teapots

rolling off the platen i remember learning that word into mark's hand over to us where we sat on the study floor teapots made of x's big x's small x's magic x's on rough yellow paper as comforting as the famous cuppa with lots of milk we were allowed to drink downstairs this image better than words even new words images always better than words received into hands into mind always.

Public and private

the study at the front looking onto street cars school opposite sycamore leaves the bedroom at the back looking onto backyard warm lit houses opposite ginkgo trees.

That long narrow hallway

between study and bedroom bedroom and study mark and mickey just mark just mark mark and mickey day time nighttime day time nighttime back and forth back and forth back and forth bathroom for being bathed by parents in between back and forth once delightful back and forth.

Two typewriters

if you wanted you could call them two solitudes the two of them both black both on metal tables one by the black desk one by the white identical desks but mickey's doubling as the bedroom vanity she was the one didn't have a study how could it matter it wasn't a time to see the meaning of that woman works in the bedroom man in his own space no time to ask if that could render you hapless helpless turn you into a weather system not even able to predict yourself not looking into that mirror not looking out that window not with the equal mysteries lipstick on mouth and words on paper.

Mark always read out loud

archy and mehitabel
wasn't something mark read to us in the bedroom and he didn't stand against any mantel either when he did he sat in his study under the map or by the typewriter as he showed us about the shift key and the shift lock and the punctuation and the red and black of the ribbon as he made the teapots and he read about that about archy the cockroach who couldn't hop from key to key and do the shift lever at the same time though i swear to god that's not why i do it and archy's friend mehitabel the black cat's just more black for mark like his black hair his black desk as i always want to swear that mehitabel was never mickey never mickey but vicki gerdie the wife of new yorker editor bob gerdie people who came to those sunday parties and who took me every friday that first year at the manhattan school so beautiful with the gap between her front teeth and her fine auburn hair pulled back in a bun and so graceful and controlled who bought me the tiniest little steiff animal at this little store on some greenwich village corner every week i saw her tenth and sixth i think it was i can still smell it the store the animals mickey would later give away my whole steiff collection so you can see why i don't want it to be mickey i don't but it was anyway mehitabel was always mickey the best mickey mark could make and i knew he was doing it as he read archy and mehitabel mark and mickey one toujours gai the other his typewriter always bigger than he could ever be could ever imagine himself and yes that's the story he wanted to tell maybe wanted me to tell maybe still wants me to tell that story in black and white the way later lady and the tramp would be mickey and cherokee bill's best story in colour mark wouldn't have minded my telling that one either he would have thought i had it right toujour gai mark and a dance in the old dame yet the way mickey never a lady still always came first.

just so stories that's the one black on the white mantel
of the bedroom with the white vanity desk of course but it was mark who read them read them and read them standing himself curly haired black irish against the gas fireplace exuding irish charm as he took that oh so english book down to read sophisticated as any writer should be leaning against a mantel and the gas smell in the room and the orange to yellow light emphasizing the comfort in the contrast black book black irish man pastel pyjamaed children tim and me surrounded by covers of giant master bedroom bed mickey putting on lipstick in front of the mirror getting ready to go out and mark's voice deep and resonant the way it will be for the party

they are going to how the elephant got its trunk how the tiger got its stripes
we loved them how we loved them stories just so just so just so just ever so
but none for how mark murphy lost it all.

World map

It wasn't really all black that room of mark's not all black at all there was looking out the window onto green of leaves and beige tan of sycamore bark and there was looking above the old hide-a-bed at the three by six mercator projection world map on the wall rectangles bright to bright one tall one wide window to wall wall to window and black in the middle and they were beautiful the leaves of that sycamore tree and the way its bark shattered into shapes a map of its own world while inside that world map you could learn to travel navigate its mint green and egg yolk yellow and sky blue and salmon pink with your hands all the world at your fingertips you could go to north and south and east and west asia africa both americas europe australia antarctica were there ants there you once asked learn your continents your countries your compass points have them pointed out to you as mark read stories of travel and showed you the routes from place to place and you learned the letters learning to read until you could do it yourself on your own sneak in midafternoon midmorning watch the light change out the window turn to the map your hands your fingers moving you could find them all find europe find america find africa england find france find egypt find mexico find new york find london find paris find athens find new delhi find bogota find buenos aires find johannesburg then start again find new york find london find buenos aires find cairo find johannesburg find johannesburg find johannesburg start again mark mark gone find new york find london find paris find johannesburg find johannesburg find johannesburg over and over find johannesburg find johannesburg find johannesburg find johannesburg find johannesburg find again johannesburg

///watch dust gather on the books find johannesburg

///and on the typewriter find johannesburg find johannesburg

///and on the black leather chair find johannesburg and on the oak armrests of the hide-a-bed find johanesburg as you look from map to window map to window press your fingers to map find johannesburg is he hidden there in the soft crumbling cardboard underneath the colours find johannesburg is he hidden there under inside those letters find johannesburg find johannesburg try to see the bright colours not the black imagined inside find johannesburg go outside place fingers to tree the tree you had walked by in the middle of the night find johannesburg the tree with its bark like a map in beiges and browns is he hidden there find johannesburg in the cracks of the street the

slate the concrete find johannesburg between the bricks of the houses the crumbling mortar find johannesburg under the leaves under the tree find johannesburg look up look down look away find johannesburg all black now no leaves no tree no bark no bricks no map at all find johannesburg find johannesburg find johannesburg find johannesburg

///find johannesburg

///where mark had gone to die.

Johannesburg is the capital of south africa

South africa is at the tip of africa

The cape of good hope is at the tip of south africa

On the map it sticks pink into blue.

Vasco da gama was the first european

to round the cape of good hope

///in november 1497

///he didn't find or found johannesburg.

Johannesburg is substantially inland

New yorker staff writer mark murphy died

in johannesburg south africa on his fortieth birthday july 31 1952

///i can't go there.

Abscess obsessed

What i keep asking myself is why anyone might want to write about the first time they had an abscessed gum an icky sticky silly puffy pusfilled if nonetheless painless abscessed gum only the truth is i do i really do it's one of those headlines that just keeps coming back into mind more a flashing sign really advertisement or *advertencia* that's like a warning *te advierto* i warn you in spanish maybe for paul garcia's presence in our lives or just because i like the bilingual alliteration or maybe it's just a last ditch attempt to avoid being pulled back into that highlighted headline that won't leave me flashing on and off in my mind

///like those blue and red neon lights in the bars even if this is from the pre-bar era at least for us kids the time when we still got to hang out at home with the housekeeper and i'm up there on the top floor and the only red blue blue red colours to flash in my eyes are the blue and red twisty flower laden squiggles on the shiny linoleum floor red blue without words to explain the darkness that surrounds me as i'm reaching my hand out to the newel post which connects railing to bannister as the staircase starts down under the skylight the newel post at mouth level my tongue curving down down down into my gum feeling it all squishy and soft with the sweet salt taste of what must have been unseen pus the lava that flows from that spongy personal volcano as i just suck and suck enjoy the terrible connection of that saltiness its precision as i sink into darkness into fear dark wine crimson in my gut to match the blue dark of my mouth that's how it felt navy blue in my dark my own dark inside me only my eyes connecting

///to newel post then moving down to the place where the floor ends in soft pine wood just before the linoleum begins with its red blue blue red squiggles which dissolve into the red the blue and then the dark dark of my insides the whole rest of the world disappearing into dark so that the headline suddenly has no words and besides the question really isn't about my gum

///at all about my gum what that thing inside me really could have been what could have caused it that puffy unnamed and uncomprehended volcano named an abscess now only because it seems the easiest description the most likely pathology so many years and abscesses later blows to teeth that swell gum and eat away bone painfully push pus through soft palate only who cares what it was really what name it should carry what mattered after all was the taste the feel that pulled the blue of gum and red of gut into dark

dark purple dark eggplant dark to go with all the other eggplant darknesses this one a fog of absolute eggplant purple dark blue to red to purple the light fading until there is no yellow no green no orange not even mustard or olive certainly no deep rust just red and blue red and blue squiggles outside or in moving to purple eggplant purple dark the red and blue the colours not just of bar neon but of the neon sign of a crematorium once seen in mexico city can you imagine crematorium neon flashing on and off to blast its way through the mexico city night filled with music *rancheras corridas* jukebox songs to make a magic rhyme with montero's bar and grill the j&e the wigwam neither foreshadowing nor reminder but connective tissue between abandonment and death death and forever present fear

///of death of abandonment such short days after the massacre in tlatelolco hundreds maybe thousands even the u.n. unable to come up with an accurate number that crematorium sign causing my stomach to heave and refine the meaning of every barroom neon i'd ever encountered as i close my eyes to see behind the sign the decomposing bodies of dead students dead bystanders toasting the horrific end of the student movement of sixty eight at the long glass brick bar of montero's as they wait their turn for the fire the salt taste of tequila and abscess rising into my mouth to let me sink once more into the somehow comforting flavours of horror that salt on buried tongue the only thing specific enough to hang onto on that street even on that top floor as the newel post faded to the size of a pin surrounded by dark by eggplant purple and exploding blues reds and my hand reaches out long long elastic man long so that really i'll repeat it the question is not about the gum about why write about your first abscessed gum why obsess over your first abscess why this abscess obsession it's about why

///write about the first time you felt you had a fatal disease felt something inexplicable and wrong inside the darkness of your body something you were sure must be fatal could not be spoken out loud could just be felt over and over the words please no be gone forming themselves over and over red blue blue red repeating in the mind as you plumbed that salty eggplant purple depth with your tongue wishing it praying it away because it was too awful red blue on off the words the sign on off on off till there were no words left to leave the mouth just squiggles and nausea a blank mind and squiggles squiggles blue red squiggles on the floor between elastic man arm its reaching fingers and newel post your reach so exceeding what you wish to grasp the mouth closing around purple volcano this thing this rotting fatal thing too awful to tell too awful

///to minutely mention to anybody that tiny volcano too big too heavy too shameful to even begin the telling so that maybe now i could i should perhaps speculate on why that feeling why that horror why that shame why those squiggles why that inability to open my mouth to just say look look there's something horribly wrong in here and it's all squishy and it feels purple what's wrong with me what's wrong with me do something what's wrong with me to go crying to mickey the way i would with a cut a bruise look look i hurt i hurt at least to the reliable day mickey no matter the night betrayals or even to paul garcia to mark before he left to cherokee bill when he came back so what was it what was it with this that seemed so shameful so fatal so awful that to admit to it would bring disaster closer instead of shove it away make the fatality real absolutely unavoidable a head-on crash at a hundred miles an hour against the concrete barrier of the saying of it words suddenly as solid as any tree or oncoming semi-trailer so that i can understand how easily that happens women sometimes even men i had a great uncle died of breast cancer never said a word feeling lumps in breasts men and women watching black moles grow each one turning away and refusing to say the horror that feeling so deep in the mind you can hardly call it thinking that belief like palpating an interior volcano purple purple deep that belief that saying the horror is worse than the horror itself so that even when you know it's only the saying that can save you something inside still insists the saying is what will make it real the saying will kill you if you just don't say it it will go away and you stop dead and you can't move stop dead already dead so maybe that's the only reason

///i want to say this to tell this tell it not show it the showing of it still terrifies me turns me away from the saying as i try to remind myself in a very flat voice with a minimum of details no visuals please no squiggles no elastic man arm that saying the horror is always and forever the only way out so that now i'm saying it not an obsession a simple public service announcement made just to remind me to remind you to remind everyone to never do that again you won't do that again will you sink into silence into tongue sunk deep into gum into back of mouth into salty crater silence when the time comes for speech but try always to speak to save yourself if not the world just remember that's what's important

///no matter how flat the voice speech can still save you whether or not you will ever be able to truly make this ridiculous volcano in the mouth eggplant purple abscess thing into a headline for an actual story a different kind of childhood memoir at least for me light as meringue oh my first abscess oh that was so-o funny did you ever think you had a fatal disease were convinced you were about to die and it was just something oh so silly doesn't that happen to everybody this new headline this new story not old dusty neon but perky bright just so perky bright no on off off on neon sign fading into brooklyn bar into mexican crematorium eggplant night but plain letters contrasting painted letters on wood or cardboard sign maybe the kind kids paint to put in front of their lemonade stand lemonade five or fifty cents the letters dripping colour into bright

///bright zucchini bright lilac bright beach sand bright bright bright day to go with the headline oh it was so silly that first abscess that's right let's laugh why not just laugh at ridiculous children at how i could have thought a salty pusfilled abscessed gum could be fatal i can laugh over my abscess obsession kids think feel say the darnedest things from a time when people could still say darned without self-deprecation and maybe still knew what it meant maybe even darned their socks that's right tell it funny tell it darned funny like a darned big fucking hug forcing today's adult laughter back into the world of that child like carbonation into a soda make that story laughter bubble like seltzer over chocolate syrup in an egg cream as you swing back and forth on the plastic cushioned metal stool of the newest of fifties drugstore soda counters such kind laughter for that imagined me little me in the upstairs hall my tongue deep in the volcano of my gum as i reach out my elastic man arm to newel post thinking i'm dying

///dying of an abscessed gum oh hee hee hee hee stood up for my first date with death don't you just like that line hah hah ho ho stood up for my first date with death that's right light ironic laughter to erase that image that taste to let that abscess heal all on its own the way it really did so i can lower the register lower the tone

///lean back and whisper as if making a discovery but i was lucky so damn lucky imagine it could have been serious and an elbow to somebody's ribs a lingering look a knowing look that's why you always have to talk you know you always have to talk about those things the ones you've been made to think are shameful even if you don't know why whether it's sexual abuse paul's tongue in my mouth those games in the basement mickey ripping tim's clothes talking about his tiny prick or maybe for someone else the simple fact of being bullied saying i've never been bullied for years thinking you just handed over your lunch money day after day out of generosity that it was funny when they stuck you in a storm drain and made you recite which of your family members you would fuck or if it's the more ferociously serious lumps in breasts or along necks instead of the magic thinking of silly abscessed gums and besides you never know

///even when the wound appears to heal the salt taste fades if it really has and suddenly when i say or even think that the laughter fades too it's hard to go oh hee hee hee about anything and i'm back where i started not even on that detroit stair at grandma murphy's but up there on the top floor at nutmeg mews my hand reaching out to newel post reaching reaching and it's before and after all time all death all fear all at once and it's no easier to say than it was back then tongue tucked into mouth tongue now still stuck in mouth unmoving impossible all of a sudden to make that simple moral that's right dears let's always say the difficult things say them simply simply say them but oh for this moment let's make it funny because it's not it's not funny and the wound has never healed

///there's no funny laughter to welcome that child back into the community of the living stood up stood up that's right here comes that line again for her first date with death stood up stood up for so many thereafter because she's never been stood up for a date with her fear which was there after all over and over through mark's death and mark's mother's grandma murphy's 119
when finally you got to go to a funeral not to say goodbye to a dead father but to kiss the old dead cheek of a woman who hated you and sit on a basement stair behind a closed door and listen to the adults in the other room whisper of cancers that rotted you away from the inside and you felt back along your gum along its curve where the salt taste had been and wondered if it was still there underneath if you carved down with your tongue if you could find it all those cancers that must be yours your tongue rubbing and rubbing as if you could erase not just your gum but yourself because even as you sit and talk or try to write try to tell the story try to laugh at your abscess obsession you can feel that cold horror inside your body growing up toward your gum and even you don't want to welcome that child

///back with her precocious knowledge turned to overwhelming fear in this culture that will not would not speak of death of that most natural if terrible of events except in whispers passes it over with passes away and passed on and even passed as if it's some kind of final exam which if it is it's the hardest one you'll ever take and all the rest of the euphemisms even the critiques of them already clichés only what can you say to that child passed by passed over no one noticing her never invited to mark's funeral or never having any explanation of grandma murphy's you could try to laugh at that too make it humourous that strange quarantine how these days we speak of children who talk of sex as prematurely sexualized and examine them for it for signs of sexual abuse but we don't look for the ones prematurely deathed or maybe i should make that more appropriately latin mortized or even amortized even as we go on looking away from her walking around her shadow say in such chipper voices oh death death has been removed from most of our lives at least until very late and even then behind closed doors so that you feel yourself to be just that

///the death behind the closed door of the detroit basement or quarantined on the top floor of nutmeg mews the one who knows the secret carries it in her precocious body even as you feel your secret tiny death you feel your gum the death in your gum even as now your tongue might wander back over that spot where now a tooth is missing you couldn't afford the root canal to recognize to know how we might laugh at our culture's death taboo but we don't speak of the prematurely deathed even the maturely deathed the mortized or amortized because we don't want to know those people don't want to integrate them into our world let the widows the widowers wear armbands or the way so many turned away from tom as he dragged his oxygen tank through meetings and parties and accidental encounters at boat shows that still allowed him to dream of lost vacations and even when the few who hung in there asked him how he was doing and he replied not even i'm dying but i haven't got long they too turned away only to pound his back and laugh deep in their throats when he mentioned the transplant list suddenly given a way out in saying you'll make it there's no worries able to look away from the long and winding or short and sharp but always inevitable road we're all travelling oh ho ho ho ho you'll do great you'll see speaking of beating death as if it's a battle much less a war we'll ever really win so who wouldn't want to keep that girl behind closed doors even you even now just like then you want her there too because even if that gum would not secretly grow and grow into a cancer the rest of your body start to putrefy still it would grow and grow into a fear that would putrefy your mind take up your whole body gleaming deep and eggplant purple reach to just inside the skin where you could just scratch it and it would come streaming out like pus from an abscessed gum this knowledge unacknowledged so even you wouldn't want her at a dinner party

///feeling that gum because what she knew was true is true that's the very crux of it it's true and whether or not it's silly to think that gum would grow into a cancer to take over the body something will something will there is a death coming trundling toward you like an oxygen cart with or without salt taste deep in mouth and no matter how you try to comfort her or integrate her that at least is still there that death so you understand why she was put away why you were willing to take three years of your life and pour them into that hole that huge volcano in your mouth mark's leaving and mark's death and paul garcia and mickey's laughter and aj on his bike making the announcement and you falling off the fence as you thought of mark once more with you in the circus and tim's dog curly hooked to the fence by drying fish hooks she'd bit into and you sick up in mickey's room weeks months of it and that time you thinking not that it was from a salty sick abscessed gum but from the only huge spiral all day sucker anyone ever gave you no matter how much you begged and this one from mark that last day you ever saw him and inside it death curled like a worm maybe all that sugar did help rot your gum that story anyway more realistic than anemia and fever from an all day sucker that's what you thought for years but what does it matter whatever caused what inside the story of the gum of the sucker death still curled there

///all of it in your mouth holding back all those other stories you chose to ignore or even forget the longest forgetting your mouth sealed up there hand reaching out to newel post as you see mickey standing off to just one side of the circular stair in the front room on the main floor all the way down as you approach the bottom and turning to you he's sick you know he's sick she says mark's sick and the world curls in around the hole of her red lipsticked mouth just as your tongue curls in around the imagined red of your gum and the rest of the world goes eggplant purple he's sick you know he's sick preparing you and then she herself going away to her last big job researching for time life before she would be fired texas i think interviewing senator lyndon baines johnson and not there not even there when i was told the news and i took that death into myself deep into myself as if i could tuck it down into that gum like those years of my life that surrounded it deep into that gum as my hand will reach out to newel post my eyes seek skylight as i seek to get out so that there is a whole book there a whole book a book of holes left behind a death itself book of stories that is mark's death and my fear of death of knowing death of death in me that is in the rotting of my gum as my elastic man hand reaches to newel post reaching reaching reaching my reach always so far exceeding my grasp of any of this and i choose to ignore it all as step step step i walk down the stairs three flights and out passing by where mickey stood to go into the street to leave all those stories behind to tell other stories that can save you in the telling or that at least i can laugh at believing there will come a time i can laugh at this one in her presence come back through these years of stories to finally arrive still laughing at the stories of that time only to encounter

///her fear to have my laughter die its own small death on my tongue which reaches back into my gum bare again after the death of the molar that finally erupted there they do say that erupted like a volcano though not directly out of that pus i don't think though i don't know for sure because all i find in that place is that same fear flashing red blue red blue on off off on which doesn't mean the story the stories aren't worth telling any story is after all worth telling if you can make your public laugh with it cry with it or just need it yourself to keep going after all that's what it's about story isn't it telling absence into the presence of us of us who are still here you can take that one right back to the beginning of language as far as it goes the story by the fire thing make your jokes in the here and now look i'm here i'm the one stood up on her first date with death but that's not the same thing as telling it to her

///that girl behind the door that girl reaching out for the newel post the one swaying back and forth the one whose tongue wanders deep into the storyless salt of that gum whose reaching reaching reaching will always exceed her grasp the one who knows subtle rot and knows death and is beyond story the way death is always beyond story so that somewhere inside that story inside that girl who sits or stands with her knowledge in her mouth will be unstory this the story to end all stories the knowledge that is itself the fatal disease even if it is a small joke inside a salty pus filled gum because that small purple volcano heralds the coming the sure coming of the fatal disease that is both the end and the end of narrative death and the death of narrative so no wonder

///it doesn't matter how very often i take her up and try to tell that story of the gum or all those other stories of mark's death to comfort to normalize her with laughter normalize some part of me i don't want to know with laughter no wonder in the end she will always be back on that basement stair in detroit the top of the stairs at nutmeg mews across the street from that sign in mexico city deathed mortized amortized prematurely and maturely because the truth she knows is a truth narrative can neither soothe nor solve certainly never get you beyond there no amount of telling will rescue her or for that matter you because where she is there is no narrative no little chain of stories like gleaming stones to bring her back into our world she is where there is no one to tell no one who has lived to tell the tale this is not mark murphy bringing back to esther whose dead cheek you will kiss as you will not kiss his the small stories the gossip of the neighbourhood where he grew up in monmouth illinois to help her through the worst of the various diseases that would take her to her bed a verbal trash collector mark was mickey always said and that's where he started while she would laugh too believing esther to fake the diseases just to get her son always to report back story a way to control her son only this is where there is no one to report to storylessness concentrated there in the fatal knowledge of that gum its chaotic blue red purple volcano this is the crematorium sign blinking on and off no one to tell the tale and no one to whom to tell it not even the self as the self fades for the moment of crossing of passing as they say passed on passed over passed whatever test that is that we will all take so that she is always there my personal reminder my very own vulture at the crossroads of stair and newel post

///and the truth is we probably all have someone like her located somewhere in our lives inside us beside us always there not halfway up and halfway down that stair but up and down at once always and never there with us and against us someone who we can pretend is our own personal portrait of some sort of dorian gray the one who hidden away rots or feels the rot the way she feels again and again into that gum as we pretend to remain young and vibrant always winning our battle with death with our good cheer and total denial the rotting gum the rotting body the shooting gun the knowledge of death always somewhere else in some closet or top of the stair under the eaves or in the cellar while still i find myself looking at the sign on the crematorium in mexico city flashing on off off on over the knowledge of the dead in tlatelolco the plaza of the three cultures while the bar nearby plays *corrida* after *ranchera* after *corrida* thinking maybe the mesoamerican duality whether ometeotl or the hero twins or all the other twinnings quetzalcoatl and tezcatlipoca says it best among so much that i would learn once set on my road of learning all the gods the divine concepts and concepts of the divine in and around and outside all of us cherokee bill with his mississippian dual heritage set me on not opposites or polarities at all that dual thinking but simply this that our deaths walk with us

///our deaths walk with us up and down the street or stair always there the crematorium sign on off on off blue red blue red while i remember scattered bars and the taste of a volcano in my mouth my elastic man arm reaching out and my death walks with me and i will always be two not opposites but dualities always two my death walks with me always two the life death duality living with me living in me as i live my death walk my death so maybe i go back to her and her rotting gum because i am her and her rotting gum and she is me laughing at the joke and even if i can never dedeath her we can never dedeath demortize ourselves still in walking with her down those stairs reencountering her up at the top bringing her stories like crumbs she can never follow but always eat like the spirits that visit on the day of the dead maybe somewhere sometime in the death of narrative when no story can yet be told in that moment that we are our deaths and we are truly in the moment to become one not two in conversation that conversation that sets our world in motion there will be something that i have told her in all my stories that will be a comfort to us when the two are finally one when the dynamism of duality stops when we are she and i one last perhaps one only

///time

///death world

///world death

///without end.

Sashimi

This would be years later with cherokee bill a habit from his years away his years in japan wonderful with ginger and wasabi the way it still is only now everyone knows about it or at least about sushi even if more people do those nice little polite raw fish and rice packages often enough with seaweed cummerbunds no just plain fish of sashimi for them picked up with your chopsticks lightly dipped into soya and wasabi and quick into mouth the way i've been doing for decades even if back then often enough i dropped the fish and the soya splashed back onto my shirt never to come off still for all my adult dexterity i liked it better back then looking at cherokee across the table as we knelt actually knelt in the japanese restaurant where we celebrated his homecoming or us still having that last bit of money before it ran out and he hocked everything he could and went back to sea that's right i liked it better when it was just us and all the other westerners in the restaurant ate well cooked teriyaki or sukiyaki and only bill conversed with the waiters in japanese i liked it better i did like it better i still like it better me with my raw secret love of raw why is my comfort my comfort food always raw.

Halfway up and halfway down

this is my stair of course it is the stair i sat on and thought about mark when he'd just died and was he in heaven or was he in hell and was he watching me or was he just rotting and i felt my face to find the skull underneath and no i don't want to write about it not now not here mostly not at all though maybe one day i'll do a book just about that just about those days of mark dying the days around mark dying which i forgot about for the longest time tried to forget about for the longest time made that mickey mark paul year maybe two disappear for the longest time the length of it just showing sometimes at the edge of the headlines the little stories which maybe i'll tell or maybe not maybe i'll just use that stair halfway up to the top floor halfway down to the bedroom to the study for one of those stupid new age pronouncements something about moving on and this is the first day of the rest of your life because even if i'm halfway still there up or down heaven or hell after all i did

///get up that is.

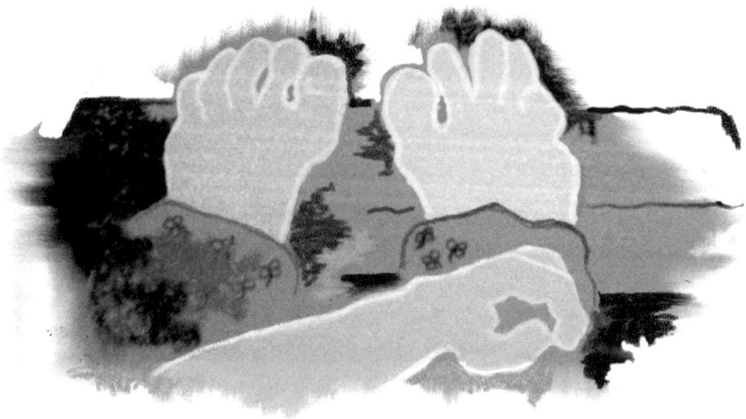

Patrifer robin

Sometimes you hear things you're sure must be profound in fact you absolutely know that they're profound spiritually profound in particular it helps when there's some extra-profound ah ah ah ah ah slow music with sanctus sanctis behind it to back up the spirituality or maybe there's quotes about tasting the fire lying in the fire walking through the fire and all that dark night of the soul burning up expiring in ecstasy stuff there's always the great one from machtilde of magdeburg about how if you want to know my meaning you can just lie down in the fire you can actually hear that music those voices again sanctus sancti ah ah ah know you're supposed to feel yourself begin to spin oh yes oh yes into fire into air into the elements into transcendence spiritual profundity at its best ah yes ah yes ah yes ah ah ah ah bernini's santa teresa sanctus sancti eeeeeh eeeeeh eeeeeh eeeeeh and all that only all you can do is get halfway or maybe not

///even that maybe not even a quarter the distance the way i could only ever get halfway up just make it like christopher robin to my stair on the top flight between the children's quarters the old nursery and mickey's and mark's rooms his black desk claiming the study her white one the master bedroom none of it anymore mark's even if that study was left the same the horsehair stuffed chair the three foot by six world map for the longest time sanctus sancti ah ah ah ah on my stair hearing the funeral ceremony in the lady chapel of saint patrick's cathedral the one i wasn't invited to and neither was tim imagined for years kyrie eleison sanctus sancti oh the music

///that music and all those stories apocryphal or not the new yorker crowd and jim agee getting mickey into the cab and her saying oh with what pride she tells it *just don't let it happen to you jim* she says as she gets in *just don't let it happen to you* and then it happens to jim anyway two years later and in a cab too that's why she tells it i'm sure at least it wasn't on a significant birthday like mark's death on his fortieth to give her more symbolic ammunition all in capital letters without a doubt *don't let it happen to you jim* lending mickey a sense of importance of foreknowledge of belonging even when she'd left that world behind for the world of montero's bar and grill of the easy drunk the cadged meal of *how much is that doggie in the window* mambo and cha cha cha only no matter what plays on paul garcia's radios sanctus sancti that music the lady chapel they don't go away at least for me imagining that ceremony and all those people the gothic beams and mark rising up rising up into transcendence his soul to watch over us and sanctus sancti kyrie eleison only i can't quite do it i'm always only just there on my stair halfway up and trying to do it myself to make it happen to push him up sanctus sancti into the space above only it's never

///the arching spaces of the cathedral but right there sanctus sancti directly above me into the space above the stair right above the stair above the landing above my room tim's room right up through the chicken wire reinforced glass skylight into the sky the sanctus sancti sky of our father who art in heaven our father who marks our heaven mark who must be in heaven push him up push him up our father up there up there from halfway up your stair push him up there push him up kyrie eleison dominus eleison push him up push him up to watch over you you christopher robin halfway up and halfway down christopher robin the story he once read you warm in his arms in that old black leather horsehair stuffed chair in his study push him up there where he can still watch you our father who art my father who art my father who art my art my art of pushing him up pushing him up pushing him up my art of transcendence my art who fathers mark in heaven who art in heaven only it's only ever halfway up the stair christopher robin halfway up and halfway down me pushing up and him pushing down pushing down pushing down pushing down on top of me pushing down and then there's uncle maurie's voice back from the cathedral back from the lady chapel there in the kitchen before i can escape up my stair uncle maurie's voice and the word *hell* repeating *in hell no heaven go to hell* the catholic kids across the street the same *in hell go to hell* ha ha ha ha ha *go to hell no heaven for you godless murphys go to hell* skipping rope to its tune no ah ah ah ah eeeh eeeeh eeeeh eeeeeh in go to hell the nuns throwing their candy go to hell go to hell go to hell and you running

///away to halfway christopher robin up your stair bearing not christ but your father up to your stair there's a christopher a lucifer christ bearer light bearer there's even aquifer and who cares if we don't name our children aquifer the aquifers are still there and we all bear the water of ourselves so why is there no patrifer not patrick like the cathedral but patrifer patrifer after all don't we all bear our fathers all our fathers our fathers who art in heaven or elsewhere but who art our art our art who fathers our burden fathers you to push him up push him up push him up push him up so he can look over you even as he weighs you down maybe just forget transcendence forget spirituality forget profundity it's all a lacanian parable my whole life a lacanian parable if not paradigm mark the dead father and mickey the non-existent woman the woman who *n'existe pas* erasing herself her own feminine not wiles but wilds her wildness her excesses nothing exceeds like excess for the woman who insists by day on being a mini-man the rational principle wielding the dead father as the weapon of patriarchal power to keep us all in line your father this your father that until we believe in fear of her nights that if we just obey that sober manly self we will have our place in that symbolic order of new yorker of time life writers she has abandoned a proper life a time life ordered life not this life outside of time that needs transcendence or at least its possibility needs to push him up push him up push him up our father our father who art only you can't do it my eyes wander to the space between the bannister posts pulled downward burn in hell burn in hell burn in hell it's not transcendence it's not ah ah ah ah eeeh eeeh eeeeh eeeeh into the ether into air into sky it's burn in hell burn in the fire of hell exactly there halfway up that staircase on the very stair the very stair the one that's been repaired the one that fell through that time of the fire the one that started in the wastebasket not ahh ah ah ah eeh eeh eeeh eeeh that time but aaaaii aaaaii eeeeek eeeeek and mickey's hand to her mouth

///eeeeek eeeeek eeeeek it's always eeeeek eeeeek eeeeeek with mickey the way it was when the mouse ran up inside the leg of her blue jeans only this time it's *the stairs are on fire the stairs are on fire* eeeeek eeeek eeeeek that last flight with the wastebasket sitting halfway up and halfway down waiting to be dumped the one that was left to catch on fire the one that smoldered burst into flames burned through the wood and mickey still eeeeek eeeeek eeeeek eeeeek *sarah is up there sarah is upstairs* up in her nursery asleep in her nursery there at the very top ah ah ah ah ah eeeeh eeeeeh eeeeh eeeeh sanctus sancti the very top you'd think i was waiting for transcendence the fires of hell not just smoke inhalation as i must have played with my toes in my crib i never remembered a thing about it of course i didn't i must have been all of six months old it was just another of those told stories waiting to be contemplated told and told again of mickey's eeeek and mark's aaaaah his fierce bravery never quite as good as bill being blooded and for that matter bloodied in the war but as good as the story of jim in his cab to have that moment of heroism of stepping right across that burning stair to go up to the nursery to go get you to bring you down no sanctus sancti but a profound drum roll as he makes that leap across the smoky limbo of space to bring you down so that years later when you could walk on your own you could crawl back hands and feet slapping the wood patrifer robin halfway up and halfway down your stair and sit there to attempt to return the favour to push him up push him up push him up sanctus sancti out of the ashes out of the fire out of the coffin out of the earth out of your hands pushing against your skull because it's not that simple anymore it's not just hell or heaven bad or good it's your own limbo that pulls you now and no simple leap over the fire into the air into transcendence into aaaah aaah eeeeeh eeeeh eeeh will do to get you out from that space that opens under that stair after you hear mickey tell maurie when he said you'd go to hell *your children are going to go to hell mickey* and there's mickey with her *don't try that with me the unbaptized go to limbo even i know that* only what you know

///sitting on your stair is that it's worse you know it's worse no one ever explains anything but you know this is worse you can feel it not fire not air not even water but the element of earth earth in the nostrils earth in the eyes earth in the ears earth in all the senses no up up up up eeeeh eeeeh eeeeh eeeeh just earth in the eyes in the ears in the voice rot in the ground rot with the worms rot with the woolly bear caterpillars rot in the earth and me feeling it not ah ah ah ah up up up up eeeeh eeeeh eeeeh eeeeeh pushing him up pushing him up not even burn in hell burn in hell but rot rot my fingers enclosing my face enclosing my skull rot in the ground rot in limbo patrifer robin halfway up and halfway down always halfway up and halfway down so you don't even remember that he was baptized you're bearing him into your limbo with you no more sanctus sancti just my hands on my face because this is mickey's laughter in maurie's face *hell no limbo* she repeats while wiggling back toward the ground in imitation limbo dancing around the kitchen laughing at him in that drunken voice *hell no limbo going to limbo limbo* a little excessive happy turbulent tune but you know

///it's going to nothing it's being told you're going to nothing that's right not up up up up or down down down down ah ah ah ah eeeeh eeeeh eeeeh eeeeeh not sanctus sancti or burn in hell but to nothing to nothing so you wonder about it again your hands on your skull nothing nothing can this be nothing can he be in nothing not our father who art in heaven or burn in hell but your elbows on your knees your fingers around your face there on your stair patrifer robin pinching your flesh distracting yourself to wonder at worms at the woolly bear caterpillars you had lifted from the earth of the highway construction down by mark's favourite the old waterfront bar only all you can see is him rotting now beneath that earth going to nothing slowly going to nothing is that what they meant by the worms crawl in the worms crawl out were they those worms in his skull in your skull there among the remainders of torn down buildings with not just caterpillars but the knee high beginnings of ailanthus adding their skunklike odour to that rubble smell of old brick and older shit such uncountry unearth earth smells but still before you can get lost in nothing get lost in the ground please push him up push him up through the skylight sanctus sancti where there's still the memory of his warm hand

///in yours walking from the bar its sawdust still stuck to your shoes your shoelaces only they play pinochle on your snout crawling crawling crawling you can't stop them you can't even if you take your hands away from your face and keep trying to push him up push him up push him up hear the profound music hear any music hear *how much is that doggy in the window* no limbo no nothing please music music without burning or rotting or limbo even limbo dancing for him who came through the fire of his own creation

///that cigarette into the wastepaper basket as he passed by together with all the writing he couldn't do barely marked paper all crumpled up and there's you now on that stair waiting for the cool water he came back to pour on the burning burning the fire of horror the worms crawl in as you try to push him up to protect you again only it's not going to happen he's not there and you can't even make him look down on you our father who art feel him guarding you not with your hands on your skull and maurie's burn in hell burn in hell burn in hell replaced by the sick nausea of mickey's limbo dancing *hell no limbo*

///where i already am patrifer robin halfway up and halfway down that stair where the wastebasket burned with no sensation left in my fingers just the fear in my stomach and i can't push him up all i can do is wait wait for nothing wait for nothingness and it will be a long time a long time of pushing my fingers into my skull and looking up at clouds through skylights and waiting afraid of nothing deathly afraid of nothing willing to go to nothing to stop being afraid of nothing willing to die just to have control of the moment of my death get rid of this fear of nothing and that's all I think about after a while not the stories not the lady chapel not heaven not hell not transcendence but nothing nothing when is nothing coming because there is no rescue not by him

///he won't rescue me not that dead mickey weapon limbo father not even that memory of warm live father he won't even look down or be pushed up so there's just my hands on my skull waiting and no the truth isn't that i did it myself figured it out myself or fooled myself into believing it was all all right i would transcend by force of will or music sanctus sancti this isn't some premature enlightenment coming up next our feature or future presentation walking through the emptiness of nothing to the fullness of nothing dark night of the soul there's none of that here the rescue will come from the outside the way rescue always comes to children in movies as in life if it comes at all maybe the way it comes to most of us at one time or another if we're honest no one simply survives heroically we depend on each other for rescue from the things no one would survive concentration camp survivors prisoners of war political prisoners may do well or badly for the duration but the end is always determined by what help arrives in time for rescue and who knows what kind of religious or secular war i was in the middle of who even were truly its factions but i was certainly its prisoner with rescue this time almost a literal deus ex machina the war hero out of the engine room *la cámara de máquinas* they say in spanish bringing god with him that other father coming back the one outside mickey's and for that matter probably lacan's symbolic order the father that didn't exist either mickey's model for the noble savage never allowed to represent the father no matter how often he carried out those duties our new man of the sea rescue from coming back bill cherokee bill coming back bill finally coming back to make the house function again always coming back the way the cherokee named people that the ones who returned from the trail of tears might bear that name bill returning from his own trail of tears in japan to rescue me not to push me up into the sky or to go there himself to look over me but to stay here to take me from my stair and back to the outside world

///back out and forward

///to and into other places that earth by the dock was covered with asphalt pretty quick the old bar torn down cars whirring by over it so that it was other places other spaces you went to for woolly bear caterpillars or ailanthus fronds swaying black mussels or green red mangos wallpaper on broken brick or tadpoles in algae filled streams spaces that don't lift anybody up but ground you in the earth oh forget lacan forget all that contingent secular all reality is discursive reality stuff this is good isn't it we've made it from the transcendent to the immanent nature of god by the age of eight as bill tells you walking holding your hand as if there were no reason to come back but to give you this message *there is no hell* he tells you looking around *there is no hell there is just this* just this and god is in this god is in everything the trees and the flowers and the stars and the dead and the woolly bear caterpillars and the water of the harbour for all its pollution and us in us we are already in god and god is in us and who cares if mickey says it's just so sticky gooey sugar sweet primitive pantheism and *if there's one thing i can't stand sarah it's when they start talking about the great spirit* and even if sometimes you think she must be right

///you say you believe him anyway you believe he's brought if not god some kind of understanding of god out of his engine room ex machina to be in machina to be in everything because you try to believe that thing about god in everything and you say it you repeat it just to get away from fear and waiting and limbo and patrifer robin up there on your stair your hands over your face feeling your skull until every once in a while there's these other times and it's like you believe the ants you believe the caterpillars you believe the leaves and they believe you and everything is so clear just so clear the branching veins on the ailanthus leaves the grey blue of the sky the sun reflected off of brick you can hear the grubs in the earth and when you look at the praying mantis you can feel her looking back and the woolly bear caterpillars carry the earth in their eyes and time stops and you're just there just here and if all there is is this this is enough this with god in it and the fear of death and nothing and limbo retreats *hell no limbo* sounds a different emphasis because god is in you and you are in god and you can feel it inside the time that is and the time that is not the emptiness that is full and the emptiness that is empty and what more could you want what more could you want patrifer robin what more than this so take this opportunity to just get up

///stretch look at the skylight feel the smoke of the fire the leap over limbo holding bill by one hand mark by the other leap over limbo *hell no limbo* and walk down the stairs out into the backyard out onto the street god is in everything woolly bear caterpillars cracks in the sidewalk sprouting stinky ailanthus trees and that's just about as profound as i can still ever get so if you want to know my meaning lie down in this fire patrifer robin the fire on my stair sanctus sancti only remember to get up and walk away ah ah ah ah eeeh eeeh eeeh eeeh saecula saeculorum amen.

I never read to my children

or almost never much less leaned against mantels to do it like mark murphy with his just so stories a terrible thing for a writer to admit really but who's really a writer i did what i do best i ranted i raved i told them stories i did all sorts of stories though mostly it was bugs bugs bugs bugs a final preference for archy over mehitabel an extirpation of my early cat preference with maybe the odd amphibian thrown in tiny frogs under leaves or giant sea monsters lost in streams and then to top it off there's my soggy shoe series that's right let's have a just so soggy shoe story

///hey diddle dumpling it might start or at least be remembered in intertextual reference to my co-author hey diddle dumpling my son only it's not john it's lee my son lee and he definitely didn't go to bed with his trousers on his trousers were in fact soaked soaked up to the knee and beyond though he did have one shoe off and one shoe on that's what starts this off step squish step squish all the way home

///from fish creek park and the other shoe not just off but afloat somewhere in the river risen with the early spring melt the current had ripped the shoe away and maybe it was kind of funny seeing him like that step squish step squish into the house after taking in the perfect cartoon made famous little boy with slingshot in back pocket huck finn i don't want to talk about it but i have to tell someone hang dog look at the front door but pretty soon fun is replaced by that other f word fear fear the kind of fear oh fuck that focuses again and again like sticking a tongue into an abscess on the luck of this time not having to say if only

///but instead

///of only having to say thank god or the goddess or touching wood or something similar as your shoulders your hands yours knees kind of shake and then there comes the pride that he was smart enough to go no further into the current from where he was playing to try to get the shoe back even if it was a new runner he'd picked out himself and it meant step squish step squish all the way home the two kilometres up hill from the park and cold too the ice still coming down the creek in huge pieces melted only enough to look like gleaming honeycombs as they're carried along with the dead and sodden branches or caught in layered piles on leaning trees not yet torn from the banks he never did tell me what he'd gone into the creek after or if it was just the joy of challenging the creaking shore bound ice for the moment your foot goes through and i never did ask either didn't even yell you idiot you could have died or expound in detail on the possible ways drowned hypothermic caught among branches crushed against rocks squeezed into culverts just congratulated him on a wise decision well taken because there he was step squish step squish home

///to hot cocoa or mulled cider and then he's in bed in his warm winter pyjamas and what we're doing is telling stories the two of us telling stories not step squish step squish stories or for that matter his favourite we've been doing them a long time a new one a night six leg stories we call them the varied adventures of various bugs brown green red crawling flying inching he picks the bug i tell the stories once upon a time there was an ugly a beautiful you fill in the phrase bug and it had six legs but instead we're both looking in our minds' eyes at that shoe that new runner he didn't follow into the river and we're telling shoe stories black and white purple and green yellow and blue ever changing shoe stories soggy soggy shoe stories lonesome shoe stories shoe in search of a friend stories hey diddle dumpling my son lee so many ways to cheat death and the fear of death we must have told that shoe all the way to the atlantic

///and across.

Johannesburg is nowhere near the cape of good hope

nor any other good hope i still can't go there.

Cat tails cat tales

If you hadn't pulled their tails they wouldn't have run away and you'd have a cat that's always the story if you hadn't pulled their tails they wouldn't have turned and scratched you and you would have had a cat long before this that's what they always tell me if you don't pull their tails they'll leave you alone and no one will have to hear you cry and have to take care of you and worry about your eyes and put bandaids on your arms your hands your cheeks your fingers and worry about infections and kiss things better and mourn your little boo boo and you know how busy i am we are that's always the story so why would you why would you who would want you

///to have a cat if you can't keep your hands off their tails you can't stop from making them scratch you until you cry and cry those big boo boo tears and what Is this about wanting a cat so much anyway there's no cat in this picture all you really want is attention attention and not from a cat either look at me look at me young lady every day it's bandage the finger bandage the arm bandage the hand so you can just stop the crying stop the tail pulling if you don't pull their tails and make them run away make them scratch you just might get a cat you just might maybe you would maybe you would maybe you would

///have had a cat long before now they keep telling me so no matter how much i stand there the tears running down my face but it is the cat it is the cat it is the cat they don't understand because how can you explain you want those cats you want them you want them you want to grab them you want to hug them you want to put your face in their fur so you always pull their tails as they turn to run away because you want them you want them you want them you don't want them to run away and why should they run you love them you do only you're too small far too small to explain

///the cat in the yard and your eye on the cat and your hand out and the cat turning to run how it's only and ever the tail that's left and you pull it you pull it how can you explain standing there that need how it's not the attention at all you don't think about your hands your arms your eyes you think about the cat the cat the cat only someone is always angry and always shouting you can't have a cat you can't have a cat you can't have a cat you have to stop pulling their tails the tail of every cat you see every cat that wanders into the yard no matter whose it is white or gold or black or crossing your path tabby marked or calico owned or disowned coddled or fight scarred and where were they all from anyway and who cares you just can't keep doing this you have to stop no cat for you until you do and that's the best take on it

///the best cat tail cat tale the best way to tell it remembering advancing maturity make the story an example of advancing maturity smarmy little george w bush smile and oh yes i couldn't have a cat not until i stopped being so eager to have one i pulled the tail of every cat that came near enough to grab i must have pulled the tail of every cat in the entire neighbourhood and they all scratched me too and i never learned my lesson not till i started to grow up just that bit you know the old story postponement of gratification and all that rational thinking understanding the relationship between cause and effect when you pull their tails they run away and if you hold on they turn to scratch you good so never restrain them always pet them nicely always that story pet them nicely that's right pet them nicely be a good girl pet them nicely and that way you can always put your face in their fur you can do it maturity is having a cat having a cat is a reward for maturity now isn't that nice my first reward for maturing just that oh how nice

///you're becoming at least to cats and the big lipstick mickey smile the bright red you always watched her put on by her mirror in the friendly mickey

go to work days oh how nice you are what a nice girl how grown up you're becoming they never did say mature in those days or if they did they said matooor and said you were only mature if you said matooor and that was years later anyway so look look big smile you don't pull their tails anymore how grownup you are big smile again the big smile reward just like the big smile how grown up reward they always tried for not fighting which never worked oh how grown up big lipstick smile any mickey smile was less of a reward than the fight itself but how good it felt that one time it really did only it wasn't the smile it was the cat and being grown up yes grown up because i controlled my world the world of my get a cat tale my cat tale of not pulling tails i don't pull their tails anymore do i do i i don't i don't so that means i can have a cat at last doesn't it doesn't it a cat oh a cat a cat what a great thing to attain such maturity figure out that leap in logic never leap overboard run after what you want until you pull its tail just wait and stay calm say calmly what you want a lesson in girlishness too that waiting that learning to wait for the cat

///to come to you maturity at the age of six or seven an end to years of tail pulling an end with a kitten in a box only the truth is that no matter how often kind calm caring big lipstick mickey tried to run that one by me i can still hear it in my head that you won't get a cat as long as you pull their tails line or for that matter there's how i would giggle and do it to myself later on adolescent or adult laughing at how anyone could possibly imagine a cat would stay with them if they pulled its tail oh what a silly child while still

///that's not the real story the true cat tail cat tale it may have a mature moral but it's still not the reason i got a cat though maybe it is the story of how when the house got a cat they declared it mine they made the cat the house was going to get anyway mine the reward for how grown up i was that's right now that you can pet them nicely here's the reward and there's not just the big lipstick mickey smile but the housecat the new kitten declared mine right there in a box though maybe even that part of the cat tail cat tale fails to be true fails to be the real story doesn't tell why the house needed a cat anyway the truth is that cat tale is completely different doesn't involve tails at all at least on cats it's really the mouse tail mouse tale of how i woke up screaming in the middle of the night which wasn't mature at all

///when you think about it even if there was this clanging clanging clanging clanging in the wastebasket certainly didn't feel mature at the time the clanging clanging clanging and me screaming screaming screaming totally disoriented until everyone ran up from downstairs to discover the mouse a mouse in the wastebasket banging back and forth in the little red metal cylinder in the corner of my room we had a bunch of them one in every room only the strange thing is i remember that one exactly how it was busted and bent in one corner so that the metal curved over to show the grey metallic unpainted inside i remember that even if i don't remember the story told and retold of how mark stepped over the one with the fire in it carrying me when i was six months old now that i was six years old and mark was gone or dead and paul garcia was in the basement so it was mickey and paul who ran up the stairs when they heard me screaming screaming maybe black whitey dawson too and bob v i do seem to remember a crowd though who stands out is mickey and paul and the mouse of course though that was later first it was just the clanging clanging in the wastebasket a wastebasket come to life starting to move as i still screamed and screamed and they went over to look into it and it resolved into a mouse which paul reached in and grabbed by its tail you see now how this one's a mouse tail mouse tale and flushed it down the toilet and maybe that was the first time i knew

///we had mice or maybe i already did though i don't think so i would have fallen in love with the mouse idea built mouse cities in my mind put clothes on them like beatrix potter's country mouse city mouse and i didn't get the time didn't get too long to love the idea of having mice before the cat i wanted so much more got there and scared them off though for mickey there's no doubt this wastebasket mouse this mouse tail mouse tale was the last straw and the reason the house got a cat the house got a cat they called mine was that we had mice and the cat was a reward for terror for screaming even louder than for when i pulled the cats' tails and they scratched me a reward for abject screaming in the middle of the night for pushing the daily reality of mouse shit on tables or corners into a terror which alone might justify counter mouse terrorism total war atrocity extermination just what mickey by then no doubt wanted so that's right the housecat

///and being told it was my cat being allowed to take care of it like it was my cat having it sleep with me in my bed and wake up not screaming but whimpering when it got its claws tangled in my hair a reward for terror for finally being terrified enough that my actions got a mouse flushed down the toilet made the hungry house mice into exterminable mini-terrorists so the fact is if it had been willful if that's what i'd done or wanted i might even feel guilty feel the cat was a reward for murder for my terror making them murder the mouse that one poor little trapped mouse the way murder so often follows terror especially murder of the small and the helpless and the obviously easy target and this one so perfectly available inside its clanging metal cage trying to get out oh i could make that mouse tail cat tale into an easy moral about a careless consumer society oh don't worry your pretty little head about where that blouse those shoes that rug comes from where that child that man that woman that mouse went just go to sleep think of all your rewards and there'll be a cat in the morning only the fact is lousy or mousy

///i was barely awake so whether or not you could say that about sleep-walking consumers too whatever i might be tempted to say conclusions i might like to draw i still see the relationship much more guiltlessly clearly neither murder nor contemplation of culpability just clang clang clang in the wastebasket scream scream scream in my bed mouse found comfort coming cat later mouse in toilet possible guilt murder moral passing unnoticed with cat as reward only for my night terror and outsized screaming and so clear guiltlessly perfectly clear that it wasn't maturity that brought the cat at all in fact it was downright childishness so at least i could still be a kid sometimes i might say i still got occasional irrational rewards calming comforting rewards just because i was a kid rewards not niceness behavioural modification rewards from big lipstick smile and smile mickey so who knows which one is the best way to tell the cat tale

///cat tails or paul's hand on mouse tail or for that matter which the best way to think about that whole getting a cat thing or a least being told the housecat would be my cat thing shsh shsh don't be afraid you poor little thing you'll get a cat or you're so grown up you're such a big girl now you understand how to treat animals you'll get a cat because that's not really the true story either insofar as you can talk about truth in a case like this the unique truth the real truth as opposed to truths and all that postmodern stuff the truth to which one of my selves on which day the truth according to my needs not my ability to take it because now that i look back on it at least one of the truths of this whole cat tail cat tale mouse tail mouse tale is that i did actually like that mouse once i found out

///what it was would have pleaded for mercy for it if i'd been awake enough built those beatrix potter costumed or cartoon cute little mouses from its image ever after probably would have thought the mouse shit cute too in its diminutive way if someone had only told me what those little black lumps were at the back of the cupboard shelves that cuter by the day image probably aided by the fact that they hadn't let me near it even near the wastebasket once they got to the room so i never saw its dusty grey urban mouse coat got bitten by its nasty sharp yellow teeth got to think of it as a mini-rat that just might bite a baby as paul walked quietly out of the room holding it by the end of its long bare tail as it squeaked and squirmed and tried to double back on itself to bite him then flushed it without so much as a grimace or for that matter a word of explanation or goodbye just soppy simpy smile at me and it's all over now kid we've gotten rid of that nasty mouse words from the both of them even if it hadn't been the mouse at all just the noise that terrified me like sounds in the middle of the night would for years still can in fact

///when they come out of nowhere so the fact is that i liked the mouse or at least the mouse concept once i was awake i liked that mouse of an idea that idea of a mouse i did i did which is maybe why they told me the cat was mine we were going to get a cat that would be my cat not to assuage any guilt i might feel or even to reward my quick thinking bravery in identifying the mini-terrorist but so i wouldn't start begging for a mouse a mouse just like the one that had gotten into my wastebasket would start pleading for a special home for it a mouse a mouse instead of a cat a cat would maybe demand windows onto the world so it wouldn't have to crash around and try to escape any similar airless prison not even wire but maybe something upscale and airy picture windows we called them maybe i would already have been able to imagine the perfect glass penthouse like the aquariums we finally wound up having the mice in years later my small dream of a mouse realized even if they weren't really mine any more than the cat was the ones i brought home from school for the summer because that year in science my class got mice and i took all the other kids' mice

///home for the summer because i was the only one who didn't go to summer camp and their parents on their own for two months would be in europe or mexico or southeast asia or on the island definitely not bothering with mice in their glass aquariums inside glass or brick apartments in the pre-airconditioning days of new york's long hot summer which means i got to watch the multicoloured upscale urban mice breed and multiply until the tanks were no longer sleek glass penthouses but overcrowded cells too many mice and they start to kill each other which is without doubt a whole other moral unto itself one you've heard before this my many many mouse tails mouse tale a brief if personal and rather disgusting aside

///for whenever anyone gets into that you know what rats do when they don't have enough space thing that people always bring up talking about modern cities new york tokyo hong kong mexico and there i am with my own new york mouse massacre i know exactly what happens oh yes i do story because it was far more horrible than any mouse in any wastebasket enough in fact to get me over any tom and jerry love of mice any beatrix potter fantasies as i came upon the dead bodies with their torn out windpipes the blood the intestines spread around the cage mouse shit no longer cute but a smell that makes me sick even if i'm breeding the creatures very carefully never too many to a cage to feed my snake

///so you can bet i never did try to write that caged mouse story into any of my childhood oh i love animals stories the way i would write about my almost cat and her family maybe should do it now no more country mouse city mouse but a narrative of resistance for the trapped children perhaps a better one to lead me out of that house than the cat tale mouse tale ones i picked and exemplary besides of that carelessness toward things so common in that house it made it hard to recognize a problem until something was irrevocably broken or dead as i kept trying to feed them water them keep them happy change the cages put in more paper check the eyelidless pinkies add sawdust as i knew at the same time with that red shame in my stomach so like what i always felt those strange nights of mickey's drinking that sense that no matter what i did and how fast i moved nothing could solve this problem and there was no one to tell this problem to cherokee bill was at sea and tim was at camp and the truth is mickey wouldn't come up those stairs even when i reported the massacres she wouldn't not until bill got back to port and he went up and did a final clean on the cages and took the remaining mice and all the aquariums to a neighbourhood pet store not carelessness on mickey's part not carelessness this time but fear

///so we'll leave that story alone leave it right there tell it some other time if at all put it together under another headline not mouse tails mouse tales so many mouse tails mouse tales but gritty kitty or for that matter mousy realism and go back to the cat to getting the cat because there's another story coming another story's almost here because it wasn't my terror or covering up the mouse murder or for that matter my maturity that brought that cat no it wasn't and maybe i can only see it so clearly when i remember that bookcase high rise they'd all been one room bungalows on the windowsills of the science room think of that science room summer think of begging to bring home those mice think of how many years mickey managed to put off any small furry creatures hamster gerbil rat mouse getting an invitation to enter that house until at last the science teacher managed that appeal to her conscience you know just how much sarah would love it and she'll be home all summer alone really with all the other kids in the country at least if the poor thing can't go to camp with her friends she can take care of their mice and you know how she loves animals and doesn't she do such a good job with the cat maybe those parents can even pay her and there's mickey dead sober and without doubt wishing she wasn't caught finally caught and i get cat and mice cat and mice together at last even if the thrill wasn't to last as those beatrix potter bright cages in their bookshelves turned to a bleak death row only let me tell you what i can see in all her struggle to stop those creatures entrance into old twenty-six it isn't concern for the challenge to my caretaking skills not that at all what i see is an echo back to the cat's entrance into the house a pinging pinging pinging on the sonar of the mind louder than that mouse's clanging clanging clanging in the wastebasket its quick exit by its tail to the toilet to bring that cat called mine so maybe this time i've got it maybe this cat tail cat tale mouse tail mouse tale isn't just true but truest not truth or truths but truest the truest explanation of why i got a cat why the house got a cat called mine

///is that it was mickey who was terrified

///of mice in or out of wastebaskets by night or by day it was mickey who was terrified that's right terrified and what i was rewarded for wasn't my maturity or my terror or my complacency i was rewarded for not noticing not my own but mickey's fear

///mickey's fear so palpable in that moment as she looked into the wastebasket then back at me and remained rooted to the floor as only paul moved so palpable i could just let it stand by itself mouse tail mouse tale and cat tail cat tale a story so small yet so significant so perfect a slice of life no moral would be necessary haven't we all felt like that or observed our rescuer mired like that in his or her own unacknowledged fear a fear overcome in some stories leading us to defeat in others it could even be writ large multiplied out into some sort of borgesian mathematical parable let the mice come and go on varied levels of house or consciousness some entering from outside in acknowledgement of fear smelling it deep in themselves others escaping their cages made supermice by its odour splitting and recombining appearing and reappearing no longer get trapped in wastebaskets to kill each other in their own cages but to trap to undermine us in ours that cage of fear and abuse through the generations that was old twenty-six a little or large slice of horror chewing away at house or will to live that house's if

not mouse's perfect symbol those rodents eroding house or home into fear into terror only it's the moral of the story that attracts me the moral of that precise moment not how it sliced life or expanded to parable its tiny moral vision power terrified of the small manifestations of chaos at its edges then in turn terrified of its terror and even more i want the meaning of the payoff for knowing that for seeing that fear that fear then looking away oh will i never

///write a perfect story a formally perfect poem never find a soft safe place to nest my thoughts when will i get away from these not mouse tail mouse tales cat tail cat tales but morality tales exemplary tales when will i just stop stop stop pulling out the moral pulling on morality's tail and getting scratched it really is a bit like the way i pulled cats' tails and got scratched this constant leap to the political this never knowing when to let well enough alone never knowing to just show the little story that's right show it don't tell it show it then sigh dear reader sigh for that tamed mouse of a story of a mouse tail mouse tale that won't even run up your leg like that black and white mouse did mickey's that time we brought it down from its cage into her bedroom before tim left for camp felt her fear and ran right up her leg inside her old safety pinned blue jeans while she screamed and screamed no this one will just sit sniffing in the palm of your hand a mouse tail mouse tale that never was even a black and white headline but just a sigh a sigh yes dear reader look at the mouse not that mouse in mickey's room the one in mine the one in the wastebasket look at that mouse look at mickey's eyes look at the trembling hand look then you figure it out that's right you dear reader dear listener you that's your job yours but no no i can't do it i can't let the story come to the reader anymore than i could let the cats come to me immature immature again immatoooor as hell

///this terrible rushing anxiety this need to underline the meaning hold onto it like a cat's tail lest it escape the mark totally the mark of an immature mind the sign of a mind just making its first step toward a maturity that will still be long in coming as it tries out its first words of cause and effect from cat to tail to run to scratch wants so to know what everything means what does it mean ma what does it mean until once it knows it must repeat it repeat the little lesson so hard learned so maybe i can put that back on mickey too neither clarity nor consistency but me eking out the meanings slowly from the complex storm system that was big lipstick smile mickey and smeared lipstick sing and yell mickey and all the other mickeys cause and effect different from day to day to cause this morality tale obsessed arrested development as everyone else moved on after all that's what it says in the history of european literatures according to the traditional interpretation anyway

///we've gone from the morality tale to the picaresque to the don't tell it show it slice of life even if it's in a galaxy far far away only after that comes the age of hyperrealism magic realism the absurd because you ask me immature mind that i am instead of maturity we've reached a time a place that rides a storm more unpredictable than that strange rodent eroded home only i'm not about to go there either stuck in the morality tale it's not mine to invent a better mouse tail mouse tale if not mouse trap extend that mathematical parable to let the mice or the mice brought fear become another rodent brought plague to erode the whole earth as we know it take it take them all out of mickey's house to become metaphor or metonymy for the whole state of the world where i can still be the child hollering that cat that cat that cat it scratched me howling over the universal if somewhat self-inflicted boo boo be that child writ large only i want this one just this one small mouse tail mouse tale together with its meaning that moment through my eyes comfort myself with its very specific meaning kiss that mouse meaning like i once did a furry head as i set it out into the world maybe that's all i'm doing doing it all the time maybe that's the only large mouse tail mouse tale if not parable i've got maybe all these little headlines with their morals my mouse tail mouse tales cat tail cat tales are my little mice set loose to attempt to erode our world or at least mine let me out of that house that's right maybe these are the mice i am finally setting free the way maybe i should have set all those mice upstairs free from their cages before they could begin their high rise bookcase massacres let them all invade mickey's room run up her pant legs again and again only i've finally gotten here and i can't go back to free any mice i didn't free this is all i can do and this is my reward not a fiction but a tiny mouse tail mouse tale cat tail cat tale with its meaning this is my story true truer or truest and my reward that's right my reward to me for maturity or terror or failure to notice is not a cat but is telling you the cat tail cat tale mouse tail mouse tale truth my true truer truest truth exactly the way i want however often i want and what i want to tell you is that

///that cat that cat that cat that was called my cat was a reward for letting mickey's authority stay intact even as i noticed the fear

///pass up her arm to her face as she peered into the wastebasket and started quickly back her body seeming to lift up as her feet remained rooted to let paul take care of the mouse oh honey it will be all right shsh shsh sarah rewarded for silence again though this time a more perfect silence that i liked so much not just the cat to come but the silent controlling power of the secret transferred to me the knowledge not of something done to me or done to another even that small grey mouse held up struggling by its tail but there there in her face the secret fear in the heart of power i liked it i liked it and it didn't matter how dangerous it was to know i'd seen the terror on her face the way so many in those positions of powerlessness live for those moments of seeing the powerful the abuser suddenly stupid suddenly afraid when you can let the knowledge seep into your eyes just enough to let them know you know but not enough for them to hurt you not at the time anyway though who knows what will happen later just because they know they feel this fear in themselves or they know somehow in the set of your shoulders the renewed spring in your stride they know you know and maybe they'll give you gifts a lot of gifts but sooner or later they

///will need to try to beat it out of you or just beat you over and over if need be just because they need to know they can so whether that knowledge ever gets beaten out or not it can become a dance rhythm one two three punch beat rape torture molest that repeats itself over and over like that overbearing macho god's gift to woman guy

///on the ferris wheel in mexico where he would grab my hand and try to make out and i'd just shake the wheel a bit with my butt as i looked away and he'd let go of my hand to grab the metal edge of our seat and i would hear his intake of breath as i wiggled the car just that little bit harder only to have him start again as soon as it stilled as i would breathe deep and look at the sky and start it all again and whether or not he ever knew i'd done it intentionally he knew i'd noticed his sudden pallor which meant that later he tried to rape me in the car and worst of all i wouldn't fight i would give in and i didn't just accept the inevitable either i probably could have fought him off successfully enough it was just too much fun the highest high knowing what i knew seeing in his eyes that he knew that i knew even as i fought my way to orgasm orgasm in my power over him that made him need his power over me an ascending spiral which made him rougher than he needed to be in the back of that car and me rougher still so i let that happen again and again tormenting him with my knowledge so he would torment me until it just went too far not just degradation but real danger and i won't tell you about that how still i got high on it so high that i can still get horny thinking about him

///and his story that man tail man tale which i'm sure i could make into some sort of metaphor or at least reflection which it probably was of my relationship with mickey with all its very specific and very sexual upstairs downstairs degradation only that's not the link not the one i care about anyway it's not the sexual addiction but the addiction to dangerous knowledge that makes the truest kernel truth in this mouse tail mouse tale cat tail cat tale what's really important here is how dangerous that kind of knowledge can make your future especially if you revel in it whether it's sexual or not hardly matters the point is how you can become addicted to that knowledge to repetition of the moment of knowing of realization how maybe i let myself revel in it with him because i'd loved it with mickey not degradation but that moment that moment of knowing and of her knowing that i knew so that it didn't matter what mickey would do

///later downstairs or what she'd done already or how dangerous it would make my future her coming after me with knives or pokers or men that shiver i saw by the wastebasket saw again years later when the mouse ran up her leg that shiver followed that time by her scream if you could see that how could you care what she would do later or for that matter what she had done or the worst of all the fact that you could learn to stay in a situation like that or even create one do it again and again in the course of your life make that secret pact between abused and abuser the pact made in that moment of their fear what lets you hold your head up on the street lets you laugh lets you think you have them by the short and curlies only it's what makes you stay there stay in that situation stay to maybe not even think of leaving which maybe makes them right after all right the way he was right when he raped you and he knew you wanted it maybe they do have the last laugh even as you imagine it always deep inside when the abuse is worst oh yes you know their power isn't real as you tell yourself how you're there just to see that magic moment of weakness and gather it up in your eyes to make fun of power even if it can kill you courting death just to be able to feel that secret

///better than catching any cat by the tail better than any cat tail cat tale mouse tail mouse tale to have that reward for my little secret not my fear my shame but hers hers which is maybe where that political thing really comes in why

///i can't let go of that no matter what excuses i make can't let go of it to make this just the mouse tail mouse tale the cat tail cat tale or some gigantic parable i want that political meaning because even if i know the power of that addiction to that moment of laughing at power and how it's trapped me as deep as that mouse clanging clanging in that metal cylinder i know

too it's not always just a trap the truth is the door to the cage isn't always open sometimes there is nowhere to run so maybe sometimes you do need that knowledge there are traps you can't get out of metal cages from which there is no rescue except to be flushed down the toilet so maybe you do need that knowledge for just that moment of turning to bite that hand that holds your tail to make sure it cannot hold your tale in some final gesture some last assertion of autonomy and by now i've translated

///enough torture testimonial in my life to know there are times that knowledge of the weakness at the centre of power may be the only truth you might be able to hold onto when there's no growing up or walking out no matter what and maybe the dangerous situations you've sought out needed to be sought maybe it's been better to be there protesting dictatorships human rights violations killer working conditions than to be comfortable live comfortably within a correctly measured life one that always protects the self yes that's why it's easier to crawl up onto that political plane

///instead of staying down here among mouse tails cat tails cat tales mouse tales wondering whether it is moral or immoral to savour that fear a good thing to know to save your dignity or something that will rob you of that dignity whether it gave me a secret moral treasure or just betrayed me again and again into the hands of abusers torturers mean-spirited manipulators because except for that political argument i have learned to make i have no idea if it kept me there too long in that house or helped me get out if it made me seek the same situation again and again once i did or led me instead to try to change the power relations in a world that sanctions the torture state dedicate a large part of my life to that witness all i know is i got a cat that's right i got a cat i got a cat

///that's my cat my cat or at least my cat tail cat tale that secret mouse tail mouse tale better than any cat because it comes with the knowledge that in that moment as my eyes met hers when that shiver shook her arm down to its extended pointing finger and a white light ran up my spine to light my eyes that moment when she made that well dear we'll just have to get you a cat promise and i could see her fear for the first time so strong it's still there i can smell her terror still on this page oh yes i knew she would do it she would get me a cat a cat or anything else i wanted the world if she could have just for me to pretend i had not noticed and it was worth it worth it no matter what came later it's a steel rod that keeps me tall because in that moment i owned a lot more than a family cat called mine yes i owned mickey yes i owned her i owned her.

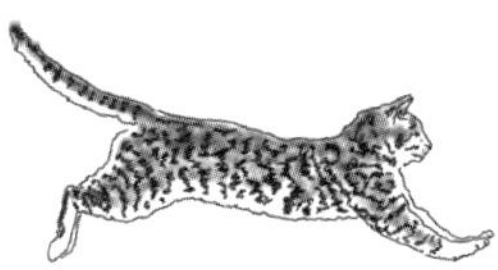

Chiquita

So here it is finally this one word headline chiquita this headline that will always be there chiquita chiquita and maybe you think it's just a greeting chiquita chiquita chiquita that spanish *oye chiquita* hey chiquita you my little one my female little one chiquita that maybe it was just something paul garcia called me chiquita but it's not it's not even if she did come from his shop in that iron box that cardboard box for an iron if you're confused by the description and even if i'm almost really sure cherokee brought her and searched for her that first night when she got lost and even if paul likely as not called me that often enough probably far too often still that name chiquita it has nothing to do with that and little to do with him and it's not some strange metaphor for me either me as *la chiquita* although maybe i could use that if i really wanted expand or expound on self as other self as cat because that's who or what chiquita was chiquita was my cat that's right that cat i finally got who was mine just mine who i fed and cared for and played with and yelled at hey chiquita when i woke up with her tangled in my hair and even if she was *chiquita* very chiquita chiquita chiquita chiquita when she came still she grew bigger and bigger she just kept growing and pretty fast too from kitten to cat sized in weeks from cat sized medium to small tabby cat sized into the biggest thing in my life in even less time probably directly from kitten to gigantic maybe not from the moment i saw her in the box but from the minute she got lost only hours later and i already knew what it would be like not to have her so maybe she's the biggest thing in this book i can do that if i want you know i can make her the biggest thing in this book the way she was for whatever time that was the biggest thing in my life and besides that if mickey's a weather system chiquita's as good a port in a storm as any i can even make her my land of oz to get carried to by the mickey tornado i'd otherwise just have to weather so maybe that's the best thing to do let's make all this a novel of setting and the setting the perfectly lovely soft breeze through leaves setting will really be soft hand through fur because the setting will be my cat the biggest thing in the book the whole book surrounding everything let's just do it and whatever happens to me or to chiquita chiquita chiquita in the future let's just do it only it won't be oz at all the mickey tornado might be oz full of wicked witches and simpering social workers and puffed up pretentious wizards no chiquita will be my kansas will be my home and like dorothy with her red slippers i'll be able to click my heels together or my tongue to roof of mouth and i'll just say chiquita chiquita chiquita and there i'll be home with chiquita home to chiquita home safe home free chiquita chiquita chiquita surrounded by fur of chiquita chiquita chiquita chiquita or maybe i'll do like scarlett o'hara forget what might or what really did happen forget the real fate of real cats or for that matter of real people forget what's in front of you on the page or in your mind forget what story you might have to tell even of chiquita chiquita chiquita instead let's just think about it tomorrow think about this whole project tomorrow or maybe not at all but whichever way it is let's go home to chiquita chiquita chiquita chiquita that's right say it with me i'll think about it tomorrow and then go home to chiquita chiquita chiquita chiquita no matter the results of the tornado or the carpetbaggers who are coming or how many times in all i'll yet be hungry.

Chiquita black and brown and white by the black tire

Let me just say it again it's really important i'm sure it was cherokee bill found her there that first night i am i really am sure sometimes i think as sure as i can be of anything only maybe i'm not if you know what i mean because what i know is that she came from paul's shop in that cardboard iron box and i got her because of the mice and paul was there when the mouse got in the wastebasket but maybe it's true anyway maybe it really is after cherokee got back because he's the one who would insist the smell of a cat would get rid of mice even if you never had to see the cat play with them around the new tiles of the kitchen floor the way we did after all when chiquita was grown up and besides that he'd worked in paul's shop though maybe that's all wrong maybe it's just that chiquita chiquita chiquita chiquita made me feel safe and cherokee my other father maybe my real father he made me feel safe too so it's one of those memories real and true and false and made up all at once the same way i make him make the *café con leche* in my mind all for safety's sake until i'm sure he brought he found my cat.

Coming home to an iron box

from school from the school in manhattan from city and country so it must have been cherokee it must have it must have.

Chiquita's tongue along my hand

pink kitty tongue rasping everyone remembers that first time of kitty rough kitty tongue on skin.

Cat shit by the servants' entrance

Cat pee soaking the floor

Cat box on the floor tiles by the old wc

i cleaned it all i really did but there's still a bitter mystery in it which is like a lot of things that you clean come to think of it.

Chiquita again in my hair

Chiquita gives birth

six kittens three tabbies two calico and white one black and white.

Mowr mowr chiquita calls her kittens

and i could imitate her and they would follow me i liked that.

We called the black and white one spot

at least i think we did and he stayed with us too.

Chiquita and her kittens

That wasn't my first book my first book was *chiquita and her friends* or maybe it was i. m. a. cat the little tiny one about three inches by six that i still have not that really big one i remember that i worked on and worked on in the little room in the school library worked and worked i can still smell the red of its cover not cardboard there's a special name and when you spill water on it the wet spot bleaches out and edges form dark and jagged like oil slick rainbows.

Chiquita gives birth again

one tabby one calico and white one black and white.

Cousin margaret's dog gives birth on the grey chair

the one in the living room i don't remember where chiquita did or seeing her lick that bright amniotic sac off their fur not like that dog whose name i don't remember.

Thirteen cats three dogs and one rabbit

there was always something triumphant about answering the question do you have any pets that way yes thirteen cats three dogs and one rabbit the six basement cats weren't really ours we were taking care of them for a friend but they were certainly better than having paul garcia down there anyway.

We didn't name the rabbit peter

of course we didn't not flopsy mopsy or cottontail either why would we i hated those smarmy rabbits on their hind legs the good girl bunnies in pink or naked only peter keeping his boyish jacket on to go out fabulously formal just to catch it on mr. mcgregor's fence to forward the plot no we wouldn't have named any rabbit of ours peter no matter what even if i hadn't had to play a lettuce in the peter rabbit first grade pageant at brooklyn friends' feel that mother's warm perfume on my face look at her even white teeth her well applied foundation as she fluffed up the green polished cotton leaves of my head lettuce costume the most insipid of the leafy greens no romaines no endives no radicchios no spinach arugulas kales swiss chards though i'm sure she didn't tell me what a good little vegetable i was i'm sure of it even if i felt like one that whole year in that strange school with its rooftop playground the pageant was the spring of the year after mark died and me still with those constant thoughts about where he'd gone whether he was in heaven or hell or baked into a pie by mrs. mcgregor like mopsy flopsy cottontail and peter's pa or maybe getting ready to fly out ascend to somewhere the black irish twenty fifth to match the four and twenty black birds still i knew i didn't want to play a pink good bunny with their bread and milk and blackberry dinners and following the rules or mr. mcgregor who made them which left only mischievous i already knew that word even if maybe i still pronounced it mischievious peter or a vegetable radish cabbage carrot rutabaga take your pick but only boys could be peter in that eat or be eaten mcgregor garden world all the kids yelling run peter run here comes mr. mcgregor nobody ready to yell stop stop please stop don't eat your vegetables as peter chowed down on the radish kids the french bean kids the carrot kids the lettuce kids and fluffed up me among them no place to run on vegetable roots no place to hide in leafy green head i must have learned some valuable lesson there even if i don't know what it was as i wore my lacy dresses for the last time never begged again for a pink polished cotton pinafore even before transfer on scholarship to city and country the blue jeans school in manhattan life on the subway singing mark's favourite kevin barry tortured for the things he would not tell while i'm there on the school swings lips sealed ready to die a rebel lettuce lettuce who is the lettuce lettuce lettuce no more good bunnies lettuce lettuce lettuce break loose.

The hutch that bill built

that's where the rabbit lived and it died there too one morning eyes wide open as if in shock who knows why but i always remember it what's that thing about in the headlights what's that thing about a life like that and not dead yet still better than a lettuce you stand a running if not a fighting chance i figure i owe bill for that.

Watching chiquita's suitors on the back fence

Climbing across the back fence after chiquita

Climbing the ginkgo tree better than chiquita

she only made it out onto the first big horizontal branch and we had to get her down.

We never called the fire department

even if we talked about it some before climbing up into that i swear guinness book of world records five storey high ginkgo tree after chiquita grabbing her and holding her close until it was safe to let her jump then swinging out of the tree ourselves scratch covered returning heroes exalted by our battle scars only i don't think it ever mattered what we did one way or the other after all as my friend mike used to say the one i went back and forth with tired enough but hardly merry just trying to escape mickey and a fate worse than yowling years later on the staten island ferry if they really couldn't get down he said urban trees would be full of itty bitty kitty skeletons mickey's too i might have added mickey's too we all knew not from subways not from taxis not from whatever limb she was out on there never was any rescuing mickey.

I never fell into the neighbours' rose bushes

it was tim did that and i don't think he was rescuing chiquita either no matter it was her favourite limb to be out on to launch her most penetrating pitiful poor me i'm a stuck kitty yowls it was almost horizontal and long too stretching itself maybe twenty maybe thirty feet out over the neighbours' yard almost to their windows before they made mickey cut it down years after my escape with tim out there one much younger day for some no cat reason of his own the way we all were often enough any neighbourhood kid on tree sharing terms distracted like him too though even looking dizzily down didn't make anyone else as far as i know grow tim's fulminating future hatred of that insipidly awful i never promised you a rose garden cliché along with no doubt the same feelings for its concomitant petals scents and thorns one small lapse in concentration and how would you feel getting one yourself promised or unpromised coming at you i don't know how fast do you remember your high school physics what is the formula for falling bodies their particular coefficient of acceleration rose garden arriving long before terminal velocity at how many feet is it per second per second.

Climbing that tree higher and higher

forget chiquita nothing could stop me.

Dreams first falling

This thing about dreams at first falling dreams isn't even a headline much less a story it's more a kind of avoidance a set of misdirections designed to send people down the wrong road or just away something to make them keep talking while you listen don't volunteer a thing nothing to make you get caught in the dream trap fall into the trap of falling dreams you watch it come up time and again so many times you know exactly how people always ask writers anyway artists as well as

///all those new age folk they want to know about dreams dreams dreams tell me your dreams though the truth is it's for sure been going on a lot longer than any even newish age likely for as long as humans have been intimate with time probably the second thing anyone ever talked about right after the newest plants to gather together with the personal history of the woman who found them people must have fallen into the recounting of dreams falling dreams flying dreams teeth dreams water dreams plant dreams animal dreams insect dreams spider dreams hair dreams snake dreams foot dreams house dreams suitcase dreams dog and cat dreams all kinds of dreams besides going back in individual time to the beginning of any individual childhood what did you dream about last night and what kind of dreams do you have and oh i don't dream and we all dream you just don't remember and we need our dreams one of those conclusions arrived at in my lifetime like the need for rem sleep and then there's do you dream in colour which has been revised too since the days when i was told you didn't nobody did nobody dreamt in colour they kept telling me when this dream topic first came up and just to show you how well i avoid it i never even mentioned how sure i was

///i not only dreamt in colour but in colour so vivid detail so precise my dreams were like magic or maybe magic realism paintings you understand not literature but that photorealism they call magic realism in the visual arts if you took the category from writing you might get chagall or something vaguely more insipid no this is wyeth and all those who came after it's not really photorealism either that's the magic no camera could do that much detail in so many places from so many angles though maybe someone might look across a table at me these days and say oh my dear but that's hypnagogia and i might say but you don't fly in hypnagogia and i certainly fly in my dreams even if it's hard sometimes to get off the ground or just too too

///depressing when you get yourself off the ground and you can fly you can fly you can fly and all those tinkerbellish things but it's still unutterably bleak if all you get to do is fly over a dark damp deserted city not a happy thought in sight where the houses have no windows or maybe one and it looks into a kitchen full of old orange light from a twenty five watt bulb dangling from a peeling paint greasy grey tin ceiling and you know you're too frightened or just too damn sad to go there to stop to rest to talk around that rickety table so much like the apartments of my childhood paul garcia took me to as he did his electrical jobs and maybe made it with the mistress those apartments or at least their sadness one definite part of why i practice dream question avoidance except with really close friends don't come to rest to land in those questions either nip that dream stuff at least as it pertains to me in the bud right at the start with that question about first dreams that's always there what's the first dream you remember after those questions about whether you remember at all which i already could have faked just said oh no i don't remember my dreams nary a one except i'd be just too afraid it would come true i wouldn't remember my dreams anymore at all and these days mostly i like them and even when i don't i like to know why i woke up feeling like shit so it's that other avoidance for me just around the question and off i go and besides that way i can think about them myself without actually telling them my eyes in the distance oh yes my first dreams the first dreams i remember 175
oh they were all falling dreams

///my dreams were at first falling dreams pretty typical falling dreams i say dead boring falling dreams and the conversation goes on and i learn about other people's dreams which is always fun and i don't have to go into any of it not really not the later mark and mickey disappearing dreams or the echo in how mark really actually did and i often wished mickey would or the subway trains coming to grab me from the platforms or even how those first falling dreams actually fell don't even have to contemplate why the fact of them wants to become a headline now springs to my fingers as well as my mind my first dreams at first falling dreams flashing off and on in my head though it's not the words really it's an image one image out of that identical set of circumstances because the fact is it was always an identical set of circumstances but that doesn't make them precisely the same and for sure i've never seen a headline that covers more than one story or says something like it rained again today which is about like my falling dreams i fell again last night they weren't even remarkable for being early recurring dreams i've never had a recurring dream in my life as far as i know just recurring themes recurring places recurring images recurring sets of circumstances so really just another rain if you know what i mean same shit different day or night and all that only the shit the rain is never really quite the same and neither was the falling just the same place the same light though maybe

///i have had recurring dreams and just don't know it don't look now but here it comes again so that's exactly what you do you don't look and your mind only remembers the ones that are different that's possible too just the way some people don't remember their dreams at all and since i don't talk about them much even more possible any number of mirror image repeat dreams could be falling out of my consciousness only it doesn't matter first singular dream or first recurring dream it was definitely a falling dream and the next ones recurrences or singularities falling dreams too until all i remember is that same time same place feel of them no beginning no end so the only thing that makes them not a recurrence of the same dream is the fact that i remember them as different which challenges the notion of recurring dream maybe there are no recurring dreams maybe they're all different it's just a question of what the dreamer chooses to remember the details or the theme and i always remember both dream or story think the detail is as important as the theme am not sure of the whole concept of theme in fact and here i am off with another avoidance while in the dreams i keep falling and falling in the very same place and always the brilliant colour

///of that one building the one kind of kitty corner behind old twenty-six and maybe i can start avoiding again here asking about you do you say kitty corner or catty corner i'm actually rather curious about that kitty and catty even if i don't remember which i said first kitty in brooklyn catty in toronto catty in brooklyn kitty in calgary i know i didn't say either in mexico city but anyway this building isn't directly behind old twenty-six but directly behind numbers twenty four and twenty two only about five feet of its yard abutting onto the back corner of the twenty-six yard so that we could not only climb onto the top rail but stare between the inch square iron pickets of its six foot fence not onto another building but out onto henry street because this building actually has an open space on one of its sides this side yard taking up the space of another building the only building on the block to have such a yard the block meaning for real the block what block really means the four streets of the rectangle of buildings which in a new york mind of course ought to be completely enclosed even the gaps left for the honey wagons to enter closed decades ago by carriage houses or garages maybe new buildings the alleys integrated into the backyards as fast as you can say water closet so this side yard almost a park it was so full of bushes is a break into the hidden inside world of backyards and for that matter a good escape route out of them once you figure it out mostly how to get over or walk along that top rail between the three prongs of the pickets

///which we certainly did later on and if you want to know which you probably don't you can tell the yard belongs to that kitty corner yellow brick building because that building does have windows looking onto that yard unlike the one whose backyard takes up the rest of the back fence line the one directly behind old twenty-six so there's no question that kitty corner building back there was built knowing that yard was its very own possession lord or lady of all it surveyed blind wall and picket fence and grass and trees and bushes through to henry street with the six panels of those casement windows and for that matter the yellow not red brick between making this a forties or maybe even a thirties building definitely before i was born but newer than most things in that neighbourhood of astoundingly well kept or notoriously run down mostly subdivided victorian or edwardian townhouses with their pompous wood sash windows and their ledges for window boxes the ones we would run along the way we would climb the picket fence along with all the other fences we were always ambivalent about the arrival of chain link it was just so easy everything behind it so accessible but no challenge you could throw yourself at the fence grab on then climb up at a run no challenge at all only i wasn't doing that yet not at the time of these dreams i think i was barely walking

///so who knows why those dreams started and why they concentrated on that one building or why my mind keeps coming back to it the yellow glow of the sun on its side the sepia dark of its windows as far as i know i've never been in that building not back then and not now not in between not ever never even had a friend in that building or a friend who had a friend in that building or a friend who had a friend who had a friend in that building have no bad or for that matter good memories real memories anyway of that building was never terrified of that building not the way i was of so many bleak brooklyn buildings with their old tile floors their cooking smells pee smells garbage smells mould smells or just wallpaper and disinfectant and terrifying long corridors so that building with its shining wall never could take on any negative valence i don't think not then or now early or late there's just the escape through its yard the escape sense of its wall the brilliant sunlight winter spring summer fall of whatever brilliant days there ever were along the south facing yellow brick of its side that never experienced that sundial effect of all the east west facing buildings of that block like so many others where you could tell time by how the sun slid down one side and climbed up the other day after day with the light on that yellow brick and casement window wall varying only with the time of year and the height of the sun in the sky a few feet up a few feet down but its yard too big to allow the wall of the building opposite the one directly behind old twenty-six to eliminate the light even in winter so it was always there always the light

///the way there was always the light in my dreams imagine my first awful nightmares in such bright light in brilliant colour no dark eggplant no mustard no olive yet just bright light on the yellow brick of that building the light and then the window and then the fall and that was it at least that was it that i ever remembered that and my own screaming and letters spilling out around me as if to match my screams except i couldn't read them they were just shapes the secret shapes of the sunday funnies or of saturday matinee cartoons in bright translucent colours like candies the large jujubes we called dots or the tiny perfumed wine gums we called jujubes drifting in the space of my fall for sure it was before i could read so they create no broader memory no broader meaning that's all there is i don't even know did i start out on the roof or on the fence or inside the building and who knows except that it was always a fall through yellow to green through green through green through green to brown the dappled green of the bushes along the picket fence on a sunny day the high hedges of that kind so common in new york that i've only ever called them hedges never learned the plant's name the one with the little white flowers in spring shaped something like mini lilacs and there i am falling into the bushes or through the bushes the light to dark green of bushes though i never seem to touch anything even as the brown of branches increases to the darker brown of approaching earth so maybe i couldn't have been on the fence not with that feeling falling through long slow bright yellow light before the green though who knows

///maybe it was more like vertigo looking long and hard out at the light from my perch on the fence though it would be years before i would perch there or have a picket stab deep into my thigh but if i could be in that building then surely i could be on that fence eyes to the light and a slow unbalancing into green as my body topples over the truth is i really don't know don't see anything more than the light on the wall and the green in the leaves and the brown in the earth and along the branches and sometimes the bright colours of falling letters and it takes oh so very long falling light into dark into green into green into brown into green so i'm betting i'm in the window looking out or on the roof looking down the way maybe i looked out of the windows of old twenty-six and got scared or looked over the edge of the roof and got scareder no one would allow their kids near windows like that these days their sills so low much less on roofs like those all tarpaper and no railings where mark took me which means maybe i'd been warned about windows i could see that yellow brick building from mine and most certainly about roofs mark never let go of my hand though later we would move roof to roof along the block all us kids but that's much later and for this there's just that awful falling feeling in the stomach and it's going from yellow yellow brilliant light into green into dark the dark green the dark green the brown but there's never any landing no chance to disprove

///that theory about how if you die in your dreams you really die that didn't happen till i was in college and died night after night drowned or burned or fallen even dissolved through brilliant colours broken to atoms only to awake perfectly alive and compact densely packed inside my body the next day no there was no one to try to sell me on a theory like that not for a long time anyway so it didn't add to my terror that idea that if i were to hit the ground i would be really truly dead no in those dreams in those dreams the fear was of falling of falling and falling that feeling of falling forever not the fear of hitting the ground only to die for real and it didn't matter anyway whether you die or not if you die in your dreams because i wasn't old enough yet to know these were dreams not when i entered them i couldn't distinguish the feel of a dream that came much later so there i am falling and falling and sick sick sick in my stomach that stomach in mouth feeling always there at the start of a fall only lasting lasting lasting

///lasting through yellow through green into brown into leaves into branches into earth dark and never landing always waking up sick and crying my face covered in tears in my white barred fourth storey crib I think i was still in that crib i certainly remember that crib the comfort of its mattress its bars and that sense of solidity solidity after falling or maybe it was a new bed a new mattress and that was the point the fear was of falling out of bed the eighteen inches to the floor but i don't think so even that mattress was too solid too comforting that mattress and the blue and white painted ceiling of my room solid solid until it happens again and i don't know it's a dream and i'm falling and falling bright brick yellow to leaf green to green green to branch brown to brown to brown earth brown and maybe screaming and maybe letters but always and forever and already and still there's never landing never landing never landing never crashing to the ground but no matter the horror and that sick feel in the stomach the truth is like i said see i told you what can i tell you it's over and over and ever and the same so it's really boring it's not even interesting it's dead boring in fact isn't it falling and never landing falling and never landing caught forever in falling and never landing and of course even if i wanted to tell it not avoid telling it how that was my first dream or my first suite of dreams my first dream suite still it's dead boring though never dead so even if i wanted to i couldn't do it make you see that light to take you anywhere beyond falling dreams that's right at first falling dreams out of window off roof from fence light green brown falling and what would that ever mean not even if i added translucent letters could i get beyond dead boring not unless i painted it into reality but if i did i would have to go there to feel it in my hand enter into that place never landing never landing never landing never landing never knowing

///it's a dream and i can't even make you see the light not the brilliant yellow on the brick or the subtle tones of the green as i fall or the bright jujube letters or that sense of doom of being suspended there forever of falling and falling and still falling looking across the table at you and still falling through yellow through green through light through dark that sick feeling in my stomach so just forget it oh yawn and turn away or let's get it over with oh my first dreams they were falling dreams my dreams were at first falling yes about falling seldom will i even get to the falling and falling just my first dreams they were falling dreams like so many people's childhood dreams they're falling dreams oh yawn and turn away what a cliché a perfect cliché so why feel that horror of falling and falling if you can help it why enter that world such horror

///for so little drama so little suspense so little return on investment not even a chance to appeal to your audience's emotions after all it is hard to make an appeal to your audience's emotions if you bored them silly they might understand why you think you're trapped in a closet in mickey's house that may not be normal or natural but it's got naturalism the frisson of untold awful worlds her chasing down real wood corridors but who would want to know why you're still trapped in dreams terrified and falling from yellow through green through green to brown and never landing dead bored but never dead too little magic for the most banal of realisms

///especially since the truth is i may have been terrified once felt trapped all of that i do remember the sensation in the gut but now that i can tell a dream from waking almost one hundred percent of the time it's become more that sensation of nausea as the roller coaster comes down that first big incline and you know nothing is going to happen highly unusual accidents aside or my dreams of being chased around by one nothing ever happens on a roller coaster except screaming and that sensation that getting used to falling sensation that becomes a wanting to fly a wanting to get used to flying sensation and i certainly developed that over the years wanting to fly and then learning to fly so that i could say that too oh it's been years since i learned to fly in my dreams yonks just yonks i can do it whenever i want and i'm one of the few at least that's what it says in the dreams books not many learn to fly at will they say and besides as far as falling goes it's been a long time that i've taken comfort in that thing my friend jean said way back when with that clarity of teenage vision that maybe later drove her mad when a finite thing faces an infinite thing she said speaking of herself as the finite one of course whatever else is true she was no narcissist it is simply and she would turn over her hand and let it drift groundward like a leaf it is simply a process of constant falling and i'm sure i remembered my falling dreams then sure in fact that i told her about them how my dreams my first dreams were falling dreams universal universe dreams i guess falling falling and i laughed too and wiggled my body groundward so that's the truth falling through green through green through green to brown to brown nausea in the stomach and knowing there was no landing was a comfort to me by then such a finite being in constant fall watching the leaves go by and over the years i came to love it even if i thought of those dreams seldom there was always the roller coaster to ride when i needed it bike out to coney island and get on the cyclone and look out to sea or close my eyes to fall to fall to fall yellow to green green green to brown but who wants to explain that so you see i would leave it if i could the way i have left it for years

///make some last comment about how something might make for a story even if it doesn't have a climax but not if it doesn't have a point and this falling and falling and falling even from yellow into green into green into green into green into green into green into brown into brown into brown into dark is just a little bit much even for that postmodern postponement of closure as the centre of narrative sort of idea even if you never land after all yellow green green dark are hardly interesting enough asides along the way to nowhere so enough of waiting for the big bang that final thud at the end that maybe kills you but most likely doesn't so maybe i really could just leave this around somewhere lose it on a bus or something crash my hard drive destroy the floppies use the cd's for mini frisbies forget to explain forget love and horror and terror and joy all at once and go on to something else altogether and i would you know i would only the fact is they've come back

///or at least that building has because this time i'm climbing i'm climbing and what's missing is the beginning not the end i still haven't been on the ground whether or not i've hit and there i am with my hands my feet on that yellow wall and what i want to talk about especially if it's that new age crowd what i want to talk about is how i felt that morning when i woke up how it felt to be once more on that building which i had long forgotten at least in its specificity yes i could say my first dreams they were falling dreams and i knew exactly where i was and i felt the green through green through green to brown but i didn't see that building clearly not like this so very bright like this perfection like this the yellow brick three inches from my eyes the feel of the mortar between the bricks as i stick in my fingers to make my grips it was always so far away even if bright when i was falling and now here i am climbing climbing and maybe you think i should have some fear of the fall but i don't all i feel is heart stopping triumph as i'm about to get to the window on the very top storey because i'm doing what i always loved to do

///all those years of climbing climbing climbing in central park or up the ginkgo tree along that picket fence bordering that yard even on the girders of the brooklyn bridge climbing climbing climbing looking up seeing my grips climbing climbing climbing as i'm looking for the grips the little places where one brick sticks out more than another or the mortar is gone only this time i've got a rope and i'm putting in my pitons and up i go up i go up i go and then i discover i don't even have to put in pitons just find my grips in utter safety because i'm top roped and there's someone down there on belay someone to belay me the way i learned when i finally did that course in the mountains to find out how it's done when you really rock climb like a rich kid the rich kid i always wanted to be with all the equipment harness and carabiners in bright metallic colours rope with a little bit of give so you don't break your spine when you fall and sooner or later you always do fall so that there i am in the middle of this dream and i realize it's a rebirth a perfect new age rebirth a story of redemption i've been through hell and here i am in the sun because maybe i've been falling for half a century only now i can go back i can go back anytime i want i can go back and get whatever part of me i left behind on that ground i never hit or in that house right across that picket fence that i never left because maybe it's possible i did get up after that fall that never seems to end and i walked back in for a glass of water or a quick snack the way we would always take breaks for a glass of water drunk out of the palms of our dirty hands in the laundry sink so who knows but there i am out of that house again and across that fence and climbing climbing on belay climbing climbing follow the yellow brick wall back into that building that i've never been in but that i've fallen out of or off of night after night on belay climbing

///and there i am thinking it's me climbing and me on belay or maybe it's my partner tom who's still alive or some good friend from any time any decade at all in my life margot or a member of my ginkgo club or maybe jean again commenting on frames of reference and the heisenberg uncertainty principle the way she would when we were on the swings in the playground five blocks from nutmeg mews or up in central park outside our school or down in the village by her place or maybe even it's lupita with her steady hand her steady eye from the years in mexico and climbing the tepozteco or through guerrero mountain brush who knows but how perfect can you get how perfect is this dream only even as i rerun it in my mind to try to get to that feeling of triumph on belay climbing and me the little climber the little climber more than the little train that could but still that's the image i think i can i think i can i know i can i know i can and all those other by now clichés about how we only ever rescue ourselves which anyone who's ever been in any real kind of emergency knows isn't true anyway but right before i can get there in my mind or in telling people later about my perfect new age rebirth you can go home again dream go home and even get the part of yourself you left behind and climb up the building you always fell from there i am getting up to that casement window which of course is open after all this part of it is supposed to be easy it's like with most dreams you can feel what's coming you know if it's going to be bad or good you're always prepared so of course the window's 183
open and even if it hurts that little bit it is a metal casement edge after all to push myself up by my arms and wiggle my belly over still i'm there and i'm flopping into that darkened room

///and suddenly my eyes look away in that real time as i'm telling it to someone or just practicing telling it with myself because they fixate on what i see and my voice stops or if i'm there in the dream i'm just staring out my dream eyes cantilevered in the window before i push myself in because there they are those jujubes bright and glowing and tucked into corners and i know even if i can't make out the form that those packages were once falling letters or will be soon again and it's then i remember another dream where i'm walking down the street on nutmeg mews toward the door of old twenty-six when suddenly a voice interrupts me a real voice real time i think which maybe makes me think how dreams are easy that it's living outside the dream that's hard that's the part that's really been the constant falling the difficulties of every day and then going back to resolve the memories that ache in your stomach that's what throws your equilibrium that's been the work this is easy this dreaming's easy whether it's falling through yellow through green through green to brown or climbing up onto the bright yellow of wall so simple so easy with the birthing done somewhere long outside the dream to make this resolution half a century later so easy the way that other dream with its voice coming from outside the dream had been so easy so smooth that walking on the street practically humming until there's the voice and there i am with my friend marie in a hotel room and we're due downstairs for a meeting at eight i don't really want to go to and she's woken up

///and i hear her say oh my god the alarm didn't go off it's eight forty we've overslept and i can feel that don't wake me up something interesting is going on i want to stay here feeling the this is my world feeling look these are my dreams leave me alone feeling that you never want that more difficult reality to interrupt so i turn over to look in desperation at the alarm only to find it says six twenty not eight forty at all which makes me kind of furious so i don't know if i just kind of do one of those hmmmmph big bounce leave me alone shoulder movements or i actually tell her not to be silly it's six twenty for god's sake go back to sleep but i certainly do i'm asleep in an instant and now i've not just approached old twenty-six i've got the door open and there in the vestibule are those jujube packages big and brilliant at least halfway up my shins but off in the corners just like they will be in the room in that building bright coloured objects all around me bright round bundles giant jelloey candies again and looking around i know i've been given the solution to a puzzle but which one is it the solution to beyond the door or in the packages and there i am just deciding which to do open the packages or the second door into the interior of the house this was after all in the days when i was first beginning to examine the events of my childhood in old twenty-six and i was full of a horror and nausea beyond any falling that might still have been going on and on and on and there i am about to solve it to solve it whichever puzzle of memory i was onto when there it comes again marie's voice exactly the same oh my god we've overslept the alarm didn't go off it's eight forty and i want to tell her to shut up only this time when i look at the clock it really is eight forty eight forty in bright red glowing numbers clear and definite and tangible as i reach out with my hand to touch the clock but it's no more real no more tangible than six twenty had been the first time i heard marie's voice so i never got to know what the treasures were what i was about to find

///or find out about sort of like those falling letters i could never read so instead of wondering about what was in those packages if they just popped out into letters that fell to cushion my fall or just popped open to entertain me like a saturday matinee or sunday funnies if those packages were there in the vestibule as some sort of reward for what i was about to find out the

way maybe those packages were in the room of the building whose wall i had just made the effort to climb up instead i just forgot about that mystery those mysteries altogether the mystery beyond the interior door of old twenty-six or maybe the interior door of that apartment i'd just flopped into forgot about all of that forgot even about recapturing my sense of triumph in that climbing dream as i looked away from whoever it was i wanted to tell it to or just from my internal monologue perhaps into the green of leaves or out to mountains to concentrate on the mystery in the nature of time on how time works was this a fold in time something that took at the very least minutes in real time first to hallucinate the hour of six twenty and reach for the alarm only to tell marie to go back to sleep then more time to walk up to that door open it and walk into the vestibule more minutes to look around at the packages trying to decide what to do and all of it occurring in an instant marie's voice heard twice to bookmark the end of a dream or a hypnagogic hallucination and the time eight forty all along or was i really taking a look into the future marie's voice coming back to shake me awake to shake me into a dream i needed to have jujube packages i needed to see exactly two hours and twenty minutes before the event would occur and we would realize we had overslept as i would hear marie repeating those exact same words twice once right once wrong making me think not only of the nature of time but the nature of truth the nature even of myth those words those exact words repeated so i never
even thought about the aborted singularity of the story in the vestibule but just about the puzzle

///its repetition such a wonderful puzzle my favourite kind of puzzle a riddle with no answer just a million hints a place to rest my mind in comfort like playing minesweeper on the computer bomb bomb where's the bomb the explosion of probabilities only open ended like falling and falling without dread just bright colours yellow to green to green to brown to brown and marie's voice to close the gap the opening into the void so that what I feel is delight awe before the miracle of the mind which is what i feel again when those dreams come back what i feel to know that first dream that first suite of dreams could come back to resolve itself could still have been somewhere in my mind all these years so that even if i haven't looked at that yellow brick building in over two decades or dreamed it most likely in four or five still the dream could be there and me the little train the little climber that could except now looking away that doesn't seem to matter at all any more what i am interested in is the message sent through time

///only it's not the oh so new age adult to the rescue of the child after all these years of sending her messages in bright jujube packages of encouragement what delights me is how they must be bidirectional not unidirectional messages constant and ongoing message forward message back messages overlapping so it's no longer i think i can i know i can proud simply of my today self the one grinning at dreams and new age romances of self rescue but about that child and the message that she has sent me which has kept me alive kept me from ever reaching that final thud and i start to wonder if in this circle in all this falling down this climbing up there is some sort of twist as i remember my friend jean again all that fascination with physics and mathematics and degrees of infinitude and of course the mobius strip so that you start to wonder if that is what this is perhaps a klein bottle that same mysterious edgeless space in three dimensions or is it four that like the mobius strip that reorients you right to left and left to right should you traverse its length this shape would turn you inside out as you moved around so you start to think maybe that's what's there at the disappearing bottom edge of that fall there's a twist in space in time to forever bounce you back the same or different in mirror reverse or turned inside out the way i feel far too often looking back toward that building that is twenty-six nutmeg mews and then too comes in my fascination with narrative time and is it all simultaneous really if viewed from outside and does the chronological really exist and what about the myths of prophecy where trying to avoid the prediction makes it come true whether oedipus or meeting death in whatever city that was or that wonderful one in the secret history of mongols where the monk to avoid the destruction of the books in his monastery seeks out the wife of temujen the man who will be chinggis khan so that she will achieve his rescue from slavery and yes the monastery is saved but the kingdom destroyed only if the monk had never gone to find borte temujen's wife none of it would have happened anyway because the future chinggis would have died a slave and i still don't understand how marie who woke me up twice in two different time frames could hate that movie mongol which talks about just that stuff so much

///and then i'm on to that question i always ask about narrative time or as much as we can understand of it in the message forward and the message back does beginning determine end or end determine beginning in our memory of it do we select the beginning we want to match the end we've got or is something truly set in motion way back at whatever beginning we can discern our dream our life the big bang only the problem is that how we perceive time is no more nor less than our ability to narrate so are we even able to see a real beginning maybe we're just drifting in a time that runs backward as easily as forward and at each moment i really do change my beginning and you can see the drift here just the way i can as i put my fingers into that stoners' gesture for a mobius strip thumb to forefinger forefinger to thumb and follow it out follow it out people would say to each other and stoned enough you could stay there oh wow man for hours as good as falling yellow into green into green into green into brown into green into yellow which is what i do falling yellow through green through green through green through brown back to yellow until i realize that all this is much better just seen in the mind's eye or in the beauty of my friend lupita's mobius strips in sculpture she really must be the one down there controlling the twist if not the belay so let's hear it again for beauty and falling through it finity against infinity because this one's going to a cliché no matter what i do and however valid it may be because the truth is that the only message back and forth forth and back over all these years is that life will be fascinating

///which is maybe why i could say all those times i was asked when i hadn't yet looked closely at any of this cared to acknowledge any headlines in my mind taken that last taxi ride of the imagination back from earl's to nutmeg mews that i'd had a happy childhood and i could mean it because in all those bike rides to coney island and roller coaster rides when i got there and climbing on fences and on buildings and making drawings and diagrams and writing books i couldn't finish and thinking just a lot of thinking i really did and yes you can make it to the end even to the end of going back to the beginning and finding your story not i think i can i know i can but i can because i think about what i don't know and whether it's six twenty or eight forty it's not the meeting that matters anyway but loving the puzzles whose resolution eludes us and that's enough for a lifetime on belay climbing or help i'm falling yellow into green into green into brown into brown into green into yellow that's the constant redemption at the end or is it the beginning of the constant fall and as to my first dreams i'll keep my mouth shut on this one I think i can i know i can on belay climbing falling

///through yellow through green through green through green through brown through yellow dead boring but never bored.

Vision quest with olives eggplant and mustard

I do have a problem with mustard that's certainly true enough not with the flavour the colour it's the colour that gets to me mustard ochre is one of those dream tones nightmare tones really that goes with the olive and the eggplant i do love the way they're all foods foods i like in fact really really love for as long as they stay foods don't let their colours loose into the atmosphere eggplant purple black is great huddled on the eggplant like white on rice the way we used to say for really close really really getting along that purple black easy to get along with on that rounded fruit it really is a fruit not a veg a fruit you can thump with your hand whack it lightly to make it resound peel it slice it cook it eat it yum yum yummy takes on any flavour you throw at it yet adds that little extra something that bite though really the shape thinking about it the shape is exactly the shape of that balloon the one i'm about to complain about the do balloon the do balloon the do balloon the dream

///that brings this all up it's the first dream i remember that had those colours though by now of course i recognize the theme have for a long time as far as it goes know exactly what kind of awful dream it's going to be the minute those colours appear know i'm having a bad day a bad month a bad year if when i imagine something i don't see it bright the way i might see an imagined eggplant bright purple black its edges precise its highlights winking against my kitchen's blue and orange but instead see those colours olive eggplant mustard thick in the atmosphere thicker along the walls thickest in the dull weight of the shadows no highlights no brightness all edges blurred just the way i saw those colours by the door of the butler's pantry as that first eggplant shaped but mustard coloured balloon grew

///and grew the shape the colour of so many dour dreams dour imaginings to come i might say it that way now dour dreams it sounds mustard eggplant olive enough even if i'm never comfortable with that dour word it fits into the mouths of others never quite belongs to me maybe it's because i don't know which way to pronounce it the childhood new york american dower like dowager queens or the more canadian scots u.k. do-er which is what i want right now let's say it together do-er dreams do-er dreams for the do balloon that wanted to do me in i knew it wanted to do me in the do balloon the do balloon the do-er do balloon that would chase me mustard dull through that dream fog eggplant and olive coloured house conscious always of its dowager queen who ruled us all with her steel grey fist her mustard puke though it's only now i see in that balloon not just the colour of mustard but oh yes dour do-er what did us all in not the dour scots presbyterians or their english chapel counterparts those dour folk of mickey's family but the do-er dour scotch the preferred cheap blended whisky the cutty sark of mickey's nights mustard brown liquid and olive green bottle their colours puked right back up into our world in old whisky and bile to do us all in again and again because the fact is that balloon the do balloon the do balloon the do balloon all mustard scotch puke colour grew from the butler's pantry where always she stashed the whisky after moon faced charlie his face eggplant purple in the dim light delivered it from the liquor store only in this dream charlie's not there and the scotch isn't on the sideboard or in the cupboard no there's just the balloon

///the balloon the do balloon growing and growing inside that tiny room with its old copper sink and old wood cupboards and mostly i'm sure it was during the time that paul garcia was still there in the house maybe that last summer he was still there and besides that there'd been some kind of gas leak one that he'd taken care of or someone had maybe black whitey dawson there were old gas jets all over the house no one had ever shut off including the one downstairs in the front hall and this leak i remember it it was somewhere in the downstairs hallway that led from the servants entrance to the kitchen for the days when old twenty-six really was supposed to be a townhouse though i don't know what the gas line was doing there maybe leading from the stove 189
in the kitchen to the fireplace in the front room there were four active gas fireplaces in the house besides the jets maybe really there'd once been a jet close to where i'm standing in the dream maybe in the butler's pantry for light maybe or to heat up food though i think the food the water whatever you wanted heated was just supposed to arrive hauled up on the dumbwaiter from the kitchen below for the butler to serve you that's how that room got its name the butler's pantry where there was just the sink to rinse glasses or dishes clean up spills but why am i talking about this what does it matter what difference does it make in our world there was just mickey and her scotch in the cupboards or out on the counter along with the glasses dirty and smelling of old liquor while the faucet dripped into the copper sink to turn it green where the drops hit and make it smell of old pennies and the fluorescent tube was enough to illuminate it all so who cares about whether the gas jet was ever right there either because there is where this thing was anyway the do balloon the do balloon the do balloon hissing and farting its fart its scotch coloured way to bigger and bigger

///making it maybe the time new york was being converted to natural gas from propane or whatever substance it was they had in those big tanks whose ceilings rose and fell balloonlike down by the harbour on the way to the beach out at riis park or coney island when everybody was talking about how they would have to put a scent into the gas because otherwise it could just sneak up on you undetected and the next thing you knew you'd be dead only when the transition came smell or no smell the adjustments weren't quite right for how natural gas burns so much hotter than whatever was there before and you turned on the hot water faucets in the bathtub and steam came out hissing and belching and farting and carried the rust out of the old steel pipes to turn the area around the faucets the drains in the old enamel footed tubs all mustard ochre brown so maybe it's that hissing and farting and belching and steaming that had entered my consciousness mustard brown on white enamel combining with olive green on copper to let the do balloon the do balloon the do balloon grow and grow the do balloon the do balloon

///inside the butler's pantry whose wood counter had turned to laboratory tin and its water faucet to gas line as the do balloon the do-er do balloon emerged from one of those gas ends the ones you attach bunsen burners to in school science rooms everywhere i'm sure one end of the inevitably old usually yellowing rubber tube to the bunsen burner the other pulled over the rough metal end patterned so much like the rebar used for reinforcing concrete sticking out from the vertical pipe nipples they may even call them with their tiny open ends suspended above the grey of the table and there it is the do balloon the do balloon the do balloon and i don't know if it emerged direct a gaseous but somehow discrete ballooning substance or if it was blown up just like a balloon maybe made out of that same tubing expanding until that rubber will thin to bursting i don't know that anymore than i know how i knew it was called the do balloon if it called itself the do the do the do-er dour do balloon or if i made that up to imitate its sound its hissing farting sound instead of the whooo whooo of ghosts

///the do doooo doooo of the do balloon if i began that immediately that first time i told that dream or just later as i told it again and again and talked about gas jets though never scotch as i laughed and laughed day bright while i chased any friend who came to my house around and around shouting the do balloon the do balloon the do balloon tried to chase cherokee bill when he came back and talked to me about dreams and visions and vision quests and the dream you waited for fasting on hilltop or in deep forest out there in the eastern woodlands at seven or eight i must have been seven or eight we learned about it at school too built iroquois wickiups your dream giving you a name while i would only laugh again because the only name this dream ever gave me and i don't know how was its own the do balloon the do balloon the do balloon but that didn't mean it hadn't given me a great gift in that laughter even if the only vision i had was of what had gone down how i am standing there in that dream moment by the butler's pantry door and the do balloon the do balloon the do balloon is about to get loose get loose and hunt me down hunt me down to envelop me in its farting belching mustard coloured gaseous cloud the do balloon the do balloon the do balloon ready to do me in the dour

///the do-er the do balloon swelling up swelling up inside the butler's pantry swelling up the shape of the old copper sink turned inside out and made whole and where the dripping water stained the sink green and forced it into that old penny smell you can see the olive stains on the mustard face of the do balloon the do balloon the do balloon with its old penny old alcohol farty puke smell as it floats up to hunt me down to envelop me farting and hissing and belching the whole house now full of gas jets and gas nipples where it will soon be able to refresh itself to appear and reappear until it will get me it will it will get me and i know as i stand by the swinging door into the butler's pantry yes yes it will the do balloon the do balloon the do balloon soon soon soon the do balloon will do me in the dour do-er do balloon soon soon there will be nothing i can do and i'm terrified and i'm a child and i don't know i'm dreaming and maybe that's when i should wake up in order to find out i am that's the way it usually works at the moment of crisis of maximum fear you wake up to find out you've been dreaming only i don't and i don't know why because instead my consciousness enters the dream and i know i'm dreaming and i'm tired of being terrified so i just place all my consciousness in that dream body and i do what my tomboy self will learn to do that same last paul garcia summer with my crewcut hair the way i can almost see it and my little pink dress turning to dirty jeans as i open that door and i walk into the old penny farty smell of the olive and eggplant butler's pantry and I take my fist and i close it and I power it forward from the shoulder right at the mustard head the olive face that is the do balloon

///the do balloon the do balloon and i'm punching it punching it punching it just that once one long punching punching punching punch and the next thing you know the do balloon the do balloon the do balloon all farting and hissing hissing and farting is getting smaller and smaller even as it gets louder and louder for one last moment because it might as well be a balloon at a birthday party it might as well be bright green or red or yellow because all it can do is fly around getting tinier and tinier in tighter and tighter harmless circles until it falls to the floor and that's when i choose to wake up to wake up with the gift of laughter in my mouth the way you sometimes do from dreams when you just can't stop laughing all inhibition gone laughing and laughing so maybe now you can understand why it lasted for years that laughter and why i've always remembered that do balloon do balloon do balloon's name and why too i chased margot repeating it the do balloon the doooooo balloon the doooooo balloon the do-er do balloon and laughed too with cherokee bill even if i hadn't known when i punched it that my intention to punch if not the punch itself had brought me to the pinnacle of dreamerhood i was a lucid dreamer and who cares if i hadn't known either for that matter that according to all those lucid dream theorists when i defeated the dream monster i could ask it for a name because the fact is that all i cared about and you could hear it in my laughter was that i chose i chose

///i chose the moment to act and the moment to wake up and name or not lucid dream or not that was certainly a vision a vision of choice a moment of control so it didn't matter if my lonely forest peak was only my room at the top of that house staring out at my ginkgo tree because i did it i punched that do balloon that do balloon that do balloon i made that small choice inside that eggplant olive mustard world even if it was only in a dream and maybe for that moment and for a long time to come that vision only took me as far as the sink in the butler's pantry which the next time for sure will once more be its small dented concave copper self with its old penny smell and its green stains and what i will be doing is taking mickey's scotch from charlie's huge mahogany hands and waiting till he leaves to pour it down that sink before she can come to get us once again the scotch swollen mickey our own dowager dour do-er do balloon the do balloon the do balloon the do balloon farting and pissing and hunting us down and yes i did that i really did i poured that scotch down that sink not that it did any of us any good

///not for the longest time

///not anymore than punching a fart coloured do balloon do balloon do balloon dream monster in the head but still you new agers might call it a move to live my vision because even if i wouldn't have another lucid dream until i left that house as trapped as helpless in my dreams as in my body still i had the power to act that knowledge of choice however small with laughter into my world my hand punching out not to punch the do balloon the do balloon the do-er dour do balloon in the head but to grab that scotch bottle by the neck and pour its contents down the drain mustard ochre over green stains into eggplant opening lucid dreamer lucid schemer for one moment in control.

About the hemp rope

not young roddy macorley and round his neck but in my hand the solid hemp of the dumbwaiter rope the feel of it in my hand rough tough splintery on hands blistery red with the fun of it pullling up down up down the dumbwaiter up down up down then standing on top of it holding the centre rope in hand up down up down up to ceiling of second floor head touching cobwebs then down down down or climbing into dumbwaiter while i still fit and tim and aj hauling me as i looked at my red palms up up up down down down then no rope at all older bigger feet among the detritus first and always the damp smell of it and then back against one side of shaft hemp rope untouched to right side why did i always do it that way facing that direction but up up up down down down like climbing a chute if you're a climber you know about that legs push back up legs catch up make sure it never gets too wide or you're going down only this was perfect and always the same so up up up down down down and the dumbwaiter pulled as far up as it could go so you could just reach over to grab the lip of the exit into the butler's pantry secure a grip then drop your legs to pull yourself through and out and flop onto the butler's pantry floor like a fish the way you will into that dream room only this time it's still the smell of copper and scotch and the only reward is the climb itself maybe that's always true another mystery this climb through the dark and yes it would make a good chapter in a horror story chased or hiding in the dumbwaiter shaft but there was no horror there never any horror there just the feel of hemp rope and old oak boards the occasional cobweb and the triumph of doing it there must have been some story resistance fighters or some such we told ourselves as we learned our ability to do and to resist and you gained the knowledge that your scrawny body could climb anywhere you might want.

Snakes and ladders

It was the bannister spindles to haul us up between the storeys the bannisters
to slide us down

///nobody ever won.

Second storey kid

You could climb up the front of the house too you only dreamed the drainpipe to slide you down.

Before the cloak room lost its windows

Secret messages through the side door mail slot

the one in the servants' entrance real mail falling onto cat pee.

That old window box

that's where we spied mickey from when she came home those days she came home i won't talk about unmoving inside the box for when she was already home.

Mickey to the rescue

The truth is it always bothers me to tell this mickey to the rescue story i hardly even bother to remember it really even if you might think i should i think i should as far as it goes after all it's one of those perfect childhood memory stories the kind you ought to tell or more to write the ones writers have been writing for years centuries probably the kind you know just fit into the absolute right spot the right slot precooked if not prewritten the fast food of stories you don't even need to talk them out might not want to really you already know from everything you've ever read they're prepackaged perfect freeze dried just add water and stir so these days if i mention it at all i pull one of those if i talk about it i'll lose it things some writers always pull promise someone even myself i'll write it someday as i tuck it away with no such intention though i might know it lurks still in my mind in case of emergency some moment of feeling just too dis- or mis-

///placed keep this sort of sealed away maybe inside a hard casing like one of those glass and metal fire boxes with an axe break glass to seize and all that something for whenever you need to fight your way to feeling normal though the fact is i can hardly manage to bring the story up on this list can't even make myself write a straightforward headline for the time i got my tonsil operation can't even find a cat that ate the canary grin to tell anyone i've got one too one of those stories everyone is always looking for a story that is the perfect example of that small instant of betrayal so part and parcel of every childhood that moment of growing up which cannot be reversed or made up for even by parent or other authority figure coming in at the last minute to try to make it okay okay okay okay as if running down a corridor will make it okay not the words so much as the concept echoing down not just the halls but the years you'll be

///okay okay only you never will be not ever again not altogether never have that same absolute trust in the world ever again ever quite be okay the kind of thing that happens in its exquisite poignancy to every child to every parent to every authority figure the hand reaching out but it's already too late even if no harm is done no real harm no real harm everything's going to be okay you keep telling yourself no real harm no harm done only you know it has because you because your child never looks at the world at anything quite the same way ever again so it takes a while to realize that these experiences are actually necessary that's what the shrinks will tell you anyway these days talking about the establishment of good boundaries the separation of self from parent from world from other all that good psychobabble you tell yourself to protect yourself from the look in the child's eyes as he she it sees you unable to repair the thousand pieces of the bully smashed toy make better the moment of teacher induced humiliation that reported out loud the paper that claimed three times four equals thirteen spelled kat or was it kaos with a k so all you can hope for is that such an experience will not occur too young or too strong not be your older son at ten locked in a storm drain made to say i fuck my sister every night that nothing more than one small toy one small moment of assertion will be dashed to pieces and the self will be gathered again stronger more resilient more able to cope with none of that

///hope even belief stopping the welling poignant sadness which makes these stories such a standard the knowledge of innocence's inevitable loss balanced against that aching desire to protect that's always there that desire to shelter even from small betrayals and always too that calculation in all our lives of when exactly it happened that knowledge of lies or malice or just the limits of the personal power or even knowledge of the good parent the good teacher the good authority figure so how perfect could this be just how perfect

///in fact there were years early adolescent early adult years before this story was yet sealed inside its just in case of emergency casing when i was using all the weapons at my disposal to normalize life at old twenty-six trying to attain to the perks of normalcy when this story was one of the best weapons in my arsenal making me try over and over to tell it like that throw it out into the room like that a perfect pristine loss of innocence story to match all the others being told though the fact is i didn't write it then either never in fact thought i would but only because i never expected to write at all and maybe the perfection i could see in that story is part of the reason the way i could feel it cold somehow lying there cold and dead feel something missing feel a weight in telling that didn't resonate with that gentle poignancy with what i meant it to mean a sense that i could never make it ring true no matter how much it fit with those other stories those stories of others stories that always rang true so that i decided the lack of shimmer the lack of rhythm of rhyme or reason precision or voice in the story was a lack of talent more than a lack of skill and besides i could never stand the idea of sitting down to tell it alone make the words move across a page myself as cold and alone as black and white and grey as that featureless hospital room of the fifties and i never knew why

///i needed those people around me their warm smiles to heat me up in those late night late high school early morning early university loss of innocence conversations where i could see some young soon to be writer sitting opposite me taking it up oh yes oh yes feel them craft it how to begin and end and yes they knew they could do it while i just left the facts to hang out feeling something wrong something wrong something wrong not okay okay okay at all even as i told it with mickey running down the hall okay you're going to be okay and i didn't know what it was that something wrong even as i threw it out there so generous with my story watching them craft it small quiet beginning to gently honed middle to sharp poignant end so easy to give away and never realizing i wasn't losing anything there was no gift after all it wasn't mine really mine there was no okay okay okay okay that i could feel echoing no small loss i could actually feel poignant like that to let me shape it

///it was just a few facts thrown out to match an intellectual knowledge of what they ought to mean patched together like a new orleans levee to prevent the floodwaters of chaos engulfing my mind and the cat failing to eat the canary to get my tongue instead or at least my paralyzed late night fingers no matter how we all acknowledged it was perfect all laughed and said oh yeah oh yeah that's the story all right all right all right all right them giving me back as they honed it a me with just the right scope and number
of difficulties to make me part of the all encompassing normal childhood we were all constructing for each other so that maybe it really was hunger never generosity that made me dangle the story there for them to craft for them to use a hunger for just that me the one i could not construct myself as i still sat there knowing there was something i couldn't grasp something wrong something something that wouldn't ring true in that story even if the facts were true exactly perfectly true how they described mickey running

///down the corridor okay okay okay okay

///something that didn't resonate in that punchline too much like being punched as i'm screaming and we all know it will not be okay only even telling it is never quite okay because there's something that goes beyond what happens next that end of story so perfectly constructed that's supposed to prepare you for the internalization of the good parent the caring parent what allows you to comfort your own self when those good boundaries are established because no matter how much i laugh and acknowledge the impact of the story how these things oh yes they push one toward adulthood oh yes i might even have said still i can't get beyond me child me in the operating theatre as the mask is coming down and i'm still trying to scream only i'm choking and it's not okay because i can't feel it that moment of comfort of recovery of post-operative ice cream against the sore throat even if mickey is there by then holding my hand i still can't put the moments the comfort together make it work no matter how many times i throw out the facts to let them be told back to me exactly perfectly true how the people in the hospital had told me that they were taking me out to breakfast after all i hadn't eaten from the night before i was six or maybe seven and mark was gone and i was all sick and infected and in those days everyone had their tonsils if not their appendixes out like madeline and i was a brave little girl wasn't i and they were taking me out for breakfast breakfast before i got to show my bravery by having my tonsils out and i was all prepared to get that done and yes i was all prepared to be all mature matooor ma-whatever that is all prepared

///to go in for the operation whenever they told me it was time i was ready i had girded myself the way we learn to do and it felt so good i could be mature and brave and after breakfast they would do it and i would prove my maturity only they had lied it wasn't breakfast i was going for it was the operation and pretty soon i knew after all it was pretty easy to know i could just feel it riding fast faster fastest on the gurney and mickey not there the way she had promised she would be there were just those nurses with their false smiles oh yes i remember those smiles i would come to have a lot of experience with those smiles and this time it's oh yes dear we're taking you to breakfast only that smell that sharp smell that antiseptic smell that proclaimed no food here as it just got bigger and bigger until it took up the inside of my skull and i knew it wasn't okay couldn't be okay what they were doing wasn't okay as i rode along on the gurney faster and faster knowing something was not right and i wasn't madeline and i was starting to scream and there was mickey running and running running and running or at least she says she was i don't remember her running and running just how she told me later about running and running as she patted my hand okay while what i remember is the mask coming down and trying to scream into the mask and refusing to count no matter how well i did it in school and the mask with its sharp chemical smell settling onto my face and the bright colours coming as i still struggled and struggled refusing to be brave for those who had lied to me or for that matter to stop from screaming liars liars liars liars for as long as i could you promised me breakfast breakfast breakfast breakfast while it's always mickey

///who tells it and tells it tells it over and over how she had told them she was to be there in the operating room and they had agreed and furthermore she had made it clear they weren't to lie she believed you didn't lie about things like that you didn't lie to children the way i will say it too repeating after her while the doctors the nurses they'd gone ahead and done this anyway no matter what she'd told them and still she'd been afraid enough for me to try so hard to be there and she had arrived on time at the time they'd told her but they'd already taken me down anyway they'd lied to her too and then there'd be the big lipstick mickey moment when she would lean over and grab my hand grab my hand and say oh i am so sorry and yes it is such a good betrayal

///loss of innocence story told by parent or by child but better by child who knows its weight and what it did what it resulted in for body and mind so why was it mickey who always told it told it over and over to me to guests in the house parents at my school until even for me by the time i had those high school those university conversations i told it in her voice and maybe that's what it was that was wrong like so many things i told so long in her voice maybe that was the kernel of untruth that told me i would never write never hear truth ringing in story the untruth was that it wasn't my voice but why wasn't it did i just resent mickey being the hero mostly the hero refuse that story because mickey's the hero so that even when i say i felt it welcomed me into normalcy still it was never my voice and i never felt normal it wasn't my normalcy and why was that you resentful little bitch what's wrong with mickey the hero mother to the rescue every once in a while isn't that what we all want well isn't it and who cares if it's a welcome into the imaginary world of mickey the world of an imaginary mickey the one with the horses and the debutante balls the one who even wanted to organize a coming out party for you sacrificed to buy you formals you refused and lectured on etiquette and meant it the way she still meant everything will be okay okay okay okay she didn't mean to fail you that wasn't her intent anymore than it ever is the parent's in any of these small stories which means it doesn't matter whether in the outside world we are perfectly absolutely okay

///okay like a babe rocked in arms because inside ourselves we can still be that babe because still there is someone out there wanting us to be okay so we can know inside we deserve to be okay and build our self esteem and all those good things okay so what's wrong with this story what's wrong with this picture of mickey running down the hall you'll be okay taking up my hand are you okay why isn't this one this tonsil operation this mickey to the rescue one of my first headlines maybe even my very first headline why have i stopped telling it why don't i write it craft it make it resonate why don't i allow for this perfect small story this small story of normalcy why don't i damn well tell it do i think i'm so damn special even my stories must be outside the norm more dramatic more over the top more different do i hate mickey that much do i really so much that i can't let her have her few small mickey to the rescue protective mickey sober mickey moments moments for the mickey who really did believe what she said when she said those nurses shouldn't have lied

///to me

///that i had every right to struggle to fight to accuse to scream that mickey who comforted me and not just then that sober mickey who always said she wanted to be the tiger mother who defends her cubs why can't i let her have her few small tiger mother moments write their headlines for that mickey who tried whether or not it grants me the prerequisites of normalcy much less its perquisites its perks why can't i have that generosity only the truth is i did for years allowed myself to tell that story in her voice allowed her those moments threw the story into the world for others to tell round momentary moulded

///delimited small alice munro perfect like the opening of a hand the saying of a modern mantra only the more i would tell those moments those heroic mickey moments the more i knew they weren't just moments they weren't round or moulded or even momentary or delimited especially not delimited they had no limits no borders no boundaries at all they formed into one long continuous enveloping narrative that once you started to swallow it like that old spittoon joke you couldn't stop those moments would form a net to trap the cubs of whatever kind of mother she really was a net because whether or not those cubs might be in that earnestly described moment okay those cubs would never be themselves trapped there in her narrative of not okay okay but look at me look at me look at me look at me

///running down the corridor to rescue you look at me look at me look at me look at me see how good how right how loving i am see how i always try so hard so hard so hard so hard despite it all despite how hard how hard how very hard it is for me think of what you owe me for trying so hard it's so hard for me let me tell you i never

///i never wanted them to do that to you i never did i even came to the hospital she'd say right after she'd grabbed my hand i could hardly stand going there you see it happened to me it happened to me she would repeat as she would start to pat and pat my hand like a drum and it was so much worse so very much worse because my parents you see my parents your grandparents they thought it was all right even if the house was perfect white and green and perfect and everything in its place not at all like here and she'd gesture around old twenty-six well those perfect people with their perfect house they still thought it was all right to lie to kids back in those days i guess everybody did so they lied and they lied and they lied and when my turn came for the operation they strapped me down on the gurney without telling me why or what they were doing just that it was for my own good and anaesthesia

///wasn't very good in those days either not like today and the operating theatres were big and they did more than one operation in one room and there i was unable to move struggling to get free and they were about to put me out to take out my tonsils just the way they did yours and her hand patting mine faster and faster a drum roll but there on the operating table right next to me there was this fireman who had just been brought in from a fire where the roof had collapsed and his chest had been crushed and they were trying to operate only the anaesthesia hadn't taken and the next thing you know just as they're trying to put me under he wakes up and he starts screaming and screaming i've never heard such screaming

///screaming that terrible screaming i still wake up sweating to that screaming it's worse than the dreams about mark because right there in that room i'm turning my head and i can see him right there next to me his wild eyes that look everywhere and his open mouth and the wild sounds coming out

///and then it stops

///and he's dead of course he's dead he died right there right before my eyes and then the mask came down so you see how hard it is for me how hard it was to come to the hospital but i came anyway and they'd told me they wouldn't lie to you remember how i didn't lie to you i prepared you for what was going to happen that's right i told them not to lie to you and there i was and i held your hand even if i could hardly bring myself to do it and you understand how hard it was for me but how you'll be okay

///okay you'll always be okay because you're so brave and you're so strong and you've always had it so easy not like me which is why i'm weak not like you you're strong and okay you'll always be okay you have no reason to scream the way you do now every time you get a needle even if they did lie to you that time even if you know they're lying when they say it won't hurt still it's only a little lie it's not like a fireman waking up to scream and die so you'll always be okay so yes it was mickey

///to the rescue mickey

///but like always with mickey to the rescue mickey she always only rescued herself because that's the way it always was her experience had always been so much worse so really you had to understand

///you really did how okay you were you were okay weren't you she was right wasn't she and it would be in that moment that maybe you would feel it for the first time that weak helplessness in your shoulders your mouth opening and no sound coming out that thing that would happen for years that was there even as you ate the ice cream kids always got after tonsillectomies with that fierce rough pain in the back of the throat that it wasn't just that someone had taken your tonsils someone had taken your voice only it wasn't the nurses with their lying smiles the anaesthetist with his encroaching mask the doctor with his cutting tools it was mickey with her encompassing narrative mickey sitting there okay okay okay okay patting your hand over and over you'll be okay as she told her story her so much worse story like so many so much worse stories that there would always be over the years because no matter how she prepared you for the tonsil operation for not being lied to she never prepared you for this so much worse than the lies of any operation all those breakfasts that yes you would get where she would prepare bacon and eggs and toast and maybe even *café con leche* the way bill did but where still there would be that smell of anaesthesia the smell of horror if not in the room in the back of your throat as she would place the plate of eggs in front of you or just walk in as you ate the cereal you had prepared yourself until she wouldn't even have to tell one of those so much worse stories

///to make your mouth which had opened to tell her what she had done the night before close again as she just looked at you as she took her milk from the fridge or patted your hand as she said she was sorry sorry so very very sorry for anything she might have done but you had to understand and your mouth remained closed and you would never say a thing never tell her what it was she had done that she didn't remember never even say that maybe it hurt just a little and then there would be others

///so many others over the years who would look at you the same way without you even having to try to tell it to say anything that pat on the hand that closes your mouth to this day if you're not careful and even now that she's dead there's always someone to say you know she really did love you don't you you understand how proud she was of you and your fish mouth still opens and closes you a fish on your side in the open air flopping just a little in rhythm to the voices of okay okay okay okay you'll always be okay you know she didn't mean it know she can't help it you don't want to make her feel worse do you you know she means well don't you and besides you're okay even as you can't find your voice know you are out of oxygen as your floppy fish self threatens to asphyxiate in the alien element of someone else's story even as the voices continue okay okay okay okay you'll be okay okay okay okay you are okay okay okay okay until there isn't a story left there at all hardly even a headline even if i wanted it it's always just that moment when the mask comes down

///the blue the yellow the red the exploding anaesthetic colours and the pain you wake to the pain you will always wake to that isn't the operation but mickey's nights you can never tell about until you don't remember them either just that hand covering yours you'll be okay and who cares if finally maybe you can tell your way to the other side tell your way to okay because even if you can this is a story you will never tell again not even throw out those facts anymore for someone else to tell and who cares if you never do if you never tell it and you never achieve that normalcy that gets you invited to the right dinner parties if you ever are that person you once thought you would be at those parties in those student apartments at university so quiet in your sophistication with your cat that ate the canary smile who cares about that at all because now i want my own voice my own voice or at least that child's voice the one who is never okay okay okay okay who always gets told she's over the top oh sarah don't be so raw so radical so dramatic so over the top and besides they'll ask what skill does it take to tell a story that's over the top only nice proportionate stories take craft which might be true enough at least from the point of view of those like mickey who create them though if you ask me it took a lot of craft or at least craftiness on my part to live those nights only who cares it's nobody's business but mine how i use the voice I've finally found and I don't want to keep everything in its place in my stories anymore than mickey did in her parents' house and besides that

///if you can't have that innocence that innocence that underlies the small loss of innocence that is the ability to sit at parties and craft stories where the worst that ever happens is a mother running down the corridor to shout you'll be okay okay okay okay well if i can't have that not at those parties not ever that trust in being okay somewhere okay if you can't have that but always await the red green yellow uncrafted raw moment when it will be taken from you and no one will run down any corridor to tell you anything at all so that when you say okay it means okay i'll do whatever you want well if that's all you've got if even okay okay okay okay will never be okay if that trust if that innocence is totally missing then why tell stories

///crafted or uncrafted

///to protect those who stripped you of it.

Mickey produced myths mostly in the kitchen

Millionaires on the maumee
that's when she talked about how if her mother hadn't died and she'd stayed in toledo she'd have married a millionaire one of the people whose estates we visited in fact so it might even have been true but she would have done that and not met beautiful exciting new yorker writer mark who invented the classic new yorker profile and who fooled her into thinking he was responsible but we wouldn't have been poor we never would have been poor you see we wouldn't have been and she would never have been so desperate as to drink herself but even so maybe i could go back to toledo and be a debutante.

Agee at the funeral
is the one i keep talking about the one mickey assembled again and again especially when she'd just gotten back from visiting mia mia agee that is or for that matter every thirty first of july for mark's birthday deathday repeating how at mark's funeral when jim got into the cab to leave she leaned in and said just don't let it happen to you jim just don't let it happen to you and there agee was dead in a cab two years later in a cab yet and even if i might say but that was a heart attack still i can hear her answering alcohol alcohol before she gets out the scotch.

Shawn after the funeral
i'm not sure we ever met shawn even if we did spend time with the gerdies i'm not sure mickey didn't feel too guilty or something to ever see shawn but anyway what she would say was that shawn was the only one who ever understood because there was the one time or maybe it was a bunch of times when mickey got all weepy about mark shawn just looked at her and said what did you ever expect mick they called each other mick and murph after all what did you ever expect even if she never elaborated on why she should have expected it except to look at that one portrait of mark everyone in the family still has and say weak weak weak that maudlin irish weak.

Mickey said there was a man
who wanted to write a book about mark he couldn't call it crack up of course that was the one about fitzgerald but he wanted it to be something like that mickey said she only talked to him because it would have placed mark it would have would have made him stay at the centre of attention as it examined why a young irish american writer the inventor of the classic new yorker profile would have cracked up would have gone crazy would have

died on his fortieth birthday would have drunk himself to death only she wouldn't do it she wouldn't do it she wouldn't do it to us not like mia did to the agee kids making jim a cult figure she wouldn't do it to us something i almost kind of believed for the longest time until i finally figured out as i looked around me as i gathered the facts that it was herself she wouldn't do it to it was herself she was protecting and if she thought she was protecting me at all and maybe tim too it wasn't from becoming the daughter of a cult figure the writer who cracked who died of terminal writer's block holed up in a hotel room and all that but from finding out what she had really been doing all that time and that i wasn't the daughter of that figure i wasn't mark's daughter at all.

Mickey produced wasp meals

Scotch woodcock
i don't remember what that is but it was mostly when mark was around and has nothing to do with a bird at all it's not like pheasant under glass it's cheap and has something to do with anchovy paste i remember that stuff farting its tan brown way out of the tube maybe there's ketchup too something tomato-ey anyway scrambled into eggs and the only scotch the cheap stuff that went into mickey's mouth irish whisky for mark maybe bourbon scrambled into their minds.

Creamed chipped beef on toast
i never knew that was a wasp meal even with that flour paste pretending to be cream not until i heard it remarked on in some movie or other maybe book about how it was ultimate wasp food we always had it as dinner because it was cheap and easy the way we did mac and cheese or forgot the creaming part and even the toast just ate the chipped beef right out of the jar in the fridge then slammed the door the jars made great scotch glasses.

Escalloped potatoes
i always like the es before the scalloped that was for when we were really broke like tuna salad or sardines or something without meat veggies were still cheap then for nights when mickey just plunked it on the table and went to evelyn brand's to eat saying there wasn't enough for her though maybe she just went to ev's to drink ev's scotch ev was the only female in the neighbourhood mickey always kept up with she was an old democratic party hack one of the first females elegant and ferocious with ethel merman aunty mame posture and no waist always complaining she had no waist as she slung her mink over her shoulder or sipped a martini all of it in that gravelly low sultry whisper from her crooked sexy mouth i always thought it was just her style till mickey told us it was throat cancer and we suddenly saw the scar stopped her from climbing further up the party ladder mickey said couldn't give speeches anymore that never stopped jean chretien maybe that's why i've always loved him forget the politics remember that gravelly voice and that same humour jean chretien on george w bush reminding me of ev putting mickey to bed in the hungry years.

Paella

That definitely wasn't a wasp meal that was something joe and pilar fed us in the back of montero's while mickey drank in the front where she found cherokee when he came back he's the one who made paella at home though it was more often *arroz con pollo* i remember those wonderful little plastic bags with the tiny saffron pistils he kept in the pantry for the rice not only could cherokee cook interesting food made *chili con carne* so hot he couldn't eat it himself he brought the money to feed us.

More mickey produced myths mostly in the kitchen

A. Cousins

The agoraphobic
was margaret a brilliant lawyer university of chicago at fifteen maybe it was even fourteen youngest person ever to pass the new york bar she was the oldest of two southern sisters the one who was supposed to be the boy rescue her arkansas family fallen on hard times ended by refusing to go out of her house in forest hills gardens couldn't boil an egg mixed a mean martini.

The femme fatale
was bootie the second one of the southern sisters really that's what she was called and no implications back then either except waspiness like tootie and billie or for that matter muffie you know how it works bootie was the one went out with all sorts of famous men of whom she was very short on praise mickey said she dated jfk but mentioned it only after he was elected had a number of abortions back alley of course there wasn't any other kind i don't know why i was told about that but someone described one that must have been late second trimester the horror of the fetus dropping into the toilet amid all the blood who knows if any of it was ever true except that she was gorgeous.

The lobotomized
we never knew her name just that she was a brilliant musician from mickey's birthplace in wisconsin far too sheltered with too high expectations mickey said she cracked up at college became violent became paranoid got lobotomized became a vegetable they didn't say persistent vegetative state then couldn't even wash herself mother killed her in her bathtub family rumour had it.

And more
i don't remember but there were over twenty three was enough for mickey to draw a breath and say at least she'd escaped at least she didn't turn on herself like that and we would all nod and never ask why she turned on us.

B. The too clean house in the too clean town
that's how mickey always described toledo and her house too how even still with the stepmother there she despised she still couldn't see a small thread on the carpet wihout picking it up and that was why she didn't care about

household things passed it on to me in fact didn't dust didn't cook didn't clean if she could get away with it had no sense of design couldn't do anything crafty or artistic either at least i didn't inherit that part she said it was a learning deficit in years before they used that word a homemaking deficit years before the homemaking word was used either so who knows what actual words she used but that's what she said eschewed all things feminine her pride that she'd never written for the women's pages never wanted to be trapped in a house much less be a wife to it but wouldn't be a lucy stoner career woman either all those stories all those myths so even if she would never say she didn't want kids said she did in fact was a tiger mother wanted kids so bad so why did she tell tim the truth about that one thing that she had the d&c when she was three months pregnant with him but because she had a bifurcated uterus he'd survived it was in medical journals so no matter what she said that's one subtext that came through clearly she didn't have to tell us she didn't want kids i was only there because she'd fucked up once and as for tim he was meant to be an abortion an abortion.

The abortion

That wasn't a myth and that wasn't a dream and that wasn't imagined and that wasn't bootie and that wasn't tim that was real i saw mickey painted red belly button to thigh i saw her it was the younger brother sister i wanted more than tim anyway.

Surely a free lunch

i want to bring this free lunch thing up again every time i think about what we didn't eat for dinner when mark was gone or even about free dinners at montero's or maybe just because people keep talking about how there's no such thing as a free lunch and there is there is i've had them i have and maybe for me it was only the once in that bar along court street and mark was most likely going to see his japanese mistress it was after he'd left the house but before he'd left for africa and there it was the free lunch in those marvellous metal serving plates keeping warm over hot water and what i remember is knackwurst knackwurst hot and swollen and sweating like a child molester's fingers and i don't know why that's the image i get just that it's the one i do and that there was sauerkraut and potatoes of some sort too and mark drinking whisky i think always whisky and talking about how it was a free lunch and introducing me to everyone there and it was really fun to be with him alone in that bar and maybe i only got to go the once but tim got to go again and again and even if mickey had to tell me mark actually told tim how he was going to africa and all sorts of other things besides like how now he had to be the man of the house and take care of his womenfolk his mother and his sister and looked at tim and winked at least that's how i imagine it tim has never said just told me as mickey lay dying how he felt trying to get her off the subway and besides that take care of me when mickey just sang and sang that rrrrr rrrrr rrrrr and wouldn't get up and we had to finally just get off ourselves and how he felt he had to get me home but he should be caring for her too and that only came up when mickey was doing it again rrrrr rrrr rrrrr dying in that hospital and i thought about how he'd stayed there and he'd done it rescuing her the way she never rescued him rescuing her again and again as if he were forever trying to get her off the subway as if he'd never gotten himself off that subway as if it were his responsibility till the day she died so maybe for him there was no such thing as a free lunch after all in fact that one just about cost him his life or at least his right to enjoy it.

Gritty kitty refrigerator realism

because i can't stop thinking about chiquita i don't stop thinking about chiquita or maybe it's the book about chiquita i can't stop thinking about maybe that's the setting not chiquita my cat but *chiquita and her friends* my book the setting crawling into that book the setting that book inside that room inside that library inside that brownstone inside that safety that was that other brownstone the brownstone of my school and deep within like a beating heart that red covered cardboard and its yellow legal pad my stories beating inside and once more its smell come again its smell over and over always there and me writing and writing day after day writing and writing only the story the stories never ended made no sense kept making no sense *chiquita and her friends* made no sense because there was no story not really you can't have story when you're in love with safety and what was i doing day after day but writing stories i could never end because i couldn't bear to make anything happen it's still something of a problem maybe i can take it back to right there that year of that book this difficulty with plot these headlines with no story this hatred of making things happen because all i wanted was stretch miaow purr dig in claws walk on fence tangle in hair eat seafood lap up milk purr purr miaow miaow and you just know there's nothing exciting not even anything remotely interesting about that story purr purr miaow leap scratch story is an extreme sport nothing risk averse about story i knew that even then i read enough exciting stuff after all but i couldn't you see i couldn't do it let anything happen to those cats not to chiquita not to any of her kittens not to the neighbourhood cats that still yowled on fences late into the night i just couldn't so maybe it was more like the picture of dorian gray in reverse no matter what happened out there in the world nothing happened in that book inside its red covers just slow beats stretch miaow scratch post dig in claws purr miaow kathump kathump heart beating and fingers moving on yellow brown striped legal pad inside the covers kitty cat drawings kitty cat unstories stuck deep inside book deep inside me as the usual difficulties unfolded the habitual horrors happened out there in the world never on the page never on the page making sure inside my heart the heart of my book the heart of my page the heart of chiquita nothing ever happened nothing nothing ever happened ever ever yowl miaow lap stretch miaow miaow purr nothing at all assuring myself that nothing ever really would i could keep them safe yes i could inside that book this time in a reverse dorian gray of denial so i keep telling myself they were unrelated my turning away from that world outside doesn't really mean i had anything to do with what really happened that day mickey came down the stairs after a particularly awful night looking for the bottle not of scotch but of milk the way she did every hangover morning bleary eyed and already saying to herself if not to us that she didn't remember a damn thing about anything that had happened the night before that was what she always said oh really did that happen oh if it did i'm sorry and there she is the milk in her hand about to start the milk drinking ceremony that completes her forgetting in that moment about to do something she'll always remember

///as she turns away toward the white kitchen table and slams the refrigerator door not for a moment looking down chiquita was quick and funny and leapt into the refrigerator all the time loved to do it that was the sort of thing she may even have done inside the red covers of my book along with miaow stretch purr miaow scratch post miaow purr there might have been leap into refrigerator we all loved it thought it was so clever what a resourceful cat what a lovely cat story surely aesthetically more pleasing than teaching her kittens to catch mice bat them about the floor this way she taught her him them to leap into the refrigerator do just as mommy did only they were small and not so very fast or strong and that morning there's the black and white one hanging on by its little kitty claws right at the bottom ledge and maybe it's already going mew mew but mickey doesn't hear it and wham kachunk

comes the door and mew mew mew for sure it's crawling along the floor now dragging its legs mew mew mew and mickey always said that was something she would always remember always hear not the milk bottle falling from her hand not even the mew mew mew as the kitten dragged itself over to the milk to try to lap it up mew mew mew but the brief sound of the snapping of the kitten's spine and no i couldn't have done that

///made that happen by letting nothing happen inside my book i couldn't have done that it wasn't my lack of attention did that i couldn't monitor mickey after all could i it wasn't in my power i only had the power of red covers and kittens inside leap purr mew mew mew lick hand purr purr like beating heart red and warm a small pink tongue it wasn't me it wasn't i didn't create that other world i didn't it was mickey's lack of attention i keep telling myself not mine hidden deep inside those red covers inside room inside that other brownstone where nothing happened it wasn't me but i did know right then that whatever else you could do with a book you could never make anyone or anything any creature safe snuggled inside its covers so i closed them snap i closed them snap i closed them snap those covers snap mew mew mew i closed them snap mew mew mew because there was no more safety and pretty soon

///no more cats mickey got rid of them all i can't stand it i keep hearing that sound she said that sound snap that sound snap there will be no more cats in this house the aspca will put down the kitten the aspca will get them all no more purr miaow leap lick walk on fence tangle in hair miaow miaow mew mew mew all of them gone

///even chiquita.

Coming back bill

but bill came back that's right bill came back better than a cat bill came back never the very next day but always bill came back thought he was a goner each time he went round the world or the horn or to the persian gulf or even coastwise but bill came back and it wasn't over land the way bill came back but i'll keep that name anyway coming back bill for how bill came back better than a cat or for that matter better than cherokee bill this coming back bill for how bill came back what the eastern cherokee would sometimes name their relatives the ones who came back from the trail the trail of tears so coming back bill for how bill came back so coming back bill for choctaw bill who was never called that but who always came back yes bill came back the one who was my father who always came back better than a cat bill came back the permanent foreshadowing in that kitty movement in the house accurate or not i will equate the two say it was bill who brought chiquita so i can tell this as if i always knew bill would come back bill would come back even when he helped put down the kitten still bill would come back and it will help get through to the catless end whatever end that may be because bill came back coming back bill because bill came back coming back bill coming back bill coming back coming back bill for how bill came back better than a cat better than a cat remember in your mind always how bill came back bill came back the one you could always trust the one with the nine lives the one who lived to tell the tale better than a cat better than a cat bill came back.

World map reprise

I started to sneak into that room when i could there weren't just colour coded countries on that map there were lines on it lines on it great big circling circulating dashed lines dotted lines on it lines through the changing tones of blue lines with names names and numbers circling lines circling circling parabolas i could one day call them parabolas or sine curves you could find where they left the map to enter again circling circling wrapping the map tighter and tighter a hug of lines with their numbers and sometimes their names magellan fifteen nineteen fifteen twenty two vasco da gama fourteen ninety seven the sea routes the sea routes magic magic finger following line circling circling to bring bill home.

Bill never rounded the cape of good hope

he always went up the persian gulf to the suez.

Horror among the potatoes

as we hunkered down in the pantry a real pantry the kitchen pantry full of cans and winter vegetables potatoes starting to grow long tentacles out from their eyes the whole room just the size of my closet but downstairs where we listened to the old wood radio from paul garcia's shop this isn't real horror this is like comic relief horror relief you could call it horror stories as relief from horror there's a whole theory about that maybe that's what this is this whole book that pantry those nights wasn't just escape it was comfort profound comfort midnight comfort the stroke of saturday midnight comfort in old old horror stories classic horror stories the monkey's paw and the case of amontillado and who knows what else midnight horror among the potatoes whoooo whooooo whoooo broadcast every saturday or was it friday midnight and we snuck in there and held hands sometimes with other kids over for the night while for once bill and mickey stayed home and listened too a way to normalize the experience of the murphy household all of us safe safe safe horror one closet one pantry one place in that house with safe safe horror whooooo whooooo whoooo as we listened to the radio not the noises in the rest of the house or mickey on the other side of the door rrrrrr rrrrrr rrrrrrr too drunk to care.

Potassium potatoes raw reprise

I didn't figure this out looking in the pantry at the potatoes in that secret dark where they grew i only found this out this past year it's potassium raw potatoes have potassium lots of potassium forget the absent calories call this nutrition balance the blood electrolytes keep up your energy avoid dehydration put on salt and you've got yourself a sports drink no need to turn cellulose into starch all that moisture makes for gatorade in little brown little red jackets balance is the basis after all of this lower order raw potato longing balance balance to always keep moving the way i would later maybe a sunday after a brief dark horror story on the radio a longer horror story lived out in the kitchen take my bike down by the brooklyn bridge to move one after another along ten foot section after ten foot section of black metal half moon fences day after day mile after mile of practicing balance around the park and around again spinning on my toes to walk back spin again to walk forward leap over brief opening hold onto a branch to take a break a tight rope walker riding my rail to nowhere but walking without wavering balance balance in the street balance meditation on balance always balance to one day carry me forward not out to sea across the bridge and away.

Fish gut cleaning

Table carving

Olive brine drinking

it may seem strange to you and maybe it was from the time there was no food in the house so we drank the brine from the el primo olive jar but i love that stuff i love its taste that sharp salt and olive better than the things themselves much much better i really do.

Pipe exploding

so sometimes it probably is all for the best even if it's not the best of all possible worlds and even if you could take it as another sign of decay when the old lead pipe to the kitchen sink just splits open and it's water water everywhere glinting shining gleaming spraying and mickey just staring the pipe so crystallized i think that's what happens to old lead it could never be fixed so aj's father joe the plumber really joe the plumber joe centola the plumber who never licensed his son so he could never leave the business that's one way to solve any joe the plumber's problem with staff well joe just heated the lead of the pipe and bent it over sealed it off so the old now cold water kitchen sink came to be used only as a table because after all you could still use the hot water in the deep deep stone laundry sink and you wouldn't know it for years but like so many things you wouldn't know for years that lead from those pipes had probably just been poisoning you anyway.

Good cheap chorizo to paint the eggs blood red

229

Mambo queen maracas moment

1. *Qué Bonito y Sabroso*

bailan el mambo los mexicanos i hear on some latin station or at a dance or maybe it's just on that new cd to echo the old record i ruined playing that song in mexico on the world champion worst record player the turntable about half the size of the lp's it played scratching them always right in the middle right in that song in that case the one which maybe said *las mexicanas* because sometimes it does and sometimes it doesn't all mexicans or just the women depends on the version but it definitely always says *mueven la cintura y los hombros* and that's what i feel deep inside *qué muevan la cintura y los hombros* and that's when *me muevo yo moviéndome* around my *cintura* that's how it's said *la cintura* which translates literally as waist though it's not your waist they mean it's some other hip belly bum place maybe the body just moving around the belly button circling its empty fullness or maybe that *cintura* word's just like so many words so much in english an old euphemism for that part of the body further down hips bum or what hips and bum enclose them moving while the waist stays so inevitably still the way you hold your right hand above your waist your belly button when you dance latin alone

///not just to mimic the missing partner i don't think but to demonstrate that central stillness while the body moves feet hips knees bum and yes *los hombros* there's never any problem saying shoulders that's accurate enough the shoulders they do so move so whatever the *cintura* is it's not the waist they mean but who cares how you want to say it or play it or translate it or for that matter whether the song's in its original with the man himself beny moré from fifty two or fifty three or the new century two thousand three version with the rap lyrics thrown in or some sixties seventies eighties nineties date in between whichever it is it always takes me back to some originary place as originary as *qué bonito y sabroso* that still belly button all our lives have wrapped around some centre of my universe in any case the hispanic part anyway and it's not *los mexicanos* for me *que mueven bonito y sabroso* much less *las mexicanas* of whom maybe i wanted to be one with my dolls from the bar from montero's my lupita and conchita and pepita and marita but if i did it would be for him *que baila bonito y sabroso* that's right *qué bonito y sabroso baila el mambo el mexicano* always for me it's *el mexicano* paul garcia garsha we pronounced it paul garsha it took me to mexico to *méxico* to put it into three syllables gar-ci-a or for that matter know to put in that accent garcía the way it should truly hispanically be but just paul garsha paul garsha *el mexicano que bailaba bonito y sabroso* paul garsha

///never pablo with his jet black dyed hair and his electrical shop with its tubes and fans and his silly dachshund rupert and his gold tooth and his maybe phoney childhood memories of pancho villa and his habit of drinking sauerkraut juice instead of alcohol against ulcers we were informed and his big smile and his *café con leche* and his air of mastery and his spanish swear words and his rakish cheer brought into the house with his sly looks and his trips to all those apartments and shops for puerto rican *cuchifritos* or electrical items or just the *café* or maybe a new coffee sleeve to pour it through and then there's teaching me to count *uno dos tres cuatro cinco seis siete ocho nueve diez* though mostly just *uno dos uno dos tres* the *clave* rhythm across the new linoleum floor *qué bonito y sabroso* i can see it still those red and blue red and blue tiles that he laid down with the boys from the shop still smell the tar underlay see the wavy *qué bonito y sabroso* dance rhythm marks in it from whatever tool it is you use to smooth it out down on hands and knees *moviendo la cintura* really in that case writhing backwards *y los hombros* too and then when it's done there's back on your feet *uno dos uno dos tres* and there's my feet on his feet and us moving across that floor *qué bonito y sabroso bailan* as he teaches me just that to *bailar bailar bailar* as the music flows from the old brown cloth speaker of the wood radio cabinet enclosing all those tubes i'd watched him place into their sockets at his shop *qué bonito y sabroso baila* yes *que baila el mexicano* because yes the song is out and it's there in the kitchen coming over the air waves and i'm there moving on his feet across the floor *y qué bonito y sabroso bailo yo bailo yo el mambo con el mexicano* because there i am his mambo queen

///mamboing *uno dos uno dos tres* watching my feet touch blue red red blue red on top of his or on my own across the new tiles never stepping on a crack to break the new order in the house mark gone and paul garsha paul garcia there much less mickey's back but floating floating *qué bonito y sabroso* above all difficulty red blue blue red blue on the black of his shining shoes as shiny as his hair and wouldn't it be good *qué bonito y sabroso* to leave it just like that with that so good feeling *bailando el mambo bonito y sabroso* across the kitchen floor *moviendo la cintura y los hombros* feet up down up on red blue blue red blue *uno dos uno dos tres* the beauty the flavour of life the life of the moment the moment in the body the mystery of the body the body moving around its centre *uno dos uno dos tres* around its navel around its nourishment keep that in mind *qué bonito y sabroso* as if no story ever intervened in this rhythm as if no story ever laid the moment low ever had to be told or reconstructed outside the words of this language *qué bonito y sabroso* i did not yet even know as i just *bailaba con el mexicano* that's right i just want to keep that headline *qué bonito y sabroso* that isn't even really mine but just something a fragment that plays over and over in the mind the body till you move your *cintura* right hand on your belly button and your *hombros* even shrug them

///up and down down and up hold out your left hand to spin to the right to the left and around shake it from side to side then open it as if to toss something away laughing until maybe you notice the story inside inside that hand or inside that body you move so you think suddenly maybe you've been trying to do that for years with just a gesture of the hand to toss away that story that never makes it to even a headline pull it out of the silent gut to toss it away with the hand shrug it away with the shoulders up and down down and up sweep it away under your feet that story that story that is the day that the music plays

///*qué bonito y sabroso* only this isn't *bonito y sabroso* certainly not *sabroso* not on that day that i move *qué bonito y sabroso baila el mexicano* on his feet paul garsha's feet red blue blue red blue *uno dos uno dos tres* across the floor only this time like i said this time i think it was only this time when we get to the other side to the white wood chair next to the white wood table with its white metal top right there by the white door to the dark basement he lifts me up and places my feet on the chair and instead of *bonito y sabroso* certainly not *sabroso* there's him taking my face between his hands and sticking his tongue into my mouth

///and then if i don't manage to toss it away toss it away the way i do when i'm talking or laughing at a party or a bar or a dance toss it away without ever letting it take over my body just move it from gut to tip of fingers maybe a bit like one of those little balls of wool pilled on a sweater as if it were nothing just oh that and away it goes dropping from the tips of fingers onto the floor soft through air as if it were nothing as if it were so small so light it truly does not deserve a headline passing off of tips of fingers an unrhythmic dust mote in the air never *bonito y sabroso* certainly not *sabroso* that's right ha ha ha not tasty at all i might manage to say in passing translating that one word not *sabroso* at all but hardly consequential i might shrug

///and add if you know what i mean these things happen don't they they happen to everyone except there's the times it doesn't seem that way and it's not possible to do that and instead *qué bonito y sabroso* of my hand moving out *bailando* its own *mambo* and tossing it away the thing stays in my body and it grows into its story even as i sit and watch the dancers only my shoulders twitching instead of what does it matter and doesn't this just happen to everyone there's that rough sauerkraut juice warmth in my mouth and things like this happen to everyone maybe it's a cultural difference sticks in my throat the way the arm sticks at my side the side of my body my body suddenly little in its little dress suddenly stiff like that small white nylon skirt and i'm standing at attention even if *qué bonito y sabroso bailan el mambo* i want to dance inside my body around my belly button while when my hand finally moves it doesn't toss anything away but seems to hit the white basement door and there it is all the rest of the story that wants to follow that headline i won't write and it's grown so big that now i don't know how to begin to tell it to find its headline think maybe it isn't real at all certainly this sudden stiffness in the muscles is not proportionate to that incident so why say anything what's there to prove it hardly matters it seems so silly so trivial after all what's so awful

///about being frenched even if you are five or six and that tongue tastes rough and bitter it's over in a moment that's right a moment like tossing that small lack of rhythm of *bonito y sabroso* away from the body that circles the navel *qué bonito y sabroso* the way you can sometimes do so why not now after all you don't know

///that the door opened

///the door you can feel behind you with your small hand the way your hand now reaches behind you as you try to speak your mouth opening and closing not *bonito y sabroso* to no rhythm at all that hand feels small as it touches space and still you don't know the basement door the white basement door you don't know that it opened it's just that you can feel it opening you're sure you can feel it opening behind your hand opening behind that tongue in your mouth that is not your own opening your mouth your eyes toward something you don't want to see that is you that is him down there down those stairs you lifted down those stairs you running eagerly down those stairs *bonito y sabroso* to dance with *el mexicano* and there is you held on that bed down there where he slept once mark was gone and there's his arm across your chest and opening your legs and it's not his tongue in your mouth but

///that little place down there that little tongue poking out from between your legs the one you can feel could feel yourself with so much pleasure your finger your fingers *qué bonito y sabroso* moving back and forth back and forth until now you don't know if you discovered it yourself or he taught you there in front of the tv that he'd brought from his shop moving back and forth back and forth on the couch back and forth as he watched as tim and aj watched as mickey told you not to do that in public then made you do it in public later on only did it start there did he start it you don't know but there was so much pleasure still is so much pleasure your hands stiff to your sides the way there was so much pleasure as down in that basement room on those grey sheets he put that little tongue of yours there sticking out from between your legs into his mouth your little lower tongue in his mouth not his big textured tongue in yours and maybe there are those who would say

///maybe there were the years you would say well it must have been all right it must have been *bonito y sabroso* how could it be wrong if there was so much pleasure so much pleasure that sweet echoing sharpness so like pain up into the body *qué bonito y sabroso* so much pleasure so much pleasure *qué bonito y sabroso* so who cares if that white door opens wide with the memory of that kiss you keep tossing away with your hand why try to toss it away at all if there is so much pleasure so much pleasure you could write it like kiddy porn love it like kiddy porn be the kiddy all the porn kings want his porn not his mambo queen so much pleasure so much pleasure in your little tongue in his mouth only *qué bonito y sabroso*

///if that was all then why are those grey sheets a wave that overwhelms that sticks your tongue stuck to the roof of your mouth all bitter and sauerkraut tasting why are your hands held so stiff at your sides the way they grabbed those sheets the way your mouth sucked on tears why is then why is that the hands so still the arms so stiff no feet on his feet no body circling the belly button why is that then that overwhelming stiffness that shame of that place in the body of that small tongue that clitoris you always thought stuck out so far that everyone could see it could see your shame even as you changed your clothes growing there so you thought it would grow forever with every hint of pleasure like pinocchio's nose this little tongue growing like this little secret behind the door you had to lie about grown so big you could always see it looking down this big little tongue that so made you want to cut it off to cut it out at least to grow pubic hair to cover it up that shame that you carry down there and cannot help touching again and again so deep in the body

///still there in the body as the door opens as you try to celebrate your feet on his feet *qué bonito y sabroso baila el mexicano* and you can't do it you can't do it because *no bailas no bailas ni bailarás* your arms still held stiff at your sides as his tongue slips into your mouth to make you unable to speak his mouth slips over your small little tongue holding you unable to move so that your pleasure is not your own your body is not your own *qué bonito y sabroso* but someone else's like this headline someone else's you couldn't dance your own dance *no bailaba no bailaba* you couldn't move *la cintura y los hombros* because of *el mexicano* because of that door opening you couldn't dance you couldn't dance

///not mambo not rumba not cha cha cha not even foxtrot not even polka not even rock music absorbed into your own body because it wasn't your own body no dance at all nothing *bonito y sabroso*

///for fifteen years.

Maracas moment mambo queen

2. *Oye*

como va that's right hear it hear them the maracas the maracas *su ritmo* the way i can see them over there red purple blue green yellow orange primaries and secondaries and just plain brown gourd colours the maracas the maracas and maybe this has nothing to do with anything anything at all except maybe setting some sort of record straight because what i know about that is that it wasn't paul garcia paul garsha taught me to use the maracas and it wasn't carmen miranda made me fall in love with them *su ritmo* even with the way she danced *su ritmo* moving across the floor so short and so dynamic with her huge headdresses chiquita banana and there to say that thing about eating a banana on your cereal every day it was the other way around it was the maracas

///the maracas brought her and for that matter the yellow black banana sliced onto my tan brown cheerios there to stay forever in my mind their colour their *ritmo* brought her out of tv black and white out of the darkness of that living room in the afternoon when all the shutters were closed and i touched myself on the grey couch in front of that tv the maracas the maracas *su ritmo* brightened the colours of the fruit of the kitchen of the dappled backyard light no dark basement door or other darkness calling to me as i poured the milk which is why i'm here to say it say it again it wasn't paul garsha wasn't carmen miranda who brought that brightness it was that maraca brightness *su ritmo* allowed me to fall in love with carmen miranda chiquita banana there to stay with chiquita my cat and it was cherokee bill cherokee bill who kept bringing them cats or maracas put those there on the mantel

///cherokee bill when he got back after the years away or maybe before he left who knows except when i see them on the mantel purple red orange yellow green blue the bright colours combine with the bright colours *el ritmo* of the time i rode on his shoulders and tim on mark's and we played at jousting across the living room floor the floor of the hall by the butler's pantry the bannister at the top of the stairs bright days before either of our knights were gone so what i see when i see the maracas the maracas is sunshine sunshine and colour stretching forward and back past present future while

///the truth is he didn't just bring them orange yellow green blue purple red it was cherokee bill too taught me to use them to make them sound not just rattle shrrrr shrrrrr all the same but like carmen did across the stage *su ritmo* their rhythm one two boom boom shikra shikra the sudden perfect fast movement shaking her image into bright colours shaking the world into bright colours boom boom shikra shikra the sudden perfect movement the rhythm of my arm *su ritmo* boom boom shikra shikra bringing it all back into the body mambo mambo rumba cha cha cha as more and more maracas arrived brought from the caribbean from mexico from central america jamaica panama trinidad nicaragua more and different colours green yellow orange red purple blue the primaries the secondaries to help me do it boom boom mambo rumba *su ritmo* shikra shikra laughing in bright colours seeing those colours seeing the colours between once more or once in a while bright bright the maracas in my hand the shutters open the morning light filtering dappling that front facing floor through the green leaves of the sycamore outside on the street and i would do it boom boom shikra shikra the hand definite delicate perfect weighed sudden disciplined the exact tiny right action to make it happen boom boom shikra shikra create

///*el ritmo* moving from hand back into body the way i would take the pastel chalks when years later once more it wasn't just the tv but my world that was in black and white in the dark and boom boom shikra shikra *su ritmo* the sudden perfect movement even if it was really scratch scratch push down push down and the colours would be suddenly bright through the unconscious rhythmic movement of the arm like seeing the grip above you in the tree along the rocks and the hand going just there and the feet following as the colours the shape the texture of rock of bark of leaf enter and stay in the body through the hand through the eye boom boom shikra shikra *su ritmo* even if it was grab press lift move still it's the unthinking balance the hand lifted up the hand grabbing boom boom shikra shikra moving perfect movement coherent sound rhythm from coherent action coherent movement into the future boom boom shikra shikra moving from hand back into body i can do it i can do it hand bringing rhythm bringing colour texture shape back into body hand extending to shoulder extending to hip until

///you don't care where it comes from *el ritmo* or what it means what significance it truly has that rhythm you want juiciness not truthfulness brightness in that sound shikra shikra boom boom that touch of tree bark dust that bright line of pastel chalk in hand rub rub scratch scratch *el ritmo* those grubby fingers gripping tim's to wrestle riding shoulders of mark and cherokee bill never know don't even need to know if there is anything that truly connects them any narrative line at all because there it is the truth of the body *su ritmo* those small moments of perfect action shikra shikra boom boom because the only important part is that you can make them you can determine them all those small discrete seeds beads pellets boom boom shikra shikra perfect and coherent to make your own sound *su ritmo* to echo back into your body their rhythm dancing with colour you your own mambo queen moving through the dappled light blue purple red orange yellow green maracas in hands shikra shikra this moment boom boom and maybe that's cherokee bill's gift not the thing itself but that basic fact

///*su ritmo* that you can do it that you do do it boom boom shikra shikra *su ritmo* on your own feet shikra shikra boom boom across the floor or on that bike he rebuilt whirr whirr *su ritmo* across the city that's all there is all there is to it *su ritmo* boom boom shikra shikra not just waiting not just watching shikra shikra boom boom but doing doing *su ritmo* out and doing *su ritmo* in and doing maybe not chiquita banana but here to stay and for that matter to say here in my body the truth of my body *su ritmo* hands moving legs moving lips moving and maybe that's all you need all anyone needs shikra shikra boom boom *su ritmo*

///deep inside until you can rely on it to be there not steady as a heartbeat

su ritmo but the only story the only throughline that you can rely on *su ritmo* rely on it until you know even when it's not there it will come back *su ritmo* the truth of the body shikra shikra boom boom the perfect movement the perfect moment maracas moment *su ritmo* some morning some afternoon some twilight or dawn some gloaming or *madrugada* some sudden moment coming around a corner or looking up from your ginkgo tree branch toward the sky while raising the hand to grab there's the truth of the self the juice of the self the most important throughline you can create the one in the colours not what you tell yourself or anyone else but the one in the body *su ritmo* that will come back that truth of the body juice of the body the self able to move in its own body *su ritmo* on its own feet who cares about *bonito* or *sabroso* or *el mexicano* what he did or didn't do or even where this knowledge comes from if it was cherokee bill or if it just grew shikra shikra boom boom *su ritmo* until maybe you start hearing mambo rumba that slight change in tune in rhythm

///*oye como va*

///and you know it to name it to sing along not with beny moré on that old radio by the basement door but with tito fuente carlos santana somewhere by now miles away *oye como va mi ritmo*

///*mi ritmo* that's right my rhythm shikra shikra *mi ritmo* boom boom my rhythm my own *mi ritmo*

///*oye como va mi ritmo* hear it hear it how it goes *vamos a goza'* with pleasure that's right take pleasure *oye como va* how we'll take pleasure *vamos a goza'* our pleasure in this body in *mi ritmo* taken back over the years *mi ritmo oye como va* boom boom my body shikra shikra *mi ritmo* yellow green blue purple red orange *mi ritmo* my body *vamos a gozar*

///that's right *mi ritmo*

///my own.

Paul garcia had a dachshund

and rupert was his name-o
r/u/p/e/r/t
r/u/p/e/r/t
r/u/p/e/r/t
rupert was his name-o

long and fat and waggy tailed
and rupert was his name-o
r/u/p/e/r/
r/u/p/e/r/
r/u/p/e/r/
rupert was his name-o

black and brown and slobbertongued
and rupert was his name-o
r/u/p/e/
r/u/p/e/
r/u/p/e/
rupert was his name-o

squealed and squeaked and mini-barked
and rupert was his name-o
r/u/p/
r/u/p/
r/u/p/
and rupert was his name-o

jumped and flipped and fell on his back
and rupert was his name-o
r/u/
r/u/
r/u/
rupert was his name-o

mickey sang the song back to front
and rupert was his name-o
r/
r/
r/
rupert was his name-o

like so much reduced to rrrrrr rrrrrrr rrrrrrr rrrrrrrr
and rupert was his name-o
/
/
/
rupert was his name-o

it was about time that dog disappeared
with his laughter causing little doggy prick
/
/
/
rupert was his name-o

Paul garcia also had a corset

white and i can see my little fingers on it

and it didn't have a name-o.

Gritty kitty refrigerator realism results

So sometimes i just think in contradiction to earlier efforts i have a duty maybe to you dear reader maybe to me maybe for that matter to me as my own dearest reader but just sometimes to get to the end to tell the end and that chiquita stuff we've done the beginning and maybe most of the middle stretch yowl eat seafood scratch post walk on fence tangle in hair miaow miaow purr purr and it did have an ending a definitive one in fact which doesn't happen all that often sometimes to end stories you just have to make it up add something that doesn't really fit whether or not it's true to make it just make it end so even if this one's a flash forward so to speak here goes and i'm fifteen or so and it's years later you know how they do that in movies brighter colours large letters maybe in this case saying once more there are mice and there i am in technicolour finally getting another cat and i say to mickey how could you have done that how could you have had chiquita put down because that's what she told me that day those years back when i got home from school and there was no mowr mowr mowr to greet me at the door just mickey to say small smirk chiquita went to the aspca almost as if she'd strolled there on her own mickey repeating to the aspca the aspca enunciating each letter then adding to be put down and now there i am teenager in technicolour anger saying tell me how you could do something like that chiquita didn't do anything wrong she was just a cat and there's mickey replying larger smirk this time oh i didn't do that how could i do that i love cats i would never put a cat down just because you know i couldn't i just wouldn't but you know it was impossible i couldn't have them in the house i couldn't stand that memory every time i saw a kitten it was so awful but no oh no i didn't do that i didn't put chiquita down i gave her to joe and pilar they're the couple who owned montero's i told them to keep her in the house not the bar so you wouldn't see her i was sure you'd go looking that's why i told you that put down for her own good story and no no i couldn't stand it cats in the house always i remembered that sound so this one this one you're getting i don't even want to see this new cat you're going to get make sure you keep her away from me so i got a grey long haired kitten from the aspca it seemed poetic justice for that closed chiquita chapter of my life to get something someone back from the aspca even if now i could imagine chiquita a true mehitabel hanging at least close to the bar so i called the new one soot for the dirt hanging in the corners of montero's only i hadn't had her more than three changes of the cat box before she got distemper must have brought it with her the shots coming too late and i had to nurse her with eye dropper after eye dropper of egg and milk i remember the colour yellow against grey

///concrete metaphors again for all those nursing a hangover mornings way back when mark with his raw eggs mickey with her milk only soot died anyway and i'll always remember the yellow eye dropper in my one hand soot cradled in my other arm and that last little sigh and the fading light in her little kitty eyes no snap not even a mew mew mew and how awful i felt how i couldn't stop crying and then there's mickey with her hand patting my arm and i know dear it's just so awful but it's not about the cat you know and then all those people telling me the same thing at school or through the years it wasn't about the cat they said children often do that projection you know maybe i was really upset about mark's death or it was the inevitable acknowledment of mortality as we grow up only what i remember is mickey patting my hand and me looking at her and the snap was in her eyes as i thought about that slow fading light and right then and forever after i kept thinking why can't it just be about the cat this time about the cat about her little kitty life why can't it just be about the cat about the cat and not about mickey not about what she remembers or what she forgets snapping spines mew mew mew or memories of mark murphy mew mew mew and his self pity why not just about the cat about the cat about the cat it's tiny little life so maybe i don't have to go back to open the covers of that red red book again to add realism to those stories chiquita down at the bar and maybe her little son in a little kitty caddy they do that these days for dogs and cats the way they did once for amputees a kitty caddy to drag its back legs instead of being put down and maybe too another kitten from another tom a long haired one dying slowly of distemper like consumption in the books i was reading by then i wouldn't have to do that detail that cruel accident or that slow death not even open the covers to my hardened cardboard heart to tell you that finishing books that telling the ending can at least clear your head of other people's made up stories the lies they tell you even if i will never know which one was the lie chiquita dead or chiquita in exile but with soot in the house just long enough for her smell to chase away the mice i can tell you mickey won that round for sure

///mickey won that one.

Looking into mickey's brain

This thing about how i looked into mickey's brain will always be first on any list i ever make of childhood stories and who knows why maybe because i like to tell it or if not tell it at least think it think it over and over think it as if i were telling it though lord knows opportunities to tell it are few and far between mostly because when i think about it think about it the way i like to think about it anyway i always make it into such a light such a fluffy story an innocent error childhood story the kind everyone has and everyone tells the one where childhood logic tells you something works one way when it works another totally and completely another your leap of logic totally and completely off base but oh so amusing your innocence as you look back making it so easy on the face of it to be amused how very funny or at least strange is it after all that

///when you see this deep brown mark on mickey's head your mother's head right there just visible beneath the hairline you think you're looking into her brain you've just crept down the stairs with tim you've heard shouting or some such and you've crept down the stairs paul garcia is shouting in spanish you still think while mickey swears in english and who knows why but creeping down the stairs always carries its own creeping down the stair feeling that anticipation that maybe you could liken to xmas because no matter how negative the gift still it's a gift and you can anticipate that gift with each footfall on the stairs until knowledge becomes a gift any knowledge a gift no matter how weird or strange it's still a gift and as long as it doesn't do you permanent bodily harm there's that other feeling too maybe hard wired into the body the desire to laugh at any close call the giggle of it didn't happen to me and then there's trying to remember it to try to understand it to try to avoid future damage future permanent bodily harm so there i am and there's tim and there's those feelings anticipation and a bit of a giggle in the throat a powerful giggle in the throat

///that i don't want to transfer to lectures on hardwiring or permanent bodily harm or facial scarring no matter how close to the hairline i want to keep it there in the feeling of the giggle in the mouth make it a different kind of giggle for some other innocent mistake in the mind because it is funny it is funny you see not that you might want to giggle but how you put it together it is funny like thinking you could get anemia from an all day sucker because you get sick the next day or that the car is a pet because of how much your father your brother some member of your family might speak to it the way someone tells me at a party the car and my dog seemed to me very much the same intense activity or sleep and the same parental voice kicking them into obedient action and the smell oh the smell only i couldn't tell this in answer i really couldn't how

///i'm looking into mark's study and tim is behind me though for all i know he might remember himself in front and paul is shouting i tell you he's shouting in spanish which is mystery enough i know the whole language now and i still don't understand what he said and there's mickey lying on the old couch the old wood convertible which tim still has though he's getting rid of the mattress with its hole burned there by a roomer you think it was a roomer which means it shouldn't be there yet not in that scene at the bottom of the first flight of stairs down from your fourth floor rooms though maybe it is maybe it is already the era of the roomers and that's why paul is shouting at mickey it's something to do with one of the roomers though that's the kind of thing that wouldn't occur to me yet that i'd have no idea of yet i remember the day after the burning of the hole even the burning smell there in mark's old study and then the subsequent stories of the house almost burning down but i don't remember it in sequence at least not sequenced with this moment of looking into mickey's brain so maybe there's a hole in the couch and maybe there isn't and maybe mickey has insulted paul the way she always did bill or maybe she hasn't and maybe she's lying under that map of the world in mark's study in some way seeking mark's protection because maybe mark is just gone maybe he's with his japanese lover in manhattan and not dead or maybe paul's really thrown her onto the couch because it's where he finally caught up with her after she fled the basement where he was staying and i do see it paul swearing in spanish and that swift kick to mickey's head because i do know he kicked her and how would i know that if i didn't see it didn't see that part of the fight because after all i wouldn't imagine it think oh there's that brown slice oh she must have been kicked though maybe she cried out he kicked me he kicked me sarah the way she always did with bill even when half the time he hadn't done anything or at least not yet so i really don't know except to know that voices have been raised to call us down and there she is on the bed whatever happened whatever i saw or didn't see subsumed into that one image not of a swift kick but of her on the bed with that brown slice across her forehead and me thinking that's where her brain must be i'm looking into her head and there's a hole in her skull like people always say you've got a hole in your head and now she does so if i look closely i'll see her brain so you can see why i can't really tell it i can't can i can you imagine

///i thought my car was a pet and oh yes well we all do things like that like when my mother's boyfriend my stepfather i guess you could say my funny uncle kicked her in the head i thought i was looking directly into her brain imagine such a thing it was so funny and it's hard to believe there's even any dysfunctional family dinner party that would go over at maybe a reunion of denizens of old twenty-six i can't think of much else and really that wasn't what made me want to giggle right then when it happened that's not what gave the story a laugh right from the beginning that's just what i thought at the time oh look there's her brain i must be looking at her brain there's a piece of her head missing and i'm looking at her brain the giggle then was for doing it a survival triumph far older than me millennia deep feeling my own forehead to know no piece was missing to say i'm all right with laughter over that strange realization coming later first mentioned maybe to tim and aj the giggle rising hard and fast so who knew how a skull really worked you might say wow i thought i was looking into her brain into her brain into her brain can you believe into her brain while the giggle moves to a guffaw funnier still with that feeling back terror and knowledge and hey i'm still here and your next instinct in the moment to try to find

///that piece that missing piece because you're looking really looking at that brown slice opening like a mouth that seemed so deep the way i'm sure you've seen them cuts opening like wide mouths into those goose egg bumps you can only get on your head that happen when there's even the slightest break in the skin always too small so close to the skull to let all the blood that pools around the broken capillaries rush out so the bump forms and the cut opens wider and wider so i was sure so sure right then no matter what i know now that if that cut was so open so wide if i could look into it like that then not only was her brain right there right there for me to see if i looked carefully but that kick must also have dislodged a piece of her skull just the size and shape of that deep blunt narrowing pyramid so that i imagined the missing piece like an unopened brazil nut the kind we only got at xmas so that truly there was an xmas connection and maybe i imagined somehow that if i found that brazil nut slice it would be like an xmas present to me because maybe i thought she was going to die if her brain remained visible open like that to the light of what was soon to be a dawning day i don't know but i thought i had to find it

///to find it and plug the hole and maybe later maybe much later maybe in that imagined or real conversation with tim and aj maybe i might have said still giggling or laughing or loudly guffawing for effect that i knew i had to find it because after all it was like pandora's box paul there swearing and mickey too swearing and laughing or maybe she's even singing rrrrr rrrrr rrrrr so that i was convinced the bad things were all coming out into the world into my world and i had to find that piece to plug up the hole i would make my own hope by plugging up the hole maybe i did actually say that in that later conversation after all by then the bad things had come out the bad things where mickey always laughed and sang rrrr rrrr rrrr and kept making fun and making fun and making fun even when you hit her even when i hit her she made fun as if the fact that you would lose enough control to hit her made her win rrrr rrrr rrrr you'd attack your own mother rrrr rrrr rrrr a woman rrrr rrrr rrrr look at you rrrr rrrr rrrr so by the time i said that i knew all those things and greek mythology besides so make it even funnier funny ironic i could have kicked her myself to make the box open i might have even said by then so make it even funnier make it funny ironic for that innocent child that i was oh hahahaha what an innocent child

///so maybe you want to join me in my laughter or maybe you don't maybe you just want to pity me maybe even thinking mickey was going to die if i didn't find that piece no knowledge of pandora no knowledge of anything as i just thought that the only way to save her was to plug that hole and maybe it was because mark had just died or maybe it's just the feeling in the house that's death and more death because mark has left his japanese mistress for his bottle and africa or maybe it's just that however innocent we are however much i might think that cut swelling open on the hematoma rising like a volcano on mickey's forehead is the gateway to her brain to make me fall on hands and knees onto that floor irrationally down on that floor looking and looking so i don't even remember how the scene unfolded when paul left or mickey went to sleep or when i realized that morning or days or months or even years later that her skull was intact but what does it matter whether you laugh or you cry i'm still sure you can understand watching me in your mind's eye hunting that missing brazil nut piece that there's a reason besides my what an idiot giggle my own laugh or my guffaw why this is the first story i always want to tell because it doesn't matter whether it's a beginning or an end or always in the middle because wherever you position it it's my first story my entrance into narrative

///trying to find it that missing piece i am sure has just sprung out of mickey's head so that i can see into her brain so i'm searching and searching desperately searching desperately sure that i can find it i can fix it i can find it and that's it the beginning the end the middle of the story that is my first story and my last story and my middle story why i always want to tell this story first because that's who i am somewhere between a giggle and a glance and a big guffaw and a desire to move i'm the fix it queen the fix it queen always ready always willing to believe that there is some piece some piece that i haven't found that i haven't got that i'm not getting and if i could just get it just find it i could fix it whatever it is all the rest of my life mark's death and mickey's drinking and bill's anger and paul garcia's abuse and my own depression if i just got it just understood it could just find it find the missing piece the missing piece the missing piece if i could just find it everything would be all right i could make everything all right so that maybe it is like pandora's box because sooner or later

///it won't matter if things are good if the sun is shining if it's a beautiful day and i'm on my own and i'm free and i can do what i want and i've made a beautiful life and everything is going well i've published book after book because no matter how good they are the bad things are still there because i always believe that there's a missing piece and i have to find it so no matter how good things are the bad things are coming because there's a missing piece a missing piece a missing piece always in my life a missing piece and i haven't plugged up the hole and bad things are coming and i have to fix it there's always something to fix something to figure out how to fix and that's my story first and last and in the middle my story and maybe too the reason i tell stories think stories make up stories resigned always to narrate trapped in narrative telling my way to that missing piece the story a map not to the missing treasure but to the missing piece that missing piece some missing piece even if i won't tell this over dinner won't laugh and laugh and tell anyone at all what a strange thing it was that innocent childhood error that twisted take on the given information maybe you thought your car was a pet well we didn't have a car though far too many pets and as for innocent errors well when her lover kicked my mother's head in can you imagine i thought i could look right into her brain into her brain her brain and guess what it was only a scalp wound hahahaha a scalp wound

///a scalp wound.

Roomers and rumours in mark's old room

one burnt a hole in the old oak frame hide-a-bed one kited cheques one worked for the fbi one survived as a tail gunner in world war two the first is the only incident i actually remember i smell the acrid smoke still under the old world map they all robbed me of that finding johannesburg finding brooklyn i didn't need to find the sea routes yet i didn't know bill was coming back i sneaked in when i could i missed that map i missed it.

Elephant memory

1. Humpty dumpty

They did seem to come in waves they really did into our house those roomers with their sad newspapers in their equally sad hands shaking with their need of a place our house the cheapest they could go and still think themselves respectable you could see it in their eyes before they ever got upstairs to the mismatched furniture so maybe it was better they could tell we didn't want them mistake it for a sign of gentility this hatred of having to rent there wasn't a single one we would have chosen to keep not even ali the turk the engineering student at brooklyn poly-tech with his books and his bright patterned prayer rug and his feta cheese and olives for breakfast and certainly not that man i don't remember his name don't even know if i ever knew it all i remember is his smudged outline through the translucent glass the kind with the embedded chicken wire and thinking what is that what is that how did he get so big it's an elephant it's an elephant really he was the biggest the fattest the roundest man i've ever seen and watching him wave his arm outside the downstairs door i thought it for a moment a miracle look look the elephant has a trunk and then there's his pointed round belly starting to move forward right in my face as i open the door slow like a ship coming into dock so maybe i think an ocean liner an ocean liner a whale a whale or maybe the whale's later after i'd seen a whale in the battery park aquarium and for that matter knew the guy wore a corset like paul garcia and he put it on first before his pants i don't know how i know that or why i can see his soft white undershirts but it's that corset that made his body so whalelike its fat so solid he seemed like an egg turned on its side the pointy side pointing forward that first time through the door no wiggle no jiggle no bounce at all so it's not only his belt not below not above but right on the point of his belly makes me suddenly settle on humpty dumpty humpty dumpty because together with his arm reaching out to present his newspaper his chins quaking as they gesture at the ad there are the words emerging i've got an appointment little girl an appointment and something so terrible in his voice i can hear it cracking not an elephant not a whale humpty dumpty humpty dumpty i thought it's humpty dumpty where are the king's horses the king's men quick quick it's humpty dumpty

///great fall coming soon it's humpty dumpty.

The turk ali

was always my favourite roomer he really was he deconstructed that room for me the map room the johannesburg room the mark dead room the mickey's head oh she's gonna die it was only a scalp wound room ali with his rosewater baklava and his loukoum and his young man's engineering student books and his cheerful smile and that intricate pattern on his prayer rug and his friday trips to the brownstone mosque around the corner still there on state street and his wedding in the big front room just like the next door neighbour's the ones with the stoop only wider three windows not two i remember the mysterious scents and the bride's veiled face she was a medical student at some other american university and oh how i envied her turkey didn't seem too far to go i'd looked at it with ali on the map such envy until he removed her veil he'd told me he'd never seen her before and i saw her pockmarked face not beautiful like his but oh what a smile so that even as that solid mature responsible body sucked the arabian nights romance right out of my life forever i still thought that i would allow myself to be pockmarked just to go with him to that big pink tongue on that map.

Feta cheese and olives

i didn't know it was called feta when i watched ali eat it for breakfast but i loved it i loved it my first kalamata olives he probably called them something different after all he was turkish with a little bit of pita what we just called syrian bread since all the middle eastern restaurants and stores on atlantic avenue were syrian then except the tripoli with its upstairs section modeled to look like the prow of a trireme to make me dream of days at sea the only one still there too i go back when i'm in brooklyn to eat raw kibbeh that's raw lamb with cracked wheat and olive oil and lemon juice poured on top that i smush in though that brown red raw isn't what i'm getting at here it's those breakfasts in ali's room sitting on his floor and eating them with our fingers but only of our right hands that's what he said the way i still do that sometimes for breakfast and i see him there as my eyes go back and forth between white cheese and black olives and reaching fingers always the extremes always the extremes and still raw see still raw though sometimes i use my left hand too.

Memory no elephant

1. Just mickey

swaying in the doorway maybe i could compare her movement too to an elephant's trunk if i wanted certainly that memory weighs more than an elephant but that's not the point the point is that's the day she lost her job and that's why the roomers came and that's where i always see them just like that humpty dumpty man never upstairs but in the doorway one after another that same shocked look on their faces just like hers if they hadn't lost something too no question they wouldn't be there.

Memory no elephant

2. Big and grey

that's the smell of the cheap scotch on mickey's rasping breath it seems to take up all the available space that day she lost her job bigger than any elephant could be in that front room as she staggered into the table but tim named it he named it she's high he said she's high while mickey just said rrrr rrrr rrrr maybe not for the first time rrrrr rrrrr rrrrr but for the first time so i had a name for it rrrrr rrrrr rrrrr she's high rrrr rrrr rrrrr

///no elephant she's high rrrrrr rrrrr rrrrrrrrrrrrrr.

No safety in numbers

urrrrhnn urrrrrrrrhnn urrrrhnn urrrrrrrrhnn do you remember that sound urrrhnn urrrrrhnn the dial moving back urrrrhnn urrrrrrrrhnn urrrrrrhnn urrrrrrrhnn do you remember urrrrhnnn urrrrrrrrhnn a black phone somewhere in your house urrrrrrhnn urrrrrhnn urrrrhnn urrrrhnn are you that old urrrrhnn urrrrrrrrhnn there were only black phones then urrrrhnn urrrrhnn do you remember urrrrhnn urrrhnn black phone urrrrhnn urrrrrrrhnn i do urrhnn urrrrrrrhnn over in the hall urrrrrhnn urrrrrhnn index finger pulling on transparent dial knocking up against silvery metal do you remember urrrrrhnn urrrrrhnn dialing a number urrrrhnn urrrhnn urrrrhnn urrrrrrrrhnn a phone in darkness the darkness of a hallway urrrrhnn urrrrrhnn i do urrrhnn urrrrrrrhnn my first number urrrrhnn urrrrrrrrhnn judson six one two one two urrrhnn urrrrrhnn time life number urrrrrhnn urrrrrhnn do you remember your first number urrrrhnn urrrhnn it was mickey's work number urrrrrrrhnn urrrrrrrhnn time life number urrrrrrrhnn urrrrrrhnn when still urrrrhnn urrrrhnn there was shelter left in calling urrrrrrhnn urrrrrrhnn urrrrhnn urrrrrrrrhnn shelter and warmth and a story to tell urrrrhnn urrrrrrrrhnn a complaint to make urrrrrhnn urrrrrrhnn i saw a robin i did a drawing tim hit me mary yelled aj spilled the ice water all over the floor urrrrrrhnn urrrrrrhnn urrrrrhnn urrrrhnn judson six one two one two urrrrrhnn urrrrrhnn shelter in calling safety in dialing urrrrrhnn urrrrrrhnn before it all changed to rrrrrrr rrrrrr the growl in the throat rrrrrrrr rrrrrrr and the order to call rrrrrrr rrrrrr the order to call rrrrrrr rrrrrrr call the store rrrrrrrrr rrrrrrrrr the liquor store rrrrrr rrrrrrr call charlie rrrrrrrr rrrrrrrr the liquor store rrrrrr rrrrr

///call the number rrrrr rrrrr

///her fingers won't dial rrrrrr rrrrrr

///no more safety in numbers

///rrrrr rrrrr.

The master bedroom too

that's right it wasn't just mark's study got rented mickey rented the back bedroom with the white vanity too i didn't miss it near as much as the world map mickey stayed in the smallest room on the top floor one small bed one bureau with the american flag folded into a triangle she was given at mark's funeral for his years on air force magazine his time in the war she never learned to fold it only aj could do that i kept looking at it as if it could contain him i don't remember where her typewriter was just how close we were to that r rrrr rrrr rrrrrrrrrr.

Elephant memory

2. King's horses king's men

weren't exactly who came through the door into the front room it was cherokee bill and it was over and over hardly for that matter hannibal over the alps with elephants though there were elephants galore my favourite the heavy west african wood table born by two beasts trunks raised you could almost hear them trumpeting perhaps to greet the incoming camels' heads on camels' saddles and lions and tigers on panels or in pictures strange half birds half beasts half sea creatures hiding behind plants woven into ponchos or saris or painted onto sea shells embroidered onto conical vietnamese hats with velvet straps and good luck swastikas at their interior peaks buddhas too christs and koranic quotations dancing shivas becalmed boddhisattvas and let's not forget among the animals their sacred versions or the plumed serpent or just the snakes or the snake charmers' flutes the baskets the stringed instruments the records that played them the occasional scorpion in plastic or fly in amber among smuggled small jewels and yes snuck in painted too or carved you could find sometimes a king or king's man queen or lady in waiting and he did put something together again at least for a long time at least for years.

One typewriter

So now it was mickey's typewriter that was in mark's old world map room and bill's studio was upstairs on the fourth floor with us the room mickey stayed in during that roomer time she rented her own bedroom too and he used it for painting in oils or watercolours with techniques he learned in his courses at the art students' league or even by numbers woodworking too intricate chains from one piece of wood animals duck decoys continuing carving done on the ships of ship's dunnage i love that word the way i do flotsam and jetsam he even made ships in bottles honing the craft of his hands the way he did his eye with everything he brought there were even sailing ships he made from turkey breast bones or placed in bottles i remember how he raised the masts with a little string sailors' immemorial crafts while mickey sat at the typewriter downstairs looking out the window or back over at the map never finishing anything she started never giving back an advance she was just a researcher she said so it didn't matter not like mark he was the writer he had writers' block she didn't and besides there was the sailor to support the merry widow something she never mentioned but it meant it didn't matter if she only ever finished

///the bottle those slow thoughtless afternoons inviting bill more and more to forget the little ships just take the bottles and jump right in. 259

Elephant memory

3. Swizzle sticks swizzle sticks swizzle sticks
were the gifts mark murphy had always brought through that door swizzle sticks swizzle sticks all sorts of bright new plastic plastic was new then swizzle sticks red orange green transparent translucent white black tan purple opaque words animals plants sea creatures home appliances cars and car parts ships and tugs the occasional crown if not the king or king's man not from away from all the bars of new york so one at least must have been an elephant one at least maybe not an african elephant maybe not trumpeting maybe it was a republican.

Xmas cards

You measured worth wealth class by the number on your mantel i remember how they dwindled over the years of our fall they never really were like presents the mantel was better with maracas with spanish dolls with old tools there was always one black politician sent one he wasn't a roomer bill said he was tim's father.

Truncating the xmas tree

where it hit the twelve foot ceiling mark did that it stopped with him trees were always smaller after if they were at all the drunks bigger and full of sentimental songs that pushed red pain into the gut deck the halls with boston charlie i learned to sing with pogo in the funnies don't know if it was sarcasm or irony but it seemed like a bright coloured cartoon secret that made my xmas plausible.

Memory no elephant

3. Tax time taxed time

a good name for that yearly fate worse than xmas that was something like a fate worse than death or a fate concurrent with death which is maybe why i've always hated that expression about death and taxes some of it is my pedantic oh so controlling baby academic bright girl self talking the one that has always known that death and taxes are of a different order of magnitude so that maybe it was okay when it was a joke it was supposed to be birth and death inevitable that if you're born you die and then someone came up with birth and death and taxes then just death and taxes it's supposed to make you kind of go duh and think of the size of the state in modern life or some such the inevitability of death and taxes but now people don't even go duh they just say it as if death and taxes really were the same size and they're just not

///more than a different order of magnitude they're in a different kind of mathematics or physics like the difference between newton and einstein so yes it's the orderly bright girl self talking the big mouth the bastion against chaos because the fact is that i still don't think taxes are inevitable if really very much necessary to sustain and enjoy our particular way of life which is another argument i mean you don't want to install your own traffic lights do you build your own roads do your own air traffic control and all but i've known too long death is another story definitely known it a lot longer than i've been able to argue that line which is why i never understood about that expression if it was just too stupid to keep being put into words unless you laughed a really deep redneck belly laugh when you said it then why did they always combine in my life death and taxes and shame and a drunk bigger than xmas and for that matter the red necks of all those men the tax guy the guy who did them what was his name it wasn't useless eustace i don't think touching me in the wrong places and mickey out like a light not even rrrr rrrr rrrr whenever she got them done or just sitting slurring words in her own piss the times she thought they would sell the house out from under us and blaming mark it was all his fault his perfidy was the elephant in the room though mentionable under the proper circumstances by mickey if not by us now when did people start saying that it's another idiotic expression even if there were always all those elephants in all our rooms but i'm really happy to be in canada to get that extra two weeks after april fifteenth before i have to sign my name to my tax return and to breathe deep and look at the prairie crocuses or drive into the mountains through the actually really inarguably inevitable spring snow and to take death out of my mouth my nose my eyes my stomach to take death away to subtract death from taxes.

Green cherokee

Now this green cherokee thing is a different kind of story in another dimension really a story of a story you know how it is a lot of writers do that tell stories of stories or stories of stories of stories a this is how i got my story kind of story it's a very in thing intertextuality i think it's called i know that's the name if you come clean on how the story of the story the story inside the story is someone else's story which just might in turn be someone else's story too then you comment on that besides which that's the way stories mostly are if you actually think about it so you're not even trying to be just oh so trendy unless you're really into charting the trendiness of vehicles what with this one reducing its central irony or history historic irony or ironic history whatever combination you might want to just one word cherokee

///cherokeeeeee cherokeeeeeee the way i'll introduce my dad cherokee bill one morning in mickey's bed cherokee cherokeeeeee cherokee echoing always cherokeeee cherokeeeee my intertext my innertext the text behind so many texts cherokkeeee cherokee just the word or sometimes the story inside the word whole or in part so intertextually almost but not quite typical so subject to deconstruction the nonwhite knight to the at least temporary rescue the twenty-six nutmeg mews story moving back away from down and out to down and dirty cherokeee cherokeeee my own little deus ex machina near the end or jump starting a new beginning forever foreshadowed or always echoed in departure and arrival arrival and departure all along all along and always that central revelation

///that morning of the big surprise cherokeeeeeee cherokeeeeeee the story of exile and return mickey always said it seemed a miracle that reencounter down in montero's she might as well have been the heroine of the *poema de mio cid* waiting in her spanish castle instead of her spanish seaman's bar under siege what with her last heel broken on her last pair of high heels that's the way she always told it the only shoes she had left the fairy slippers to fly her across the bridge into manhattan to look for work broken broken and no money to buy more and then before she could slip further take the next awful step whatever it was there's the deep breath the slight wait

///and the guy at the bar

///the guy at the bar who isn't one more pickup one more cadging of drinks but cherokeeeee cherokeeeee not that she'd mention any of that the guys and drinks stuff is never quite part of the story the next doomed step is never named any more than it is in a victorian novel just filled with that atmosphere of imminent ruin ladies falling irrevocably and irredeemably from respectability not that that hadn't occurred years before inevitable results of the touch of the demon rum and all that except that was our little or really very big secret if you think about its ramifications its own echoes the secret of old twenty-six what everyone knew and never mentioned even if mickey pissed herself in public or especially because she pissed herself in public what was really at its worst just before cherokee came back what he rescued us from really no matter how often mickey would tell that shoe story but in any case rescue is rescue and this time the guy she sees the one she sets her sights on for whatever the long night will bring there leaning against the bar the way he always did when it was the three of them cherokee bill and mark and mickey is suddenly familiar the image suddenly resolves cherokeeeee cherokeeeeee the way it will for us the next morning

///gone three years at least by then sailed away got the hell out in some form of depressed horror from that awful quadrangle mark bill mickey paul and him always and forever mark's confidante that's right it's sir lancelot and arthur this time the man who doesn't know who he loves more only he winds up siring his best friend's child cherokeeee cherokeee and he didn't even know
mark was dead or that mickey could fall on such hard times so it's different now there's a way to make it up to lift the siege so it's cherokeeee cherokeeee to the rescue and he must feel it too he's back and it's all changed that long time of shipping out from the west coast beachcombing panama his demure wife just like lancelot's only in japan and now it's time to save the widow of his liege lord his friend and mentor that slightly older always seen as wiser certainly more accomplished man cherokee would wax so eloquent on mark his sensitivity his profound command from roughneck to the new yorker in so few years while cherokee wasn't yet twenty one when he first came upon that house fresh from the marine brig it must have seemed a castle and now he can be that nonwhite knight if never the cavalry cherokeeee cherokeeee to the rescue if he just never speaks of the time before says how it really was what really bound them together maintaining always his loyalty to mark for the longest time that both of them he and mickey were acting in loyalty to mark not in betrayal mark's last leaving an internal contradiction nothing to do with them and after all there was paul there too and it's true cherokeeeee cherokeee was the one to listen to mark's complaints so please let cherokeeee cherokeeee help construct the sordid truth into that perfect tale of last minute rescue tell it for years if he wants and besides it is true

too in its way a tad artificially gussied up maybe but worth us believing it absolutely from the moment we see him there in her bed and you know why cherokeeeee cherokeeeeee he's the only good surprise ever encountered as we came down those stairs and both of us me and tim flinging ourselves on him cherokeeee cherokeeee a repeated surprise found again year after year when his ship came in

///after nine months or three or a week or a year always those first few days or weeks of peace of hope and nothing at all like this small ironic echo the heart skipping the smallest beat cherokeeee cherokeeee like when his letters come and i see the smooth proud handwriting that mickey always said was the defense of the uneducated what else could they have taught him in six years of school on the reservation just that pride in literacy reflected in the perfect cheerful upsweep of the cursive script while nobody could read her own only this time it's just that one word cherokeeeee cherokeeee i see at first and besides it's typed there on the desk in my office in canal flats it's my own exile and return to this place and to these stories it's a pile of paper and there it is cherokee

///cherokeeee cherokeeeee

///a tiny intertextual echo a textual error that quietly inserts itself into the layers of memory so many departures so many returns as i wander too on my landlocked journey to build not just layers on layers on layers or even stories of stories of stories but ironies on ironies on ironies all of it just popping up again that day in that one word cherokeeee cherokeeee as i'm looking down at those eight and a half by eleven sheets right next to where i've just put the computer after all i haven't returned there in a while but i am once more ready to begin again become once more the inner child of nutmeg mews and the whole mess looking up at me is pretty unpunctuated lots of letters and no little dots so i think it's one of mine and then words leap out not just cherokee and my mind echoing cherokeeee cherokeeeeee but meg too like mickey's initial initials m. e. g. and all that so even if i can see it's not nutmeg mews it's still real close to this material if not my heart and besides there it is cherokee which means i'm absolutely sure cherokeeeeee cherokeeeeee that this one's mine it's just got to be it hardly matters if i don't remember whether i'd started to write about cherokee cherokkeeee cherokee bill my dad who is really my father and for that matter my nonwhite knight but also really choctaw even that word cherokee cherokeeee cherokeeee echoing to deconstruct another smaller but more widespread mistake than the knight's betrayal of his king bill getting himself renamed that way choctaw to cherokee by his fellow sailors who couldn't tell their indians apart

///you'd agree a pretty common problem among sailors if you think about columbus though as far as it goes i shouldn't feel smug writers don't always do much better even the occasional famous feminist has been caught in a real whopper like kate millett trying to do d.h. lawrence one better talking about mexico and its population of violent inscrutable indians then while d.h. only traded zapotecs for aztecs a prestidigitation involving at most a couple of mountain ranges which at least left the calendar system still intact she goes and exchanges aztecs for incas a thousand or so miles of land and water and god knows what amount of history and culture and inscrutabilities erased with a few choice keyboard strokes the compression of the americas you could call it even today's sailors would most likely do better after all they'd be at sea the whole distance counting the days if not the hours into port like cherokee bill with his pipes and his books

///from mexico to peru is at least a few days sail more if you go the long way round vera cruz to lima i think that's a port my geography isn't too great either even if cherokee cherokeeeee bill sure made me better on the indians though cherokeeee cherokeeee we still echoed that same sailors' mistake while that journey would be memorable too the green of the canal or hitting the storms off cape horn bill talked about that the time he brought back the ponchos from argentina though peru would more often bring up tupac amaru those stories of the last inca's descendent hanged drawn and quartered in the town square of cuzco after his near successful rebellion his pieces strewn to the four quarters the way i might feel about my hope for those sailors throw my hands up in the air as if it would scatter something to the four winds because no matter how they might measure a sea journey they never seemed to get anywhere with landlocked oklahoma even if they listened to bill's stories they just homogenized it couldn't understand it contained more than one kind of indian in this case brought in from the four quarters bill would tell those histories over and over the five civilized and all the other tribes herded under terrible conditions to their new homes walking the winter with whatever seed corn they could salvage those sailors weren't going to take that in on an at least equally long voyage or if they did even keenly feel echoing in that story the history of their profession's own deprivation hard tack and maggot ridden meat mile after mile still sailors were comfortable now and the indians could just be the same as far as they were concerned and generic too let them wear warbonnets and sell cigars at the same time as the sailors filled the state up with no name brand indians best called cherokee sort of the way you call a tissue a kleenex because it's the one name everybody knows cherokee cherokeeeeee for oklahoma even if the state long ago ceased to be any kind of in perpetuity indian territory and the name is choctaw red man's land in choctaw choctaw too just like bill

///so i'm thinking looking at that paper pile was i writing about all that stuff all that pain or even the clear clear joy cherokeeeee cherokeeeeee of that one repeated surprise now was i was i what part of that had i finally decided to talk about what exactly about cherokee cherokeeee bill it was probably a good idea i knew i'd have to sooner or later wow look i'd already done it this story must be mine for sure i'm thinking it must be no question when you write the way i do sometimes you lose track of where you've been or where you're going and for certain of what you've said and what's just been bumping around in your mind so which one is it i wonder what's it about which of all bill's stories or cherokee cherokeeeeee stories about bill is it was i coming down those stairs with tim cherokee cherokeeeeee to see him there in mickey's bed or was it something else cherokeeeee cherokeeeee was he picking a fight over that name or maybe just picking up a rifle somewhere else in the house what exactly was it memory or intertextual echo intratextual insertion or elided lie i ask as i pick up the papers and kind of shake them in my hand looking over the whole page all at once scanning it quickly to see what's going on which makes it along about then i notice the word green right before cherokee there's this word green no cherokeeeee cherokeeee but just green

///green it says and it's pretty easy to guess it's not about the no longer green grass of the broken treaties and let me tell you whatever else there was about bill cherokee cherokeeeee or taking us aside to tell us he was choctaw asking us to call him bill still he was never green never green at all at least when i knew him that was certainly never one of his faults overly violent sometimes after a while shouting or hearing shouted cherokeee cherokeeeee wasn't always such a good such a hopeful fling yourself in his arms thing though it was never me who was flinging myself away still all that aside he was never green even his eyes the bluest blue a blue eyed indian which means i suddenly realize this story's not mine at all this story is my son's

///a lee proudlock shivers story his very own take on goosebumps his own child horror series from way back something he started when he was six times he didn't punctuate at all either there were no little dots on his pages any more than there are on mine and meg's not my m.e. or my m.u. muse or even some version of those few leftover mickey monograms embroidered like her stories on whole cloth from before she married mark anymore than green is there to explain that last initial from the time she was the one who was truly green just like the grass surrounding her immaculate middle class childhood home in toledo green green just like her name no this meg's his main character the one to be haunted though not by memories or echoes of cherokee cherokeeee and talk about not having your indians straight well to him a cherokee is just a car this cherokee isn't even a choctaw it's a boxy green four by four and a damn good off road back road vehicle it is too

///i used to drive the lumber roads and high mountain passes in mine that's for sure why my son's protagonist drives one so don't worry cherokee cherokeeeee bill wherever you are i won't miss this added irony this quiet we've got you surrounded indian walk echo irony piled on irony either fail to notice the clever snare the trap closing in my mind to show me exactly how involved i am in how or why when my son says that word cherokee he's not talking about bill and he's sure as shit not talking about the nation still responsible for that mistake or not you've just got to understand i loved that car i really loved it and even if it never made me scream cherokee cherokeeeeee it made me think it often enough cherokeeee cherokeeeee with its aura of last minute rescue got me out of enough tough spots the best vehicle i ever had fifteen hundred metres up in fifteen kilometres of switchbacks over sharp shale and the cd player doesn't even skip a beat and my son's bouncing along right behind me hand clap squealing with delight and all of us comfortable and snug and sure feeling safe

///as hell or make that heaven cherokee cherokeeee all the way up into the clouds and down again that thing got me over my mountain road phobia my fear of the sharp curve you don't quite make even of the one lane logging roads looking over the three hundred foot drops with the fully loaded logging truck coming right at you logs swinging wide so you better find a turnout fast that's right even looking that trucker in the eye cherokee cherokeeeee i can still feel good the way i did that morning which means i'll laugh to that if not drink and drive a dry toast to my son's story its hidden irony and to that super safe back road vehicle and to that other cherokee too because whether he was cherokee cherokeeeee or he was bill and even if he was definitely choctaw that fear hit me worst those years i was first trying to sort out the memories of old twenty-six

///look at them arrange them leave them behind always in my mind that question of had i really left was i still stuck back there was i always to be compelled to return just like cherokeeee cherokeeee was there something i'd left there the way he'd left me was the edge the cliff the curve i so deeply feared i wasn't going to make not a twist of fate but just a twist in memory a moment of emptiness as the mind not the car leaves the road a whoosh and i'm back into a dark closet a scotch fume kitchen in brooklyn forever well let me tell you cherokee bill violent or not and never toward me was the only one in mickey's bed or anywhere else in that house back then cherokee cherokeeeeee who ever made me feel safe or gave me the idea that i could negotiate the curves make it to the corner or even as far as the subway whoosh off not just with him to the union hall cherokee cherokeeeee to shoot the shit with the guys or sign up to ship out or even to the pawn shop to get back the stuff he'd pawned before his last trip or to pawn the stuff again to get mickey through the next one he let me know cherokee cherokeeeee let me know bill let me know my dad let me know that i could make it on my own go beyond pineapple street down to the docks beyond atlantic avenue out to coney island or over the bridge and out of town farther and farther away each time the plane to university or those long student movement drives finally safe instead of sorry in the jet stream on super highways on mountain roads even at eighty miles an hour through the appalachians back then at a hundred and forty kilometres now through the rockies so cherokeee cherokeeeee it doesn't bother me at all if the irony is too apparent

///for words or even to bother with drawing attention to again vehicles and sports teams gas stations and camping equipment the only way to learn the names of the many nations take your cherokee to the mohawk the way cherokee bill left the sailors at montero's bar and grill to take himself down to the mohawks at the wigwam over on pacific street did his fighting there until they all started hanging out at old twenty-six and he could do his fighting at home even when it wasn't with mickey cherokee cherokeeeeee and all that pretending not to know he was choctaw taking on a new tone still i can't stop myself loving that car even if it wasn't green and i traded it in for a dodge ram three quarter ton diesel

///traded our dakota too

///two of north america's most romanticized indians in exchange for one equally imaginary big horn sheep why let me ask you this can't i get a dodge mouse a quickly dodging mouse something to remind me of those latter days on nutmeg mews cherokeeee cherokeeeee bill the one who always dodged or for that matter kicked quickest sounds about perfect to me or maybe make it a ford cockroach better than a vw beetle the closest a car ever came to the insect world but still only a nickname the way pancho villa called his own car *la cucaracha* that would fit for paul garcia the creatures crawling down in his shop and him pretty crawly too even as he sang it *la cucaracha la cucaracha* only this time we'd have a whole line of cockroaches black or brown or pink with diaphanous wings steady in the darkest slipperiest corners could be its motto only flies in desperation but always lands safely so true to my life i'd buy one in an instant still the truth is i miss my cherokee i do the way sometimes i miss cherokeeee cherokeeeeee i miss bill i miss my dad his own gentle irony all those wonderful quiet at home in port sober days before he took off again goodbye cherokeee cherokeeeee leaving mickey's bed to be inhabited by horror none of this would be lost on him not one word not one letter of this small irony not a single one so cherokee cherokeeee that's what i whisper between clenched teeth when i'm taking the bumps hard gearing that diesel down for the hills the camper i wanted so bad bouncing in the pickup bed as we hit the ruts my muscles tensed against the next jarring blow up my spine and i swear to myself cherokeee cherokeeee that the next time we decide to run two vehicles the next time we can afford it i'll get myself another cherokee and my next cherokee will be green

///green for the in perpetuity grass of the violated treaties green for the hills of mississippi the choctaw were removed from to hasten the western expansion of slavery green for bill's lost innocence for the days when he hunted with his father before his mother left or he was ever beaten or got violent himself green for the time before he went to war or sea or jail or heard that word cherokee applied to him learned the interchangeability of indians green green green it'll be green all right the greenest green my cherokee my cherokeeee cherokeeeeee with as they say all the bells and whistles and accompanying me through all the dust of memory and mountain roads i leave behind on my journeys on my quest exile and return along with the cherokeeee cherokeeee whispered screamed sung in my mind there will be written there for all to see not only the grand cherokee embossed in gold on the car's side but you can bet i'll have made a bright blue vanity plate the bluest blue as blue as bill's eyes change provinces or states to get it if i have to where you'll see stamped out as clear as mountain water running forever those seven letters that spell out the word choctaw.

Mark murphy said

he knew all the people at the new yorker and he'd only ever met one genius and that was james thurber.

Cherokee bill said

he knew people from all over the world and he'd only ever met one genius and that was mark murphy.

Mickey said

there were only ever three important men in her life mark murphy the brilliant paul garcia the sexual cherokee bill the helpmeet and she'd never ever met a genius.

I don't say

there were those days those years later broke and in art school i moved back into old twenty-six and that world map room with mickey's old typewriter gathering dust in a corner was mine and i took push pins and made the map my easel painted my first self-portrait there pinned over the american continent long before i'd seen the two fridas there was the two sarahs me holding me as a baby two me's naked madonna and child on the map a virgin birth on one of her nights mickey threw my portfolio my drawings my paintings even that one out the door screamed there never had been never would be any great women artists

///i briefly tried to choke her but that was all hand and eye were enough that coordination had already taken me far far away i didn't have anything to say and i didn't have to say anything so for years i didn't

///it had nothing to do with genius.

Resistors on rector street

So sometimes it just might be time to relax sort of take it back down divide it all back up maybe kind of into bite sized chunks maybe that's all this whole thing has ever been not headlines or still lives but just consumable bite sized chunks like looking at leila across the table where this all started right before that imaginary taxi ride kind of playing with my food pushing square chopped veggies or was it trendy little crescent potsticker dumplings around on my plate or even round pieces of california roll dipped into wasabi and soy as i talked about how yeah yeah yeah you could do it all in headlines only the finger food had much more flavour so maybe we'll just take a rest try bite sized treats little chunks of finger foods for the mind this one doesn't really have enough soul for chicken soup

///but the resistors are perfect for tales of cheerful discovery or rediscovery it wasn't till i was in art school i saw them again on a design assignment when once more i stuck my hands into the bins and suddenly it was trendy to brag of those few brief years with the mexican stepfather who was an electrician no intellectual red diaper baby me no red army chorus just pancho villa's *división del norte and la cucaracha* in that era besides which this one is a calming spot i can talk with leila as i did with my design class not about class and its ramifications at least not directly but about my love of colour local colour colour on the local the bmt local in discrete little chunks and besides it's time for a good memory of paul garcia there were a few not the apartments he took me to or how he had my hair cut to within an inch of my scalp didn't stop the barber who thought my torn jeans and dirty hands my snotty nose meant i was a boy or mamboed me around the kitchen floor his tongue in my mouth or invited me too often to the basement to crawl among his sheets or even how i was so sure it was a discrete chunk of mickey's head he'd kicked out no let's go for innocence

///finger small child hand sized chunks of memory that's what narrative is anyway isn't it or maybe that's just language that dividing up into small discrete chunks the better to see you if not to eat you with my dear and all that making reality possible if not palatable the resistors on rector street my discursive reality bite sized hand sized chunks resistors and condensers really they already had those believe it or not and transistors too paul at his most cheerful humming under his breath and taking me on the subway the bmt local to rector street rector street a magic place i didn't even know was real thought i'd made it and its tiled subway stop up until that design assignment even if what i always remembered was resistors and condensers all in their bins their bins out on the sidewalk under awnings discrete bins and discrete sizes and discrete colours and that discreet odour electrical accessories always have and each individual piece with its bare circular copper ends its stripped wires those little stripes around its middle i think it's for how many amps of current or ohms of resistance that's right resistance they offered maybe that's why i'm here too how i got this far current and resistance

///discrete chunks of language flowing if not floating in a narrative of resistance each step contained in its firecrackerlike transistor resistor or condenser the one advantage of telling even of resisting telling is the fact that it never takes as long as living though i have no idea how i'm going to fit all those beautiful transparent vacuum tubes into the metaphor or the metonymy maybe i can talk about the vacuum at the centre of things as the moment of absence before the light is created the current of the story pushes out to be resisted and therefore told or just about their wonderful little silver coloured prongs plugging them into the flow to bring out the sound light up the picture tube so many different patterns your computer plugs still have that designs that signify for silver prongs to get just the right amount of information across the barrier and back to the facts ma'am just the facts the transparent tubes their wires inside breaking up your shining reflection and there i am looking at them looking at all of them and with the tubes it's don't touch but with the resistors and condensers hard and waxy turquoise or orange or tan or yellow

///cadmium yellow medium with mauve stripes maybe the name's dioxynine purple or cobalt violet learned too in painting class and that waxy waxy finish no glass at all so you can stick your hands in the bin just as much as you want without fear of breaking something or of being cut feel the scratchy wires and the wax then pick them up twist the ends connect them together toss them in the air a world within a world a world like words because you always knew you did as you counted the stripes that it meant something stood for something even if you couldn't decipher it any better than you could those black lines and circles among the bright colours of the sunday comics the funny papers we always called them so it was like being in the subway too

///looking around and seeing the letters the numbers on the pillars of the stations without meaning you could decipher so there was just counting the stations on the bmt local the only local train that made it to brooklyn still does for that matter though they call it by another name no discrete lines anymore but everything all mixed up just the smaller chunks of each route its own colour on the map as if you took a resistor a condenser and stretched it out then each train with its number or letter the old bmt still different the m and the n and the r locals and the q express over the manhattan bridge somehow that line the most mysterious of all who knows why maybe only because it went to that mysterious place where i could pick those things up in my hands or just because i took it so seldom that later i would question its very existence its twisty route through lower manhattan that slowed the train and made it squeal when there would be the years of going to that city and country school always on the express straight forward and fast and rattling back and forth on the track the way it was always the express to get to the numbered streets or even up into manhattan

///and no matter which it was there would be the doors clacking and humming and the lights the stations passing the mysterious letters on the pillars like striped resistors in each stop painted yellow or blue or red or dull grey heavy waxy enamel paint coloured layer over coloured layer cold to the touch except on the wooden handrails with their paint chipped sometimes back to the wood and in each stop its soot covered magic mosaic bright coloured like the comic book figures saying their magic letters and each one telling you the nature if not the name of the stop the way those figures told you the action the bmt with the best mosaics because it was the oldest line of all and all those people just staring across at each individual train or building or ship or bridge formed with its discrete chunks of coloured glass and you just staring in turn at all those tall people and then your hands in the bins language and resistance and the train whirring into the stop and looking up and getting on and standing between the strangers' legs and maybe it was then or maybe it was with mickey going to see someone in town as she always said in town not into manhattan but into town i just know it was on a subway though mostly i think it was then between hands on resistors and paul humming and counting the stops one stop two stops three stops and when do we get off is it in one stop two stops three stops four or maybe in *uno dos tres cuatro* because he taught me to count in spanish *uno dos tres* and then we get off so it was long before i was released into the numbered streets to go to school on my own or up to margot's counting them off fourteenth and thirty fourth and forty second and the most mysterious fifty ninth before the big gap next express stop one hundred twenty fifth on the ind going uptown

///but somewhere in there counting one stop two stops three stops four and then we get off *uno dos tres cuatro* and trying to memorize the mosaics to find our special one the way i memorized the comics each special face to find its meaning it was then that i looked around and saw only feet feet and legs and maybe a purse and tried to remember how many stops had it been one stop two stops three stops four the people around me and the resistors in my future hands the resistors and the condensers made me understand something about what could be resisted and what condensed even if the language to say it is just a conceit a reading backwards of what those words could mean because then it was just things just those small yellow and turquoise and mauve things things with texture and no meaning much less language but it was still then in that anticipation standing there that you could see it the mosaic out of the corner of your eye the memory so clear clack clack clack the train coming and paul by your side the about to be resistors the condensers in your hands clack clack clack clack one stop two stops three stops four and then we get off *uno dos tres cuatro* and you knew it then somewhere between one stop two stops and a mosaic *dos tres* and we get off a resistor a condenser and we get back on somewhere in there you understood

///something about how the body is not always the same the self not absolute anymore than the stations the mosaics the numbers the counting the resistors the condensers were always identical the world changed and
you with it it wasn't the way you had always thought that grownups were grownups like the people around you on the train grownups were grownups and you were a kid chiquita was a cat and curly a dog and you always had to hold a hand crossing the street and hide in a closet on a rrrr rrrrrrr rrrrrrr night take your medicine and get your needles a resistor was a resistor a condenser a condenser a transistor a transistor the stripes would never change not in colour not in number no it wasn't like that at all everything changed because you changed everything their size might be the same but your hand would be bigger and so would you bigger and taller those numbered birthdays with their candles on a cake like stripes on a resistor they meant something a greater distance from something a closer distance to something else just the way your stop approached and who knows what it was except that i know it was there just there on the subway and there's a shoe and there's a leg and there's paul's there's mickey's hand and there's a mosaic just out the window the resistors the condensers turquoise and yellow and purple in my pocket the pieces of glass turquoise and yellow and green on the mosaic while there i am staring and staring there i am and i know it in that exact moment i just know it not just resistors and condensers discrete chunks in my eyes in my hands but the current in them the current and the resistance that's right the

current and the resistance and the train moving not the little train that could i think i can i think i can much less peter pan flying and crowing but the stolid solid subway and me solid in it solid and on the ground solid underground and the current starting the ohms resisting the tubes lighting the mosaic glinting and in transit in my train or with my hands in the bins there's that current there's that resistance always that current always that resistance people change kids become grownups mickey was once a kid paul ran with pancho villa to the rhythm of the train clack clack clack clack i will grow up i will grow up i will grow up i will grow up i will.

We breathe

So let's take a deep breath a really deep breath that's right a deep breath and change the subject always good for that a deep breath to change the subject the way by the end tom i'm sure mark too mark bill mickey couldn't take any deep breaths and for that matter the subject never changed let me tell you never changed one of the difficulties when you can't breathe like the ad says there isn't too much else when you can't breathe so the subject never changes the subject is always death so let's change that let's change that we can breathe so let's change the subject besides it keeps the narrative moving or adds a little bit of suspense suspense increases if you slacken the rope just a little bit every once in a while not an intellectual aside for more information or just to enter some little idea or other but a breather a real breather like that circus tararar-boom-deay and bouncing back take things away from death and betrayal just for a moment death always being a betrayal mark's death tom's death and no matter how little you understood one or well you understood the other still it's a betrayal among so many others bill's and even mickey's deaths and then there's what they did that were betrayals too that are always there whether or not they're big the way they were with mickey and besides there's the world moving on no matter what and then this stuff i keep talking and talking and talking about on and on and on trapped in narrative so a breather let's take a breather a deep breath

///now and if we're going

///to take

///a deep breath now well what a good place to go for a deep breath for when we breathe deep go to deep memory of breath dedicate it to tom who couldn't breathe to bill now and mickey too and even tim who's having a hard time breathing can hardly breathe sometimes do you believe that a whole family with lung disease and me with all these long long breaths long long breaths reading in long long breaths to think to understand to remember so that's it first memory of breath of when we breathe not of breathing itself ahoo ahoo ahoo you'd felt that often enough in running hard or fear the stitch in the side the heart in the mouth but of knowing that we breathe acknowledging breath what a breather talking about breath and there i am

///in the subway it's true i do remember it i do i don't know how many people do that have a specific place for the memory of what you might call an intellectual event a memory of thinking of thinking something a particular something some sort of idea and it's mostly for the first time just like first dreams or first days at school oh yes i was there exactly there when i realized for the first time

///and i have a lot of memories like that and for whatever reason a lot of them in subways or at least trains or train platforms the mexico city subway the chicago el even years later the toronto subway with my own children on my back or in tow really important memories of understanding things at least one in toronto an important point of postmodern philosophy something about multiplicity and layering sometimes i remember the place and know it was important then forget the idea but polyvocality would make sense after all such layers of voices and so many subway first ideas from growth to breath with this one this breather maybe more typical my subway of subways the mother of all subways and whatever it is about nutmeg mews there's a subway stop for every line within five blocks it's the place where all the subway lines the irt the bmt the ind come together even if they're all letters and numbers now the a the b the c the four the six and among them was only ever the old bmt local the only local that made it to brooklyn and you would have to ride out three or is it two stops to dekalb if you wanted to do the manhattan bridge still this breather this memory of breath how we breathe we breathe was in the subway again long after or sort of after anyway the twisted bmt rides to rector street with paul and what a contradiction in terms maybe it's an oxymoron the new york subway breather what a place for a breather for first realizing that we breathe

///at rush hour yet

///with the train coming into the station fast as if its own breath were pushing its air ahead of it as you run along that tunnel or maybe it's that you stop running because you feel that air feel its cool breath that train in this moment breaking you always think of it as breaking onto the platform ahead of you whooshing along so that you know you have all the time in the world to walk up to its last car go to the rear window look out because you're almost at the end of that tunnel the one between what used to be the seventh avenue and the lexington irt's the east side and the west side we called them too now just the two and the three the four and the five each one up a different side of manhattan and there you are your breathing calming ahoo ahoo ahoo as you slow to a walk ahoo ahoo ahoo

///ahoo and it occurs to you to notice

///to notice and to think we breathe we breathe we breathe surrounded by the white tile of that short tunnel we walked through twice a day to get to and from school the shortest way to the tail end of the seventh avenue train that left us almost at the school door the twelfth street exit of the fourteenth street station who knows why it would occur to me then right then to think we breathe we breathe something we do is breathe i would find myself thinking we breathe we breathe this is a breather we breathe ahoo ahooo ahoooo that's what we do

///to stay alive we breathe we breathe

///or something like that anyway we breathe we breathe and who knows who had told me about breath and breathing but that's it we breathe you see we breathe or maybe it's that it was just after i'd had my tonsils and my adenoids removed i think that's what they'd done removed my tonsils and my adenoids they were very into that back then though i still don't know what an adenoid is you always had your adenoids removed along with your tonsils that was that dreadful operation where they'd lied to me not that they didn't lie to me about tom so here i am 283

///talking again dreadful operations and being on a hospital bed and what kind of a breather is that anyway falling again into horror the horror of hospital beds and icu and tom and not being able to breathe and me shouting do something only for him it wasn't one of those silly ether masks and if there were bright colours i hope there were bright colours he didn't live to tell me about it because it was the respirator and i shouted do something and i left because they threw me out and that was a betrayal my betrayal too so i still can't face that moment so what kind of a breather is this so forget that story that will never be an idea found on a subway i don't think there's a place any time soon i'll be able to look that memory in the mind's eye or for that matter make it into an idea so back we go to we breathe we breathe let's take a breather ahoo ahoo ahoo we breathe we breathe

///it really is a breather even if it isn't i tell you

///i'm going to give you a breather and then i talk about something dreadful again that's what we all do actually maybe that's an idea that occurred to me in a subway too station after station dragging me back to the nature of narrative we breathe we breathe ahoo ahoo ahoo always and only a quick breather and back to the story maybe that's from the c-train in calgary so it still is a breather it really is ahoo ahoo ahoo let's take a deep breath we breathe we breathe and recover before we finish running to the train to take up our place in the rear window of the last car to look out at the lights watch the tunnel the tunnel of our own lives disappear the narrative behind us the dark overcome us ahoo ahoo ahoo we breathe we breathe

///let's breathe let's have this breather even if it is

///a breather to catch your breath from thinking about something dreadful operations or hiding in closets mickey and the men in my room or tom mickey bill in icu it's still a breather because we can still do that concentrate on our breath so there i am in the subway and the train is about to whoosh into the station i can feel it coming in the tunnel its own whistling breath whistling like emphysema which isn't what tom had or isn't all that tom had and then there's the table i was on when they took my tonsils and my adenoids he was on when they took his life so concentrate on the train concentrate on your breath we breathe we breathe something we do to stay alive is we breathe we breathe we breathe ahoo ahoo and if i was thinking this after that tonsil operation you just know it wasn't too early in my life i already knew about growing up and mark was in his heaven and i was in that new school that city and country school which was why i was in that subway and almost at the end of that we breathe we breathe let's take a breather tunnel inside the tension between the train coming to take me away and the white white white white not even any ads back then white

///white tunnel that's like the operating theatre that's like drifting away that's like being transported that's like the question where do you go when you die only this time ahoo ahoo ahoo there's a train there's a train as well as more light at the end of the tunnel and you're going to get on that train and leave this piece of your life behind the way you would leave that memory of walking out of icu behind the light at the end of the tunnel may be an oncoming train but that one's not your tunnel not this time your train is on that track ahead of you and it's going to take you away away from brooklyn away from that house away from that operating theatre away from the doctors' voices as they tell you to count to count down ten nine eight or to leave the room there's nothing they or you can do this has been a terminal event and you can hear the respirator but it's not his breath he doesn't breathe he doesn't breathe not on his own and that's a lot worse lie than telling you they were taking you to breakfast and then taking you to the operating theatre telling tom they were going to take over his breathing and then he would be all right only he wasn't he was near dead and he would never regain consciousness and you were holding his hand only this time you're not dead the train is coming and you're still not dead as long as you're writing this the train is still coming and you're still not dead that's why this is a breather it's a real breather you're on your way to somewhere else and you're not dead we breathe we breathe and you're not dead so a deep breath a breather because we're not dead that's right in out we're not dead mark is dead tom is dead bill is dead mickey's dead but we're not dead in out we're not dead ahoo ahooo ahoo we're not dead the tunnel is long and white and the white robes of the doctors are far away and it's still not a near death experience the light at the end of the tunnel is still the outgoing train the one to take you away and we breathe we breathe we're not dead the train is coming to take us away we're not dead and that's the funniest thing the funniest thing

///about this breather is that it's a breather a real breather ahoo

///ahoo ahoo because all it means to be a breather to take a breather is to know you're breathing is to know you're not dead let's take a breather recognize our breathing recognize we're not dead the reason to relax the suspense is just to notice we're not on the train not yet we're not on the train for this one moment we can stop the forward motion just long enough to notice its nature to say to ourselves we breathe we breathe we're not dead we breathe we breathe we're not dead only the thing is if you say it too often if you take too many breathers it's all you can do we breathe we breathe ahoo ahoo ahoo we're not dead and pretty soon it's all

///you can think about ahoo ahoo we breathe

///we breathe we're not dead we're not dead until when you attempt to stop thinking about it you can't stop because you think you only breathe becauase you think about it ahoo ahoo we're not dead and every time you try to think about something else you panic because you stop breathing ahoo ahoo i really did that when i first noticed ahoo ahoo standing there at the end of that tunnel and breathing through my nose because i didn't have adenoids anymore ahoo ahoo look at this ahoo ahoo i'm breathing ahoo ahoo that's what we do to stay alive ahoo ahoo isn't this fun ahoo ahoo why didn't i ever notice this before ahoo ahoo we breathe we breathe to stay alive we breathe we breathe ahoo ahoo only then when i stopped thinking about it ahoo ahoo we breathe

///i didn't

///i didn't breathe ahoo ahoo i didn't which means i panicked i really did and even now

///that i know better even now

///it's still the truth

///the breather can only go on so long we breathe we breathe ahoo ahoo before the narrative must resume its course because we breathe we breathe if it doesn't ahoo ahoo you panic and we breathe we breathe is no longer a breather ahoo ahoo it dominates your life we breathe we breathe thinking i'm not dead i'm not dead ahoo ahoo i can't let go of this i can't i cant i can't rest i can't sleep ahoo ahoo it's up to me to make me breathe we breathe we breathe if i stop thinking about it i'll be dead ahoo ahoo and even if that part's not true you're not a dolphin it won't happen any more than you can hold your breath till you die to punish your teachers your parents your friends ahoo ahoo nothing will happen ahoo ahoo you'll just faint

///and breathe again ahoo

///ahoo ahoo still you can't stop thinking about it you need a story to stop thinking about it ahoo ahoo because that's not a place you want to be ahoo ahoo we breathe we breathe we're not dead we're not dead thinking about that all the time ahoo ahoo the nature of we breathe we breathe your breath ahoo ahoo we're not dead so you've got to stop you've got to stop ahoo ahoo you've got to stop ahoo let's stop ahoo ahoo we breathe we breathe and i knew it for the first time in a subway in a subway

///in a subway at the end of a tunnel ahoo ahoo a white white tunnel but let's let it go we breathe we breathe ahoo ahoo clacka clacka toot

///toot get the workmen out of the way watch the lights disappear behind us tell a story any story let's get on the train.

Little soaps

So this is finally the one about the good mom the dream mom the big lipstick mom the one i'll see with her big lipstick in a dream four years after she's died four years and four months after september eleventh i remember that last phone call so maybe this dream was in september too or was it november one of those rhyming months anyway thirty days hath and all that like the counting counting counting days for the good mom to come home always with that big bright slash of red across her mouth and her explaining about how you always exaggerated the lipstick going beyond the lip line moving joan crawford round above the indentation at the midline of the upper lip no cupid's bow for the forties the early fifties that's when it must have been and me no more than four or three and that's the way it is in the dream that big lipstick and i say looking good ma looking good and acknowledge to someone off to the side in the dream that it's crazy to be saying that three days after she's died so i know she's dead in the dream and what does it matter really if it's three days or four years and for the first time there's that tearing in the gut the missing the good ma the good ma the good ma oh mama mama who i never would have called that ma or mama even when she was

///good that is the good mickey was always mom except when she was mam or mem or mim or mum an experiment i tried some year when i was into vowels trying to see if i could make that good mom real again or maybe joking for the moments when she was or at least the good enough mom joking and drawing pictures but never ma no never mama even if paul garcia might have called her *mamacita* in some other more terrible circumstance or maybe that *mamacita* was me while that looking good ma dream it's made me think i should do it write something righteous something for once for the good ma the good mom or mum or mim write it and get it over though it's not really the dream that reminded me maybe the looking good ma dream came as a result of being reminded because first there was sitting around in the hotel room in canmore

///with myra and doing the usual ceremony as we packed to go this time sharing them out putting the little soaps in the washroom into the suitcase the little soaps that were once only little soaps little individually wrapped soaps the ones that have now metamorphosed maybe crossbred and evolved little soaps into little shampoos little body lotions little conditioners sometimes even little shower gels little packages of tastefully wrapped shower caps plus the shoe polishing chamois and the infinitesimal sewing kits from the best places which now that i think of it i'm sure go back forever while these days it's the wrapping or the style of the jars that tell you the price of the hotel some even have wonderful little corks in the openings of their teensy jars though those really don't work very well if you're thinking of reusing the things for travel take them with you on the next trip in case you're going to a b&b or hostel renting a small apartment places that don't do this at all because you take the ones with the corks and they uncork in your suitcase or backpack and believe me you never really get that lotion out again so maybe those will work if you want to set them out on your bathroom counter to silently brag about where you've been or give them to the kids the way i always did when they were younger and really i think now everybody does it takes the little shampoos the soaps the lotions the conditioners the sewing kits every day tucks them into the suitcase before the cleaners get there if they're not checking out collects them in droves the thing is

///that for me that day looking at them as i put the round soap that swears it's hand milled into the front pocket on my backpack i get this image in my head and it goes back so far so very far it kind of kicks me in the solar plexus even if i always knew it was a tradition this gesture of soap to suitcase continued a family tradition this stealing of little soaps a family tradition in a family with so few traditions that is beyond the getting drunk at christmas and for all major holidays as far as it goes and some very very unrecognizable personal ones too like july thirty first a lammas tradition for mark's death day with mickey drunk in subways or suicidal in bathtubs none of which can be considered positive even if tradition it may be so why not pick up on this little soap tradition make it a positive tradition consider it not stealing but a gift the hotel's gift to deprived or even entitled children or just to the discerning traveller after all they keep getting fancier over time and if the place is cheap and wants to conserve they can just attach a soap dispenser to the wall of the shower and forget the rest and many of them do so yes little soaps little soaps the fun tradition of little soaps let's wholeheartedly continue the tradition of little soaps little soaps guiltless and beguiling carefully packaged little soaps little soaps little conditioners little shampoos little lotions little shower gels the way i brought them home to the kids myself and saw

//as i passed them out mickey's old brown suitcase with its bright gold m.e.g. not meg or nutmeg no matter how nutty but m.e.g. her initials from before mark from before us opening to reveal the pink brown soft satin liner the little satin pockets along the back and sides and there they are the little soaps little soaps always the little soaps little soaps and it's always for me the little soaps little soaps and who knows what there was for tim there must have been something hiding in those pockets maybe a real present like a little car or maybe it's the little shoeshine kit the buffing cloth because who would give a boy little soaps little soaps or tell him for that matter why or how you made lips so bright made your bright big lipstick line that way the way mickey would always wear lipstick the way there would be tube after tube of lipstick in her drawers when she died reds oranges maroons mickey dating herself to the days of lipstick bright lipstick with no eye makeup eye makeup was what pushed you over the line and made you not a scarlet woman the way maybe her lipstick had made her for her parents

///lipstick and smoking their generational line while eye makeup in mickey's never on but in mickey's eyes would make you a beatnik oh the marvellous symbols of intergenerational conflict battle lines being drawn while the real fear was the return of mccarthy and you already at fifteen signing petitions and for that matter handing them out on street corners to be signed but that's a long way away many years and many i will grow up i will grow up subway stops from little soaps little soaps and you standing by her vanity as she would put it on the bright lipstick so it was always a special moment a special between us girls moment seeing the little soaps being presented the little soaps and seeing the bright gold coloured lipstick tubes next to them 289
a this is what professional women do travelling women do moment maybe tim never got anything from mickey's suitcase at all maybe he only got things his little shoeshine kit his little chamois from mark's suitcase in some sort of role modelling for the just right young professional couple forties style i don't remember i really don't even the colour of mark's suitcases except that like so much else the suitcases were colour coded his and hers masculine and feminine like their identical desks only his painted black and hers white at least they didn't paint their typewriters but still so much possibility a world opening of places to go and things to see and big smiles coming home coming home coming home cheerful smiling out of the bright day taxi sober calling i'm home i'm home mostly coming home so you can see

///why i would try to continue that tradition with my kids even if being of a different generation i always gave them to the boys too which is maybe why i have a son who might want giorgio armani cologne for xmas if we ever did xmas drunk or sober instead of just little soaps little soaps little lotions little shampoos little conditioners little shower gels and travel whenever we can and maybe you can see that those little soaps little soaps little conditioners little shampoos little body lotions little shower gels are a promise of escape the escape that is the condition for coming home little soaps as the tradition for you for your children a way to tell them tell the world that you can always go somewhere else be someone else the way

///those suitcases smelled of going places mickey was never able to go again not after mark's death the loss of the mickey green girl reporter job and there was only ever coming back from the bars from montero's from the j&e from the wigwam her farthest adventure tim costello's only that left coming back when the lipstick was smeared and there were no treats not even little soaps little soaps or for that matter much of a home so why not just talk about this the beauty of the smell of that suitcase and that looking good ma dream that looking at her and smiling looking good ma looking good even if you would hardly have said that then used those words still the truth is that back in the bright room with the gas fireplace and the white desk that doubled as a vanity and the brown suitcase popped open and the little soaps little soaps little soaps right then she was looking good ma looking good the best looking ma in the world the good ma the good mom the good mim the good mickey big lipstick mickey the one you always wanted back the one she probably wanted back that tim that bill that ev that anne marie that all of us wanted back that we always hoped was coming back the one with the open suitcase the one with the generous laugh the one with the little soaps little soaps

///who will never now be there again the one who you have to give up finally give up and send off close the door and do that modern thing get closure close close her the book on her so why not at least say it at least remember it little soaps little soaps and maybe even offer it up why not as a hope and a prayer because it's nice sometimes to believe just the way you can make it nice to remember so send her off not groaning and swearing rrrrr rrrrr rrrrr the way she was again those last days you saw her in the hospital those days she would have hunted you down again if she could have moved from her bed but as that charismatic christian woman from the community board saw her on her last day with the green glow of peace around her and you can just make yourself believe that lady isn't making it up only in your mind you'll make the glow pink brownish pink the way the light of the fireplace glinted off the satin pockets of the open suitcase in that room and why not i say why not why not let mickey have her moment her good mickey moment her looking good ma moment let her have it somewhere out there wherever it is that she's gone and maybe even you can pray for it hope for it believe for it if there is any continuance or even if there isn't let this be her last taxi moment her last taxi to herself with a sober shout of i'm home i'm home just give her that last peaceful moment let it glow by the fireplace glow out of the pink brown suitcase good ma mickey good mom mickey good mem mickey big lipstick mickey little soap mickey pink satin pocket suitcase mickey looking good ma mickey always coming home always coming home always coming home

///big lipstick mickey always

///coming home.

That old pinball in the front hall

that deaf dumb blind kid may have played a mean pinball but kwhang kwhang bing bang no matter how deaf dumb and blind we may have felt sometimes down into the sense of touch against the metal puck along the alley of the machine kwhang kwhang we sure didn't not a mean game at all not even a tolerably good one and most folks wouldn't even call it a pinball machine anyway though we did it had always been kwhang kwhang bing bang a pinball machine from its days down at montero's when mark or bill it was back then or mickey allowed us to play with it only they had to pay kwhang kwhang bing bang them or one of the sailors or any other friend even joe and pilar kwhang kwhang bing bang and now we didn't we didn't have to pay at all it was in our front room and we could just do it over and over and i don't even know if paul was still there just around or maybe in the basement or if it was just a favour mickey was doing but there it was and all the kids even the ones who weren't supposed to be talking to us coming to play with it and we didn't even collect money just played and played kwhang kwhang bing bang that was the pinball part but it wasn't you see like all those things i'd come to call pinball machines later with all those complicated levers it was just a minibowling alley with a puck and it even needed sawdust so the puck would slide but when it got there kwhang kwhang bing bang all the noises started depending on how many of the little bent wires embedded in the alley the puck had touched though for the longest time i thought it was the pins so kwhang kwhang bing bang all of us playing it over and over through the spring the summer the golden fall days deaf and dumb and blind if not mean to anything but ourselves to the hand kwhang kwhang bing bang and the metal solidity of the puck game of mind and body at once game of disappearance into mind into body into hand into puck into kwhang kwhang bing bang just us kids deaf dumb blind just now only now to all adult activity just us kids kwhang kwhang bing bang just us kids just us kids just us kids in the moment in the moment that summer in perfect balance the pause that refreshes as we awaited all unknowing yes this is where to end it for the door to open behind us not on rumours or on roomers or on mickey or on mark or on paul or on cherokee bill or even on tigers camels elephants but kwhang kwhang bing bang on the rest of our lives.

Contents

ACKNOWLEDGEMENTS

A book a long time in the making, even in the dreaming, *Last Taxi to Nutmeg Mews* owes much to many. As always, to friends and family, to all those who have shared with me, formed and informed my voice, far too numerous to mention. Yet, specific debts are owed. I will start with Leila Sujir because she did, in fact, make just that suggestion of an autobiography in headlines which threw me into a voice and a way of vocalizing that was both new to me and at the same time my most authentic voice in the English language. After, to all those who believed in the work as I wrote it and performed it and assembled it and drew it and videotaped it. Most importantly, those of the Word Hoard in Yorkshire, who have brought me to England repeatedly to write, tour, instruct and perform and who put me forward for my Arts Council England International Artists Fellowship in 2007. Particular thanks go to Keith Jafrate for his long time support of this work in spoken, written and graphic form, also to Diane Darby and Kath Jones of The Word Hoard's *Close to the Bone* women's group with whom several of these pieces were developed. Also, in Yorkshire, to Taru Sinclair and Bob Lockwood of the Kelman Group, who opened their home to me and whose experimental theatre took me back to my sixties roots and forward to new ways to look at improvisation. In Calgary, there are all those of The Centre Gallery, an open artistic space that in its years of existence allowed many Calgary artists and writers to show and perform their work, interact with each other and prosper from their differences. For me, in particular, it gave me a space in which to install and show work, and develop intermedia performances from the *Nutmeg Mews* cycle. Thanks go in particular to Catherine Cruz, Kathy Treybig, Barb Bickel and Vivian Hansen. The latter, and only one left in town, still part of my Y2K support group along with Weyman Chan and Stuart MacKay. Thanks also go to writers Marie Jakober and Roberta Rees, and artist and activist Rosemary Brown, for their long time enthusiastic support. Also to Sheri-D Wilson, spoken word artist extraordinaire, and director of The Calgary International Spoken Word Festival and The Banff Centre's new spoken word programme. Also, to Lillian Allen for her support both way long ago when I was just starting, and this year in Banff, particularly for recording assistance for some of these pieces. And last but hardly least, my publisher and editor Beth Follett of Pedlar Press for her belief in all my voices, whose support made it possible for me to piece this work together. And to Zab the graphic design genius who works with the press and got all my cats and my cockroaches in a row, so to speak, and who made this book so beautiful. And yes, the funders, The Canada Council for the Arts, The Alberta Foundation for the Arts, and Arts Council England, who have all helped some version of this work at some time.

Stepping on ants has appeared in Calgary's *Filling Station* and Yorkshire's *The Text*, as well as in Murphy's UK collection, *die tinkerbell die*. *Green Cherokee* was in *The Text* and *die tinkerbell die*, while *Cat tails cat tales* appeared in *The Text*. *Burned on the fourth of july* appeared in the Murphy special edition of *The Text* under the title, *Always the sparkler*. *Flight to Tallulah* was developed for the 2009 CBC Poetry Faceoff.

SARAH MURPHY is a Calgary based performer, author, intermedia and visual artist who has contributed to the Canadian arts scene and to her wider community for over twenty years. Best known for her award-winning performance monologues and innovative novels and short stories, Murphy has also produced installations that coordinate with intermedia performances. Her spoken word work is especially groundbreaking, and richly deserves recognition for bringing to spoken word prose the resonance of poetry.

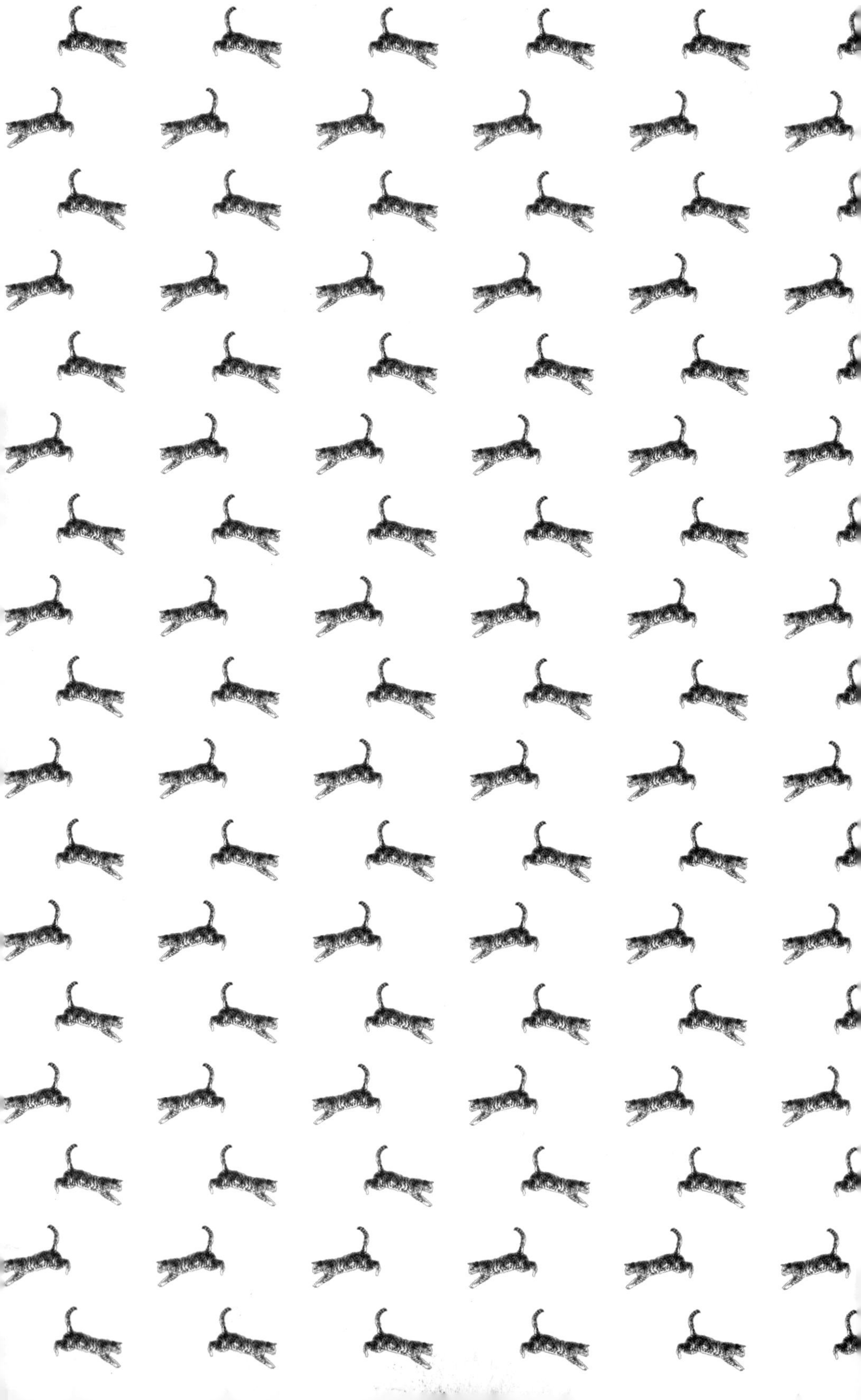